ESCAPE TO THE WEST
BOOK TWO

A HOPE UNSEEN

NERYS LEIGH

PROLOGUE

June, 1869

Sara crept down the staircase, carefully keeping her stockinged feet to the edge where she knew none of the steps would creak.

She could hear voices, but they were only loud enough that she could tell who they were, not so loud that she could tell what they were saying. At least, not with the door closed.

Biting back a sigh of frustration, she tip-toed the last few steps, her sights set on the parlor across the hallway.

A door to her right opened, practically making her jump out of her skin as Elspeth walked from the kitchen carrying a loaded serving tray. Seeing Sara, she opened her mouth to speak.

Sara shook her head frantically, pressing a finger to her lips and pointing at the parlor door. A smile crept onto Elspeth's face and she nodded in understanding. She waited for Sara to hide herself behind the huge grandfather clock next to the parlor door, gave her a final conspiratorial smile, and entered with the tray of tea and cakes.

There were a frustrating couple of minutes during which Sara wanted to scream her impatience, filled only by the sounds of Elspeth serving the tea and the occasional "thank you". Then she stepped back out into the hall with the empty tray, pulled the door to within an inch of the frame and left it there. She winked at Sara before returning to the kitchen,

1

leaving Sara to listen to the resumed conversation now audible through the tiny gap.

"Thank you for agreeing to see me on such short notice, Mr. and Mrs. Worthing. I know your time is valuable."

Sara let out a quiet sigh at the sound of Henry's voice, smooth as velvet. She couldn't deny that listening to him was a far from unpleasant experience.

"There is nothing as valuable to us as our daughter," Sara's father said. "The happiness of our children is more important to us than anything, isn't it dear?"

"It certainly is," Sara's mother agreed. "It has warmed our hearts to see her as happy as she has been these last few months. Meeting you has been so good for her."

Well, at least Sara had convinced them. If only she could do the same for herself.

"You have no idea how pleased I am to hear that," Henry said. "In fact, that's why I asked to meet with you today."

Sara's heart sped up to double time and she pressed her fisted hands together over it. She'd known this was why he was here. As soon as she'd seen his buggy pull up outside their house when they had no plans to meet, she'd known.

"Go on," Mr. Worthing said.

She heard Henry draw in a deep breath. "Mr. and Mrs. Worthing, knowing Sara has brought a joy to my life I didn't think possible. She is the light in every one of my days and I can't imagine a future without her. So I'm here to ask, would you allow me your daughter's hand in marriage?"

Even though she'd suspected a proposal was coming, Sara had to clamp a hand over her mouth to stop a gasp from escaping. Henry Hunt, one of Brooklyn's most eligible bachelors thanks to his wealthy family, handsome features and promising business career, wanted to marry her. She should be overjoyed.

2

Shouldn't she?

There were a few seconds of silence during which she imagined her father and mother smiling at each other. Or maybe they weren't sure about Henry. They could refuse him. For reasons Sara didn't entirely understand, that thought gave her hope.

"Mr. Hunt," her father finally said, "if Sara is agreeable, you have our blessing to marry our daughter."

Slumping against the wall, Sara closed her eyes.

"Thank you, sir, madam." Henry sounded like he was smiling. "I am deeply honored. Is she at home? I feel as if I can't wait another second to ask her."

"She is," her father said. "I'll have Elspeth fetch her."

Realizing her father would be coming out into the hallway at any second, Sara jerked upright and started for the stairs.

"Before you do," Henry said, "I hate to bring this up at such a joyful time, but might we talk about her dowry?"

Sara stumbled to a halt halfway across the hall.

"Uh, her dowry?" her mother said.

"Yes. I hate to bring such a crude matter as money up, but... well... I feel it's best to settle such things at the beginning. Don't you?"

"Of course," Mr. Worthing said. "We have given the matter some thought..."

Sara listened in mounting horror as her parents discussed how much Henry would receive to marry her. Her prospective marriage to the man who was, to all intents and purposes, her perfect match, was turned into a series of figures and items, a business transaction.

Eventually, unable to listen to any more, she fled back up the stairs to her bedroom and flung herself onto her bed.

She knew her parents didn't regard her as a commodity to sell, dowries were a normal part of marriage, but it was

3

still uncomfortable to hear. The worst thing about the whole affair, however, was her utter lack of excitement at the prospect of marrying Henry Hunt.

With his blue eyes and wavy blond hair, he'd charmed Sara from the moment they were introduced by her cousin five months previously. Within a week they were seeing each other regularly and it had been wonderful, new and thrilling.

And then... it wasn't.

It wasn't that she didn't enjoy spending time with Henry, he was fun and interesting and attentive and handsome, but after a couple of months she had realized there was something missing. They were the perfect couple; a similar age, financially and socially matched. Marriage made sense. She'd have a good life with Henry and he seemed fond of her. Indeed, she was genuinely fond of him.

And yet she didn't love him. At least, she didn't think she did. She'd never been in love so she couldn't be certain, but she'd read about it, and what she felt with Henry didn't come close to the fluttering hearts and sizzling touches and longing looks of the romance novels. Did that kind of love even exist? Was she a fool to think it did?

And then there was the prospect of a life with Henry, filled with primping and preening, social functions and dinner parties, entertaining his friends and business acquaintances, being the perfect wife to a man of money and standing. It would be her job to make him look good so he could succeed in *his* job.

Just the thought of it all made her feel like she was suffocating.

But her parents were so happy with the match and the last thing she wanted to do was disappoint them. If only she felt differently.

Hugging her knees in front of her, she told herself she would come to love him and her life with him. She remembered all the gestures of affection, all the chaste touches and secret kisses, all the compliments and the laughter. Surely that had to mean something. Surely it meant she could be happy with him.

A soft knock on her bedroom door pulled her from her thoughts. "Come in."

Elspeth stepped quietly into the room. "Miss Sara, Mr. Worthing has asked if you would join him and Mrs. Worthing and Mr. Hunt downstairs."

Sara drew one hand across her eyes. "Thank you. Tell him I'll be down shortly."

Elspeth nodded, moved to close the door, then stopped. "I know it's not my place, but if you have any doubts you should wait until they're gone. There's nothing much more important than making certain you marry the right man. You don't have to give him an answer now."

Sara gave her a small smile. "Thank you."

Elspeth returned her smile and left, pulling the door closed behind her.

Sara slid her feet off the bed and into her shoes. She appreciated Elspeth's advice, but she wasn't sure her doubts would ever be gone. This was what everyone else expected of her and what a young woman in her position was supposed to want. She wasn't sure she really had any choice in the matter.

When she reached the parlor, Henry was waiting for her alone. She tried to find the excitement she knew she should be feeling at the imminent marriage proposal. Or if not excitement, at least happiness. Or relief. *Anything* other than the mounting gloom she felt now.

"Sara, you look beautiful, as always," he said, rising from the couch and walking over to take her hand.

He leaned forward to kiss her cheek and she managed to force what she hoped was a half decent smile.

"I suppose you know I've been speaking with your parents," he said.

She nodded.

"And I don't think I've been very good at hiding how I feel about you."

She nodded again.

"So there's only one thing for me to say." Keeping hold of her hand, he sank to one knee in front of her. "Sara, would you do me the honor of becoming my wife?"

Say yes, she thought. *This is what any woman would want. Say yes. Say it.*

She opened her mouth to say yes. Instead, she said, "Are you in love with me?"

The smile on Henry's face faltered for an instant. "I... beg your pardon?"

"Are you in love with me? Does your heart quicken when I walk into the room? Am I in your thoughts constantly when we're apart? Do you feel as if you can't bear for us to be separated? Are you deeply, madly and passionately in love with me?"

Although she tried to sound calm, her heart thudded in her chest. She didn't even know what she wanted his answer to be. The easy answer of yes? Or the uncertainty of the rest of her life after a no?

And then he hesitated.

It was only for a moment, but she saw the flicker of doubt on his face before it was quashed.

"Of course I do, Sara. You're everything to me. So will you marry me?"

She stared down into his beautiful blue eyes and whispered the only answer she could.

"No."

CHAPTER 1

Eleven months later.

"We'll both be happy, you'll see."

Sara took Amy's hand and stood, pulling her friend up from the train seat.

Strangely, Amy seemed reluctant to leave. She was probably just nervous. Sara certainly was. She'd been eager to meet Daniel ever since they'd started corresponding, but now that the exciting future had become the imminent present, her stomach was swirling. Would he like her? Would she like him? What would he look like?

When their letters had begun to seriously approach the possibility of marriage she'd sent him a photograph of herself that she'd had taken especially, so he at least had an idea of her appearance. But there were no photographers in the small town of Green Hill Creek and, other than the basic details he'd told her - six feet and two inches tall, dark hair and eyes, twenty-seven years of age – she didn't know what to expect.

She glanced out the train window again at the little cluster of men gathered outside. Three of them had dark hair. She ruled out the one with the beard as Daniel had said he was clean-shaven. That left two alternatives, unless Daniel had grown a beard since.

Her eyes were drawn to one man in particular. She couldn't help it. Even from this distance and through the grime covering the glass, he was handsome in a way that made her heart flutter. She wouldn't mind spending the rest of her life gazing at *that* face. Although it didn't matter what he looked like because, through his letters, she'd come to know Daniel Raine as a kind, caring, wonderful man. A man she could fall in love with. A man she *was* falling in love with, even before they'd met in person.

That was the important thing, what was inside. God didn't look at the outward appearance and neither would she.

But still, that *face.*

"Come on, let's go and meet our husbands." She laughed, possibly a little hysterically. "Doesn't that sound strange?"

Outside, the station was crowded with milling passengers, some stretching their legs before the rest of their journey continued, a small handful boarding the train here. Sara grasped Amy's hand again, seeking strength from the contact. Even though they'd only met a week before at the start of their journey from New York to California, she counted Amy among the best friends she'd ever had. And right now she needed her friend.

They followed Lizzy, Louisa and Jo in the direction of the waiting group of men "Oh, Amy, I'm a little nervous myself now. If you feel me starting to swoon, pinch me hard. The last thing I want is Daniel thinking I'm a feeble woman who isn't able to cope with life in the west."

"Ladies, welcome to Green Hill Creek." The older man who was speaking as they approached introduced himself as Simon Jones, pastor of the church that worked with the Western Sunset Marriage Service to match Christian men in the women-starved west with ladies in the east wanting to start a new life.

As the pastor and his wife welcomed them, Sara's

attention again went to the tall, dark-haired man she'd seen from the train. His eyes met hers and one corner of his strong, full lips curved up. She quickly dropped her gaze. If he wasn't Daniel, she very much didn't want to be caught making eyes at him.

"Miss Cotton, may I introduce Richard Shand."

The welcome over, Pastor Jones had begun introductions. Sara looked up to see Lizzy throw herself into the arms of a very surprised looking man. Sara clamped one hand over her mouth to stop herself from laughing. Knowing Lizzy as she did, she wasn't surprised at all.

"He's going to have his hands full," she whispered to Amy.

Amy smiled. "He certainly is."

The pastor next called Louisa, who he introduced to Peter Johnson, an older man who explained he would be taking her to meet his son, Jesse. Sara wondered why Louisa's intended hadn't come to the station himself. By the confused look on Louisa's face, she was wondering the same thing.

The pastor again consulted a piece of paper in his hand. "Sara Worthing?"

Sara gasped, her insides somersaulting and her mouth suddenly dry.

"Shall I pinch you now?" Amy whispered.

Stifling a laugh, Sara gave her a grateful look and let go of her hand to walk forward.

"Miss Worthing," Pastor Jones said, "meet Daniel Raine."

She tried not to gape as the man she'd been watching stepped forward. It was him.

It was *him*.

From the moment she'd seen him through the train window, she'd known it was him. Despite there being three dark-haired men standing in the small group at the station, somehow she'd known it was him. Or maybe she'd just hoped it was him. How was it possible for any man to be so perfectly handsome? And tall. And strong-looking. And *handsome*. She almost couldn't believe he was real.

"I'm very pleased to finally meet you, Sara." He held out his hand.

His voice! It was like listening to aural molasses. Sara stared up at him, frozen to the spot. *Say something!*

Placing her trembling hand into his, she managed to whisper, "Hi."

His answering smile etched a perfect dimple into his right cheek that made Sara's legs feel positively wobbly. If he kept this up, he was going to have to carry her to the church.

Oh, why had she thought that? Now every time she looked at him she was going to imagine his strong arms holding her against his chest where she could lay her head on his broad shoulder, which perfectly matched his other broad shoulder.

She suddenly realized she was staring and dropped her gaze. To his chest. Which, despite being hidden under a red plaid shirt, she could tell was as impressive as his shoulders. Was there anything unattractive about him?

Not wanting to appear to be staring at his chest, she dropped her eyes to his boots. Maybe he had bunions. Hideously ugly bunions.

She had to bite back a giggle. There was a chance she wasn't thinking entirely straight.

Her gaze snapped back up to his face as he slowly shook her hand and then threaded it through his arm as they stepped back to join the growing group of couples. Daniel smiled down at her and all the nerves she'd had about meeting him melted away.

It was really him, the man who had so delighted and entranced her with his letters these past months that when he asked her to cross the country to marry him, she hadn't hesitated to say yes.

He was her Daniel. The man she would spend the rest of her life with.

She couldn't have been happier.

"Josephine Carter?"

At Pastor Jones' voice, Sara dragged her eyes from Daniel's face to watch Jo step forward. The dark-haired, bearded man moved forward to meet her.

"Miss Carter, this is Gabriel Silversmith," the pastor said.

Mr. Silversmith's rugged face stretched into a smile. "Pleasure to meet you, Miss Carter."

He looked a little older than the other men Sara's four travelling companions had come to marry, perhaps in his mid thirties. His complexion was darkened from the sun, blending with his hair and beard. Sara tried to gauge Jo's reaction to her intended, but Sara had found it was always hard to tell how the fun but enigmatic young woman felt about anything. They'd spent a week together on the train travelling from New York to Green Hill Creek, but Sara still felt like she didn't know Jo any better than when they'd first met. She'd found it much easier to bond with Amy, Lizzy and Louisa.

Jo smiled, taking Mr. Silversmith's hand and bobbing a small curtsey. "The pleasure is mine, Gabriel." And then she winked.

Sara's hand flew to her mouth to hide her shock. She knew Jo was about to marry the man, but a wink was so wildly forward it threw her. Maybe she'd been mistaken, maybe Jo had something in her eye. It was dusty and smoky around the train, after all. Yes, that must have been it.

"And finally," the pastor said, drawing Sara's attention away from Jo, "Amy Watts."

Sara peered around Daniel to the only man still to claim

11

his bride. He stood awkwardly, looking so terrified she felt instantly sorry for him. Adam Emerson stood as tall as Daniel with hair as dark, if a little longer, and the most striking blue eyes she'd ever seen. He wasn't as handsome as Daniel, but he was close. A small smile stole onto her face. Amy would be thrilled.

"Amy Watts?" Pastor Jones repeated.

Sara looked around, only now realizing her friend had vanished. She'd been so taken with Daniel that she'd barely noticed anything else around her.

"Amy?" she called, searching the throng of passengers loitering around the station for Amy's blonde hair and unconventional outfit. Finally she spotted her, more or less where she'd left her, half hidden by the crowd. "Amy! There you are."

Amy was looking up at a man in a long dark coat, Mr. Pulaski. Even though Sara was off the train, the sight of him made her want to hide. He'd spoken to her on several occasions during the week long journey. Those had been the times she hadn't managed to avoid him. He was quite astonishingly and persistently boring.

At Sara's call, he looked towards her and their eyes met. He smiled and touched the brim of his hat. Not wanting to appear impolite, Sara nodded in response.

Amy was walking towards the group and Sara gratefully moved her attention back to her friend.

"There you are," Pastor Jones said, sounding relieved. "Amy Watts, may I present Adam Emerson?"

As Amy greeted her husband to be, Sara's gaze strayed back up to Daniel's face. He'd told her in his letters that he and Adam had known each other since they were children, and he looked pleased for his friend as he watched Adam and Amy meet for the first time. Then he moved his eyes to Sara and she blushed and looked down, embarrassed that she'd

12

been caught staring.

She could already tell she was going to have a problem stopping herself from gazing at him constantly, but she supposed there were far worse problems than having a devastatingly handsome husband. Like having a husband you weren't sure was in love with you so much as your social status and ability to hold a dinner party.

At least with Daniel Sara knew he wanted her for her. He'd even paid for her train ticket across the country which was no small cost. Of course, she'd brought the money with her to pay him back. She'd just needed to know he wanted her enough to do it.

"Well," Pastor Jones said, "now we're all sorted out, let's get the luggage and head to the church."

They made their way to the rear carriage of the train where the trunks and cases were being unloaded. With the five of them, quite a mound of luggage was building up.

Daniel leaned down to whisper, "Whose are the blue ones?"

Sara laughed. "Don't worry, they're not mine. They're Louisa's." She pointed to a single brown trunk and matching suitcase. "Those are mine."

He nodded, smiling. "I wouldn't have minded, but I might have needed a bigger wagon."

The man who had come to meet Louisa, Peter Johnson, began loading the heavy-looking trunks onto his wagon standing nearby, lifting each one as if it weighed just a few pounds.

"Peter's the town's blacksmith," Daniel said in response to Sara's look of amazement. "Strong as two oxen, which I guess has come in useful with Jesse."

He unwound his arm from hers and went to retrieve her luggage.

Sara moved to stand next to Louisa. "Are you all right?"

13

Louisa released her lower lip from between her teeth and gave her an unconvincing smile. "Of course." She glanced at Mr. Johnson. "Well... maybe I'm a little worried. Oh dear, does it show?"

Sara linked their arms. "Just a little bit. But it's completely understandable."

Louisa sighed and chewed her lip again. "I asked Mr. Johnson why Jesse hasn't come and he just said he'd explain when we got there. Oh Sara, what if he's changed his mind? What will I do?"

Sara squeezed her arm, drawing her closer. "You showed me his letters, there is no way the man who wrote those wonderful words has changed his mind. He's besotted, that's the only word for it."

This time, Louisa's smile was genuine. "Besotted?"

"Besotted. I might even go so far as enamored."

Louisa laughed quietly. "I'm sorry I'm not going to be there for your wedding. Daniel's very handsome."

Sara couldn't help but nod in emphatic agreement. "I can't stop staring at him. It's embarrassing."

Louisa nudged her shoulder. "Don't worry, by the way he's been looking at you he won't mind one bit."

"Are you ready, Miss Wood?" Mr. Johnson said, walking towards them.

Sara could almost hear the wagon behind him groaning under the strain of carrying Louisa's trunks. She must have packed everything she owned. Sara had left most of her belongings with her parents to send on later. Looking at all that Louisa had brought, she was suddenly worried she may not have packed nearly enough.

"Yes, thank you," Louisa said. She gave Sara a quick hug and whispered, "See you Sunday," before leaving with Mr. Johnson.

Having loaded Sara's luggage into his wagon, Daniel

walked up beside her and held out his arm with a smile. "Shall we go?"

Sara slipped her hand around his elbow into a position that, despite only having just met him, was becoming wonderfully familiar. They followed Pastor and Mrs. Jones away from the station as the train pulled out in a cloud of steam, resuming its journey to San Francisco.

In front of Sara and Daniel, Lizzy was chatting animatedly to Mr. Shand, her arm in his. For his part, he was still looking a little stunned. Sara hoped he would appreciate Lizzy's constant enthusiasm as much as she had come to.

Next to them walked Jo and Mr. Silversmith, also arm in arm. They weren't speaking and Jo was looking around her at every building they passed. If Sara hadn't known any better, she would have said she was sizing up the town.

To Sara's left were Amy and Adam. They weren't touching and Adam's hands were pushed into his pockets as he looked at the ground ahead of him. Amy looked nervous, darting glances back at the station behind her. Something was clearly wrong.

Sara heard Adam ask if she was all right and Amy came to a sudden halt. Then she crumpled to the ground.

Sara gasped and rushed over to her. Adam was already on his knees beside his soon-to-be wife, looking scared.

"What happened?" Sara said as the others all gathered around them.

"I... I don't know." Adam touched one hand to Amy's face. "She just fainted."

"Oh my, is she all right?" Mrs. Jones said.

"Give her some air," Lizzy said.

"Amy?" Sara said. "Amy, can you hear me?"

After what must have been no more than a minute, but felt like an age, Amy's eyes fluttered open and she looked up at Adam.

Sara breathed out.

"She's awake!" Mrs. Jones said.

"Give her some air!" Lizzy repeated.

Adam helped her to sit up. "Are you all right?"

Amy put a hand to her head. "I'm sorry, I don't know what happened."

"You've obviously had a lot of excitement and stress travelling," Pastor Jones said, crouching beside her.

Sara thought Amy had been acting strangely since they arrived. Perhaps this was why. Daniel moved to stand beside her and almost without thinking she wound her arm around his. She was worried for her friend and being close to him felt reassuring.

"I'm all right," Amy said. "Truly, I'm fine."

With Adam's help she rose to her feet, a little unsteadily. Taking a step, she faded again and would have fallen if Adam hadn't held onto her.

"Maybe I should just take her home," he said to the pastor. "Could we possibly have the ceremony tomorrow?"

Sara felt desperately sorry for him. He looked on the verge of panic.

"Of course we can," Pastor Jones said. "That's a good idea. I'm sure all she needs is some food and a good rest."

Leaving Daniel, Sara walked over to Amy as the others backed away. "Are you well, Amy? Can I do anything?"

"No, I'll be fine." She smiled and whispered, "You go and marry your handsome cowboy. I know you want to."

Sara had to bite back a giggle. Daniel wasn't a cowboy, but as they were in the semi-wild west it was close enough.

She leaned in close to Amy, lowering her voice. "He's wonderful, isn't he?"

Amy seemed to be feeling better as they walked the rest of the way to the church, nevertheless Adam stayed close, not taking his eyes from her as if waiting to catch her if she

16

fainted again. Sara knew that was a good sign. It meant he cared about her. He and Amy would be a good match.

When they reached the church, Adam and Amy said their goodbyes and carried on towards the middle of town and Adam's home. The rest of them went inside.

The Emmanuel Church was a homely building, with flowers in pots outside the front door, tall arched windows letting in plenty of light, and cream colored walls giving the interior a warm feel. Rows of wooden chairs filled most of the building, with a raised platform at the front. The pastor and Mrs. Jones led the small group to the front where they took seats in the first row and he stepped up onto the platform.

"Welcome to Emmanuel Church," he said, smiling. "Of course you don't have to attend, but we'd love to see you on Sundays. I'm contractually obliged to say that, but it's still true."

A smattering of laughter rippled around his tiny congregation.

"When my wife and I got in touch with the Western Sunset Marriage Service more than two years ago in response to the increasing need for wives for the unattached men around the town, we had no idea of the response we'd receive, and the number of marriages that would result. It has been a joy to be instrumental in bringing lonely men and women together and seeing the happiness it brings. I am truly honored to be joining you together as men and wives, and know that you will be continually in our prayers as you start your new lives together."

"Amen," Mrs. Jones said.

Sara looked up at Daniel beside her and found him gazing at her in a way that stole her breath away. Tiny lines formed at the corners of his eyes and his dimple appeared. She decided that dimple was her favorite thing in the world.

"So without further ado, Miss Carter and Mr. Silversmith,

would you join me?"

Sara blinked and looked at the pastor. She'd missed every word he'd said from the moment she'd looked into Daniel's eyes. They could have been sitting there for hours for all she knew.

Jo and Gabriel's vows went without a hitch and Sara noted that the pastor didn't include the usual "you may kiss the bride" at the end. Although, somewhat surprising everyone in attendance including the bridegroom, Jo kissed him anyway.

Lizzy and Richard's short ceremony also went smoothly, for the most part. As the pastor said, "Lizzy, do you..." she immediately said, "Yes!" Then, her eyes wide, she slapped one hand over her mouth and exclaimed, "Oh!" and laughed along with the rest of them.

And then the pastor said, "Miss Worthing and Mr. Raine, would you join me?"

And Sara's stomach exploded in butterflies.

Over the past week, Sara had sometimes felt as if their time on the train would never end, that she would never get to meet the man whose letters had persuaded her he was the only one she wanted. Even though it had been her choice to become a mail order bride, it was still a huge undertaking to leave her family and friends and travel across the country to marry a man she'd never met. She wouldn't have done it for just any man. But Daniel wasn't just any man.

His letters had brought her a joy and excitement she'd never felt before, even at the beginning of her courtship with Henry. She'd waited for each one with an almost unbearable anticipation, and when they'd arrived she'd read them over and over until they were in danger of falling apart. When he'd finally asked her to marry him, she hadn't hesitated to say yes.

And now here she was, about to become Mrs. Daniel

Raine. In a moment of clarity, she knew she was right where she was supposed to be, where God wanted her to be.

"Sara, Daniel," Pastor Jones said as they stood side by side in front of him, "marriage is a sacred vow before God and a pledge to each other to stand together, as one, for the rest of your lives. Whatever may come, you will never face it alone. It won't always be easy, but if you love and hold onto each other through it all, it will be right."

He'd said the same thing to the other two couples, but somehow it went straight to Sara's heart when he was talking about her and Daniel. The thought that loving and holding onto Daniel wasn't going to be difficult came to her and she felt a blush heat her cheeks. Daniel's smile grew, which made her blush even more.

"Daniel, do you have a ring?" the pastor said. "It's all right if you don't, most men have the ring made afterwards."

"I have one." He looked at Sara as he pulled a small cloth bag from his pocket. "I don't know if it will fit, but I can have it altered. I just wanted to have it ready for you."

The backs of Sara's eyes were suddenly burning. She blinked rapidly and pressed her lips together, an embarrassing squeak all she could manage in response.

Don't cry. Do not cry.

Never moving his eyes from her, Daniel handed the narrow gold band to Pastor Jones who placed it onto the open Bible he held.

He then said, "Would you face each other?" Somewhat unnecessarily as they were already gazing into each other's eyes. "Daniel, would you repeat after me..."

Daniel's eyes held hers as he slid the ring onto her finger and said, "I, Daniel Jonathan Raine, take you, Sara Julia Worthing, to be my wife, to have and to hold from this day forward, for better or for worse, for richer, for poorer, in sickness and in health, to love and to cherish; and I promise to be faithful to you until death parts us."

"Sara, please repeat after me..."

Sara's heart was beating so fast she almost forgot to say the words, and afterwards she wasn't sure she hadn't made a mistake somewhere.

But it didn't seem to matter, because the pastor said, "I now pronounce you man and wife. Congratulations, Mr. and Mrs. Raine."

And, just like that, she was Daniel's wife.

CHAPTER 2

Sara stepped through the church door into the sunshine on the arm of her husband.

Her *husband*.

Although she'd had plenty of time to mentally prepare herself for being married, she still found herself a little overwhelmed. She had a husband. She was a wife. Daniel's wife.

She surreptitiously peeked up at him as they exited onto the street. Every time she looked at him her heart sped up. Would that stop happening? Would seeing his face become so commonplace that she would no longer feel that twinge of excitement? She hoped not.

From this angle his strong jaw line was particularly striking and she wasn't aware she was staring until he looked down at her and smiled. Feeling the blood rush to her cheeks, she looked down. She was really going to have to get the blushing under control.

The small group of three newly-married couples made their way back to the station where they'd left their luggage-laden wagons in the care of the stationmaster and it was an emotional farewell to Lizzy and Jo, despite knowing they would all see each other again at church in just two days time. Sara had become used to seeing them almost all day, every day.

When they'd left, she walked to where Daniel was waiting by his wagon.

He dipped his head to look into her eyes. "You OK?"

"I am. It's funny how seven days on a train can bring people together. I feel like I've known them so much longer." She reached out to stroke the neck of the horse nearest to her, a beautiful chestnut mare. "Who's this?"

"This is Ginger. She's Will's." He indicated the bay stallion next to her. "And that's River. He's mine."

Will was Daniel's younger brother who worked for him and lived on the farm. Sara couldn't help feeling some trepidation at the prospect of having him around. It was one thing to be moving in with the man she'd been corresponding with for months and had just married, but entirely another to get used to living around a stranger. Although from the way Daniel had written about him, she knew they were close. She hoped Will wouldn't resent her sudden intrusion into their bachelorhood. Perhaps they'd even become friends.

Sara greeted both horses, swallowing a pang of sadness at the thought of her own horse back at home. Although she'd known it was the right thing to do, leaving Eliza was a wrench and she missed her.

Daniel helped her into the wagon and climbed up beside her, then he snapped the reins and River and Ginger started off.

He glanced back at her single trunk and small suitcase. "That doesn't seem like much to bring with you. Is there anything you need to get in town before we leave?"

"Oh, no, thank you. I have everything I need." Sara thought back to packing for her trip. "My parents said they'd send anything more I wanted, but you said your house isn't very large so I didn't want to bring too much and overwhelm you."

He looked horrified. "Oh no, I didn't mean for you to feel you couldn't bring everything you need, I just didn't want you to be disappointed. We can stop at the general store..."

Without thinking, Sara touched her fingers to the back of his hand. "It's all right, I promise. I don't need anything."

His eyes dropped to where her hand rested lightly on his skin. Even though he didn't look at all like he wanted her to, she snatched it away, and then immediately regretted it. She needed to get used to touching him. He was, after all, her husband.

Her *husband*.

No, she still wasn't used to that.

And the truth was she wanted to touch him. The thought embarrassed her and she groped frantically for something to say before she blushed again.

"I do hope Amy is all right," she managed to come up with. "In all the time we spent together on the train, she never once struck me as the type to faint easily."

"Adam will look after her," Daniel replied, and then he chuckled. "She was probably just overcome by his intense masculinity."

Sara's eyes widened. "His what?"

He shook his head, smiling. "Just something he told me once about a book belonging to his mother he stole a look at when he was young."

A friend of Sara's back in New York was a great collector of those kind of novels so she wasn't a stranger to what was in them. She'd read more than a few herself, but that was the last thing she wanted to admit, so she kept quiet and tried not to smile. As they were leaving the edge of the town she turned her gaze to the surrounding fields.

"So you and Adam grew up together here?"

"Sure did. He's just two years younger than me so we went to school together, played together. I guess it's kind of fitting our brides arrived together." He glanced back at the buildings of the town receding into the distance behind them and smiled at her. "Don't worry, he's a good man. He'll be a fine husband to Miss Watts."

Sara nodded and they rode in silence for a while. She gazed at the landscape around her in awe; the fields and trees, the mountains in the distance looking glorious in the sunshine, everything a bright patchwork of greens and blues and browns. She didn't think she could have asked for a more beautiful place to settle.

"How was your journey?" Daniel said.

"Long and uncomfortable. And I loved every second."

He laughed softly. "I have no idea what to make of that."

"Well, I made four wonderful new friends and saw so much beautiful scenery. And I was excited to get here." She glanced at him quickly and then back at the horses in front of them. "I was looking forward very much to meeting you."

There were a few seconds of silence before he said, "I've been excited for you to arrive too. I'm not sure I've slept more than a few hours all week, knowing you were on your way."

She spent a few seconds wrestling with the smile trying to surge onto her face before giving up and letting it make her look like a giddy schoolgirl. "It all feels a little like a dream. After all the time we've been writing to each other, to finally be here and see everything you've told me about is, well, I keep feeling like I should pinch myself."

He chuckled, dipping his head and then looking at her sideways, his brown eyes sparkling. "Please don't do that. I wouldn't want you to hurt yourself when you've only just arrived."

"All right," she said, "I'll save it for later."

His answering laugh was filled with warmth and joy. It made her feel wonderful.

They continued to talk as they drove along the well-worn road running between fields and trees, Daniel pointing out landmarks or telling her who lived along each road they passed. Eventually they turned onto a track marked with painted white stones. A simple wooden board mounted between two posts proclaimed it simply 'Raine Farm'.

They entered a small area of woodland, the sunlight dappling the ground through the new bright green leaves of oak and hazel, before emerging from the trees to the sight of a pretty single storey wooden house with blue painted walls and purple flowering wisteria draped across a trellis around the door. The horses didn't seem to need guiding as they made their way around to the back and stopped in front of a large barn set away from the house, across a wide, packed earth yard. Another, smaller barn sat at the other side of the yard behind a long, single storey building.

Beyond the barns, a vista of fields and trees stretched to the feet of the distant mountains, their peaks taking on a pinkish hue in the late afternoon sunshine.

Daniel jumped down from the wagon and walked around to help Sara to the ground.

"Welcome home," he said. He rubbed the back of his neck as he glanced at the small house. "It's not very big and, well, I'm not much of a gardener. It could really use a woman's touch, I reckon. I've been buying lumber when I can afford it and just as soon as I can, I'll build on some more rooms. I wanted to do it before you arrived, but there's always so much to do on the farm and..."

Sara placed one hand on his arm. "It's perfect."

His eyebrows rose. "It is?"

She turned in a slow circle, taking in the house with its wide, covered porch, the barns and the fields. It was so far away from the modern, three storey brick city house she'd lived in her entire life that it felt like she must be in a whole different country.

And she loved every bit of it.

She smiled up at his nervous expression. "It is. It's wonderful. I know I'm going to be happy here."

He breathed out, lowering his hand to briefly touch hers. "I'll do everything in my power to make sure you are, I promise."

Sara had no doubt he would. The truth was, right now she felt like all he had to do was exist to make her happy.

A bark sounded behind her and she looked round to see a black St. John's dog bounding across the yard towards them. The dog headed straight for Daniel who bent to ruffle her head as she eyed Sara suspiciously.

"Sara, this is Bess," he said. "She might take a little while to get used to you, but if you scratch her ears she'll love you forever."

Sara leaned forward and held out her hand. "It's a pleasure to meet you, Bess."

Bess took a few tentative steps forward and stretched her nose out to sniff at Sara's fingers, her tail wagging slowly. Perhaps it was because she could smell Daniel's scent on her, but Bess' ears perked up and she moved forward, looking up at her expectantly. Sara rubbed her ears and she sat, closing her eyes in bliss.

"Looks like you have a new friend," Daniel said, grinning.

"Well, you can't be the woman who came all the way across America to marry Dan because you are *much* too pretty for him."

Sara looked up to see a man striding towards them across the yard, a huge grin plastered across his face.

Daniel cleared his throat. "Sara, meet Will."

Will brushed his right hand off on his denim trousers and held it out to her. "I'm so sorry you've come all this way to be so thoroughly disappointed at your runt of a new husband."

26

"Please forgive my little brother," Daniel said. "He's under the mistaken impression that he's funny."

"And charming," Will said.

"Yes, he's mistaken about that too."

Sara couldn't help smiling at the brothers' banter. Now she'd met them both, she couldn't miss the resemblance. Will stood a little taller than Daniel and shared his brown eyes and dark hair. He even had a dimple, albeit it on the left instead of the right.

She took her new brother-in-law's hand. "It's a pleasure to meet you, Will."

"Likewise. It will be such a relief to have some intelligent conversation around here for a change."

He winked and she laughed, her fears about any resentment on his part fading. She should have known any brother of Daniel's would be as wonderful as he was.

"Yeah, yeah," Daniel said, waving him away. "How about you unhitch River and Ginger while I take Sara's things inside."

With a final grin at her, Will headed for the horses.

"Would you like to go in?" Daniel said, nodding towards the house. "I'll bring your luggage."

She made her way to the porch that spanned the back of the house, plans blossoming in her mind's eye. She'd always loved gardening and as she walked she imagined plants and flowers growing around the house, just like in her parents' garden back home. With the sun beginning to sink towards the horizon, this time of day was her favorite to walk outside, the scent of flowers touching the air, insects flitting from bloom to bloom. Paws, her mother's huge tortoiseshell cat, rubbing around her calves whenever she stopped to admire a plant.

A feeling of homesickness suddenly swept over her, so strong she had to stop to let the pain in her chest pass. She took a deep breath, waiting for the unwelcome emotion to fade. This was her home now, she would have to get used to thinking of it that way.

Resuming her climb up the four steps to the porch, she came to a wooden bench set beside the back door. It was in just the right position to take in the view across the valley to the mountains. With a few cushions and maybe a blanket it would be a comfortable spot to sit and watch the sunset.

And it would be even better with Daniel sitting beside her.

~ ~ ~

Daniel wandered back to the wagon, casting surreptitious glances back at Sara as he walked. She was moving slowly, taking everything in as she approached the house.

He was a nervous wreck. The wedding had gone well, but now all he could think was, did she like him? Would she like his home? He had a whole list of things he wished he'd done before she arrived, if only the farm didn't take up so much of his time. He'd been so fixated on bringing the farm to a point where he could support a family that he'd forgotten to see it as the place where he'd be raising one. He hoped Sara would see the potential rather than the reality.

Looking back one last time to watch her walk into the house, he collided with the front wheel of the wagon and grunted in pain, leaning down to rub his knee.

Will chuckled as he worked on unhitching Ginger from the wagon. "I have to admit, I didn't think you'd be this nervous. It's so entertaining."

"Wait until it's your turn," Daniel said, reaching over the side of the wagon for Sara's suitcase. "Then you'll be a wreck and I'll get to laugh. What does she have in here? Rocks?"

"Never happen." Will lowered the wagon's shaft to the

ground and led the two horses to the entrance to the barn where he stopped and began removing their bridles. "Although if all mail order brides are as pretty as Sara it could almost make me reconsider my vow of bachelorhood." He smiled. "Almost."

Daniel lowered the heavy suitcase onto the ground and Bess wandered over to sniff it. "One day you'll get the urge to settle down."

"Why on earth would I do that? I get to keep all my money, don't have any responsibilities, I can do whatever I want, and when I need some female companionship..." He shrugged one shoulder.

Daniel didn't respond. He knew his brother was no stranger to the saloon in town. It worried him to see how far Will had fallen away from God, but all he could do was pray. He'd given up arguing with him long ago.

"Give me a hand with the trunk, will you?"

Will left River and Ginger outside the barn and joined Daniel at the back end of the wagon.

Will grunted as they lifted the heavy wooden trunk to the ground. "No, I believe she's packed her rock collection in here. Is this all she has?"

They each took a handle and started for the house.

"She said she didn't want to bring too much in case it didn't fit. I think I may have overplayed the size of the house in my letters." Daniel frowned as he looked at his home. "I just didn't want her to be disappointed in anything once she got here."

Will stopped, causing Daniel to almost stumble as he was forced to a halt.

"She's not going to be disappointed," Will said. "Not in the house or the farm, and certainly not in you. You're a good man and you're going to make her happy. She'll know that. And that's the only time you'll ever hear me say it." He started walking again. "Besides, with such an outstanding brother-in-law around how could she possibly be disappointed?"

Daniel chuckled, shaking his head. "Can't imagine."

They maneuvered the wide trunk through the narrow back door and carried it through the kitchen and living room and on to the bedroom where Sara was standing looking through the lace curtains covering the window, a gift from Daniel's mother when she'd found out he was going to be married.

She turned towards them as they entered and Daniel came to an abrupt halt. She'd removed her bonnet and the light from the window framed her reddish blonde hair, making it glow. For a few seconds all he could do was stare.

Until Will, stuck outside the door, nudged the trunk against Daniel's leg.

He looked down, embarrassed, and moved further into the room, allowing Will in behind him. "Where would you like this?"

Sara looked around the room. "Here at the foot of the bed will be fine, if that's all right."

Bess brushed past their legs and went straight to sit beside her new friend.

"I'll go and get your case," Will said when they'd set the trunk down, flashing Daniel a small smirk before leaving.

"Sorry it's so heavy," Sara said, indicating the trunk with her free hand while she ruffled the top of Bess' head with the other. "I brought some of my books, although I noticed all the books you have in the living room. Would I be able to borrow them?"

"No, you can't borrow them." He regretted his choice of words when her face fell. He stepped forward and raised his hand to touch her, before thinking better of it and letting it drop to his side. "Everything here is yours now. You can do whatever you want with anything you want, including taking any books." He spread his hands to encompass his small home. "What's mine is yours and you can't borrow your own things."

The smile she gave him set his heart racing. The photograph she'd sent had been beautiful, but in person she took his breath away. And best of all, she would be the last person he saw each night and the first person he'd see each morning. He gave silent thanks to God for what may have been the hundredth time since he'd met Sara at the station.

Thankfully Will chose that moment to come in with Sara's suitcase, interrupting Daniel's unseemly staring. Again.

"Could you put that on the bed?" Sara said when Will hesitated, looking around.

"Well, I'll finish up with the wagon while you two get acquainted." He shot Daniel an unsubtle look and then smiled at Sara. "I'm really glad you're here. Having a woman around is certainly gonna brighten this place up. And..." he glanced at Daniel and then leaned towards Sara as if he was about to impart a secret, "...Dan's been a wreck waiting for you. It'll be nice to have the old Dan back."

Daniel's gut dropped. "Will!"

His brother laughed as he backed out of his reach. "See you for supper!" And then he was gone, still laughing.

Daniel winced as he turned back to Sara. "Sorry about that."

"I understand," she said, her eyes dancing with amusement. "I have a younger brother at home too. Believe me, I understand."

He pushed his hands into his pockets, half relieved, half still embarrassed. "James."

Her face lit up. "You remembered."

He should have. He'd read each one of her letters so

31

many times he could recite them by heart. "It was easy to remember, with him and my other brother sharing the same name. And you have an older sister, Grace, who is married to Paul, and a baby niece, Carol." He almost winced. He hadn't intended to show off at being able to remember her family.

The smile slid from her face as she nodded, her lips pressing together and moisture shining in her eyes.

Daniel gasped in horror, stepping forward. "I'm sorry, I didn't mean to upset you. Please, I..." He wanted to punch himself. She hadn't been there fifteen minutes and he'd already made her want to cry.

She shook her head, wiping at her eyes with her knuckles. "It's not you. I just miss my family. Carol is growing so fast. I've only been gone a week and she'll already have changed."

He knew it; she hated it here and she wanted to go home. How could he expect any woman to want to leave her family and travel all the way across the country just for him?

Going to the dresser against the wall opposite the window, he took a clean handkerchief from the top drawer and handed it to her.

She sat on the bed and dabbed at her eyes. "Thank you."

Unsure what to do, he pushed his hands back into his pockets and shuffled his feet. "Would you like me to leave you alone?"

"No," she said in a small voice. "Please stay."

He sank into the pink upholstered armchair that had also come from his moth65er and rested his elbows on his knees. Staring at the vase of wildflowers on the windowsill he'd picked this morning to try to brighten up the room, he wished he knew what to do.

"I'm sorry," she said, "I think I'm just overwhelmed and tired from the journey."

"I guess this must all be very different from what you're

32

used to in New York." He glanced at the plain white walls. The sturdy but simple furniture. Himself. He hadn't even dressed up. Adam had worn a suit to meet his bride. Why hadn't Daniel bought a suit to wear?

Sara looked around her. "Yes it is, but I like it very much."

A snort escaped before he could stop it. He waved a hand around the room. "This?"

A smile crept onto her face. "Yes, this." She ran a hand over the carved foot of the bed. "It's... homey."

Not the word he would have used for his functional but uninspiring house. "It is?"

"Yes. Just a few touches here and there, some paint, and it'll be perfect. Would you mind if we had some color on the walls? Just a bit?"

He shook his head in happy confusion. Just a moment ago there had been tears in her eyes, now she was making plans for their home. Women were amazing. Strange, but amazing.

"Anything you want to change is just fine by me. Truthfully, I've been so busy with the farm that the house was really just a place to sleep and eat. I haven't done much to it at all since I bought it other than fix what needed fixing, so whatever you want to do, go ahead. Just tell me what color and where to put it and I'll have the walls painted in no time. The general store in town stocks paint in all kinds of colors. I'll be going to the market on Wednesday so you could come with me if you'd like." He was so relieved she wasn't crying that he didn't seem to be able to stop talking.

She smiled and he wished the chair was closer to the bed so he could reach out and take her hand. Although maybe it was too soon for that. But he still wished.

"I'd like that very much," she said.

"So, um, you're not sorry you're here?"

33

Her eyes widened. "Oh no, not even a little bit. I just miss home is all. But I chose to come here." She looked down, her cheeks turning the most becoming shade of pink. "And I'm truly glad I'm your wife."

All the words left his head in a rush. "I... uh... I'm really glad you're my wife too. You have no idea."

She laughed, covering her mouth with her fingertips, and the sound ignited a warmth inside him he'd never felt before. If he'd been able to look at his own heart, he wouldn't have been surprised to see it glowing.

Where she was lying on the floor, Bess raised her head from her paws and listened for a moment before scrambling to her feet and bounding out the door.

Footsteps heralded Will's appearance in the open doorway. "Sorry to interrupt, but Mrs. Goodwin's here. And she has food." He disappeared again.

"Mrs. Goodwin?" Sara said.

Daniel couldn't help smiling. Things were looking better and better.

"Mrs. Goodwin is a local legend. You are going to love this."

CHAPTER 3

Sara sat on the bench on the porch behind her new home and gazed at the distant mountains bathed in the orange glow of the sunset. It was a breathtaking sight and she wondered that she'd lived her whole twenty-three years without seeing anything so magnificent.

She silently thanked God for bringing her to this place. She was still embarrassed at her emotional reaction to Daniel's mention of her family earlier. He'd done nothing but make her feel welcome and the last thing she wanted was for him to think she didn't want to be there.

She snuck a surreptitious look at him from the corner of her eye where he sat at the other end of the bench. He seemed more relaxed than when they'd arrived at the house, one foot resting on the opposite knee and his arm draped over the back of the bench towards her. She had an almost overwhelming urge to slide closer to him where it could settle around her shoulders. She remained where she was, however, a cushion at her back and a shawl wrapped around her instead of Daniel's arm.

It was the first time they'd really spent any time alone other than on the journey home, and she was glad of the opportunity. She liked Will very much, but she found herself wanting to talk to Daniel, just the two of them.

Will had left not long after supper. He hadn't said where he was going, but Sara had caught Daniel's look of disapproval. But he hadn't said anything to her about it so it wasn't her business.

She and Daniel had been sitting together on the bench for a while, Bess stretched out at their feet, watching the changing colors of the evening and talking. It was wonderfully comfortable. Initially she'd worried it might be awkward, their first real conversation, but after months of exchanging letters it felt... right.

"I must ask Mrs. Goodwin for the recipe for her beef stew and dumplings," she said, pulling her shawl tighter around her against the falling temperature. "I don't think I've ever tasted anything quite so delicious in my life."

Daniel's eyes went to her shawl then moved to the space between them and for a moment Sara thought he might move closer. She was disappointed when he didn't.

"Mr. Goodwin is a very lucky man," he said with a smile. "I suggested to her once that if she opened a restaurant people would come from miles around, but she said she just enjoys cooking for her neighbors. She's convinced an unwed man can't cook for himself so she likes to bring us meals every once in a while. I'm ashamed to admit it, but she's not far wrong where Will and I are concerned."

"Does that mean she won't bring you meals anymore now I'm here?" She held one hand to her chest in mock horror. "I'm so sorry."

He chuckled. "I think I'll live. And I recall you mentioning your cooking skills in your third letter. I'm looking forward to sampling them."

Sara suddenly wished she hadn't tried so hard to impress him. "Well, I thought I was a good cook, but having tasted Mrs. Goodwin's stew and dumplings I'm not so sure."

He gave her a smile that made her heart shiver. The ethereal light of dusk had turned his sun-kissed skin caramel and glistened in the dark waves of his hair. And to think she'd thought Henry handsome. He didn't even come close to holding the tiniest stub of a candle to Daniel.

"I'm going to love your cooking," he said.

"But you haven't even tasted it yet."

"Doesn't matter. I know I'm going to love it."

The way he was looking at her, his eyes glowing with warmth, sent her heart from shivering to thumping. She suddenly wanted to kiss him so badly she had to scrunch her toes in her shoes to keep from throwing herself across the space separating them. He held her gaze for so long she felt sure he was going to take the initiative and move closer.

And then, to her horror, she yawned.

She slapped her hand over her mouth, her eyes widening. "I'm so sorry! I'm not bored, I promise."

His laughter warmed the chilly evening air. "I'll try not to take it personally. You've had a long journey. I'm surprised you're still awake. We should probably turn in anyway."

He stood and opened the kitchen door, standing back for her to walk ahead of him into the house. In the living room he lit two lamps, set one on a sideboard, and carried the other into the bedroom, placing it on the nightstand.

Pushing his hands into his pockets, he turned to face her. "The bedroom is yours. I'll be sleeping in the living room until we... well, until we know each other better."

Despite the low light, she was sure she detected the hint of a blush coloring his cheeks.

"I'm pushing you from your bed?" she said, mortified.

"Don't worry, I'll sleep fine. For the first year I lived here I didn't even have a bed. Just had my bedroll on the floor. To be honest, I was always so tired back then I could have slept on a rock. I'd take the other bed in the bunkhouse, but Will snores so loud after he's been..." he paused, looking like he was searching for the right word, "...out, you'd swear the house was falling down. And I'll feel better knowing I'm

37

close if you need me."

She bit her lip. She hadn't known what was going to happen on their first night together and she'd been a little nervous about the prospect of them sharing a bed, but she certainly hadn't wanted him to be left sleeping on the floor.

"I feel bad I'm keeping you from your comfy bed."

"Please don't. I promise I will be just fine." A smile curled his lips. "And it's not like it's forever." His eyes darted to the bed and then lowered to the floor.

This time it was Sara's turn to blush. "No." She looked down at Bess who had followed them inside and was now sitting between them, her eyes flitting between the two of them as if she was following their conversation. "Does Bess sleep in here?"

Her ears pricked forward at the sound of her name.

"Oh, no, she sleeps in the barn. She's done that ever since I got her when I first moved in here. I tried to get her to sleep in the house, but she likes to be with the animals. I think she thinks she's guarding them or something. Apparently she thinks I can take care of myself."

Sara reached down to stroke her silky head. "I always have wanted a dog. I'll bet she was good company."

"That's why I got her. It was lonely out here by myself, before Will came. A neighbor's dog had puppies and I took one look at Bess and that was it."

She imagined Daniel holding Bess as a tiny puppy and melted a little.

"Anyway," he said, smiling as if he knew what she was thinking, which he couldn't possibly. She hoped. "I'll let you get some rest. Sleep well, Sara."

Goodness, how she loved hearing him say her name. "Goodnight, Daniel."

He walked to the door and glanced back at her. "You'll never know how grateful I am you've come all this way to be with me. I'm really glad you're here." And then he left.

"I'm glad I'm here too," she whispered to the closed door.

As she took her nightdress from the suitcase lying open on the bed, her eyes strayed back to the living room door.

How could she have *yawned?*

CHAPTER 4

When Sara woke the following morning, the sun was well on its way into the morning sky.

Finding her watch in the pocket of her dress, she was horrified to see it was after nine and she'd overslept dreadfully. She hoped Daniel wouldn't think she was lazy.

After washing and dressing as quickly as she could she opened the door and peered out into the living room. A bedroll and pillow were folded neatly in the corner, but Daniel was nowhere in sight. She stepped one foot out the door before stopping and looking down at her bare left hand. Shaking her head, she returned to the bed and took her wedding ring from where she'd left it on the nightstand. At least Daniel hadn't been there to see her forget it.

She slipped the gold ring onto her third finger and held her hand up to admire the way it looked before returning to the living room. In the kitchen she found a blue checked dishcloth draped over something on the table. Propped against it was a note written in Daniel's familiar handwriting.

Good morning, Sara!

I know you must be very tired so I didn't want to wake you. Will and I are working in the fields today and I want to get an early start so I can get home before the sun sets. I'd like to show you around the farm a bit, if you're feeling up to it.

If I had the choice I'd spend the whole day with you, but there's always work to be done! Tomorrow after church we can have the rest of the day together. I'm looking forward to that very much.

We've taken our lunch with us, so don't worry about cooking. Please feel free to do whatever you want today, except work. You need to rest, so as your husband I'm ordering you to enjoy yourself! By the way, that's the only order I'll ever give you. I won't be the kind of man who treats his wife like a servant.

Bess is going out with us so don't worry that she's not around.

Have a relaxing day,

Daniel

Sara realized there was a smile on her face.

She was sad to have missed him, but the letter went a good way to making up for her disappointment. She read it again, twice, then she took it into the bedroom and placed it in the drawer where she'd put all his other letters to her. They were among her most cherished possessions and one day she planned to show them to their children and grandchildren.

A thought came to her - had Daniel kept her letters to him? She looked around the room for likely places he would keep such things before stopping herself. She wasn't going to snoop. Yes, they were husband and wife, but snooping was definitely an activity you didn't engage in until at least the second week of a marriage.

He might keep them in one of the drawers he had kept for himself in the bedroom.

But she wouldn't know because she *wasn't going to snoop.*

To distract herself from temptation, she returned to the kitchen and picked up the dishcloth on the table. Underneath was a plate of sliced bread, butter, and a jar of honey, along with a glass of milk. Another piece of paper leaning against the glass read, *Remember, no cooking! Dinner is in the pantry.*

Laughing, she investigated the small pantry and found a tray loaded with smoked pork and boiled potatoes along with a jar of preserved tomatoes and two boiled eggs, plus a handful of apricots. It was a simple meal, but she didn't mind. Another piece of paper read, *Have a good day. I'll see you later.*

She held the note to her chest and sighed, well aware she had a big, silly grin on her face. She couldn't wait for the afternoon when he'd come home.

After the bread, butter and honey breakfast, which was delicious and she decided to have as often as possible from then on, she went exploring.

Sara's mother had taught her and her sister how to cook at an early age, so even though they had a cook, she knew her way around a kitchen. Every young lady, Mama always said, needed to know how to cook, clean, run a household and look after her husband so that he could provide for and take care of her. Having staff didn't mean Sara would never have to do those things for herself. Of course, Mrs. Worthing had never imagined her daughter would be living all the way across the continent in the wild country of northern California, but Sara was grateful she'd been prepared to be a wife.

What neither her mother nor anyone else in their household could teach her, however, was anything about farming. She didn't have the first idea about what it took to be a farmer's wife, but she was determined to learn.

The first thing she did was set out to investigate the barns, passing the large pump for the well which sat not far from the house. On seeing it the day before, Sara had been relieved to find running water inside the house as well. She hadn't relished the thought of having to fetch her water from outside.

The smaller of the two was set back behind the bunkhouse where Will lived, its brown roof looming over the smaller building. The thick wooden walls were weathered to a silvery gray that shimmered in the rays of the sun, beautiful

42

in its own way. Sara imagined a simple trellis covered with climbing roses brightening its walls and wondered if Daniel would mind. Pink would contrast wonderfully with the color of the wood.

She tugged on one of the huge doors, expecting it to be difficult to open, but the hinges were well oiled and it swung with hardly any effort. Inside, dust motes hung in the air, a shaft of sunlight from a window high up on the wall making them sparkle and dance as she walked in.

To her right were stacks of lumber which was probably the wood Daniel was going to use to enlarge the house. Next to it a ladder ascended to a hayloft and most of the rest of the space was taken up with shelves of boxes and jars of seeds, tools, and some paraphernalia she assumed had something to do with beekeeping. Most of it she had no idea about. She had a lot to learn.

Beyond the small barn was a large enclosure surrounded by stout wooden-framed fencing filled in with wire mesh. Within the fence was a chicken coop and at least thirty chickens contentedly pecking amongst the grass and dirt. They paid her no attention whatsoever as she approached. Sara had plenty of experience eating chicken but absolutely none with the live variety. She supposed collecting eggs wouldn't be difficult, but would she be expected to pluck and prepare one? *Kill* one? The thought made her shudder as she watched the brown and white birds using their claws to scratch at the earth and then gobbling up anything they found. Hopefully Daniel or Will would take care of that part.

The chicken enclosure stood next to the pasture. River and Ginger were out with Daniel and Will, but the large grassed field still held one occupant - a golden brown cow. It lifted its head from the grass and turned its gaze on Sara and, after a few seconds of study, plodded towards her.

Sara stepped back from the fence a little as it

approached. Cows were another animal she'd had plenty of culinary acquaintance with, but that was where the familiarity ended. Up close, they were disturbingly big.

The cow reached the fence and hung its head over the top, staring at her with its huge brown eyes.

"Hi," Sara said, "I'm Sara. I guess we're going to get to know each other over the next few days."

The cow continued to stare at her. It was unnerving.

Being the only cow there, Sara assumed it was for milk, so it followed that at some point she'd have to milk it. She looked at the udder hanging beneath it with some trepidation.

"I'm just going to say this now, so we understand each other," she said. "When I milk you for the first time it's going to be awkward for both of us, but I hope we can become friends anyway."

An ear twitch was the only acknowledgement the cow gave.

"Well, I'll let you get back to eating."

After a moment's hesitation, she reached out and gingerly patted the cow between its ears. It shook its head, stared at her for a few seconds more, then turned and plodded away.

"Well, what were you expecting?" Sara murmured to herself. "A deep conversation?"

She continued past the pasture to the larger barn.

Not only was it larger, it was also clearly newer, its walls still a relatively fresh shade of golden-brown. She guessed the small barn had been here when Daniel bought the farm and this was his own addition. Inside was a much more impressive space, large enough to house a series of stalls for the animals and leaving plenty of room for a workbench, a threshing floor, and some farm related equipment Sara didn't recognize.

44

Looking around her she felt a sense of pride at all that Daniel had accomplished on the small farm. And he'd done it all in anticipation of having a family. In many ways, her arrival was the culmination for him of years of hard work. She'd never before considered how much her coming here to be his wife must mean to him.

"Oh, Daniel," she whispered, tears pooling in her eyes even as she smiled. "I hope I can be everything you've been working for."

At the sound of a horse approaching outside she quickly wiped at her eyes and went to the barn entrance, wondering if Daniel had returned early and hoping he had.

Outside, a single-horse buggy was circling around the side of the house. It came to a halt in the middle of the yard and the driver waved to Sara as she jumped to the ground. "Good morning!"

Sara wiped her hands on her skirt and walked over.

"You must be Sara," the woman said, smiling. "I must say, your picture didn't do you justice. Daniel must be thrilled."

"Uh, yes, I am. And thank you." Should she know who this woman was?

"Oh, I'm sorry, I haven't introduced myself." She stuck out her hand. "I'm Mrs. Raine, but you can call me Abigail. I'm Daniel and Will's ma."

Sara's stomach dropped to her shoes.

Daniel's mother. Her mother-in-law. Here. In front of her. Now.

Mrs. Raine, Abigail, laughed. "Well you look like you've just found a skunk in the larder. I guess this is a surprise. But you don't have to worry, I already like you."

"I, um..." Sara looked at Abigail's hand, still outstretched between them. She rapidly shook it. "I'm sorry, Mrs. R... Abigail. I don't mean to be rude, you just caught me by surprise. If I'd known you were coming I'd have given you a better welcome."

She waved a dismissive hand. "There's no need to stand on ceremony with me, Sara. You're my son's wife. We're family now."

"Of course, yes." Sara smiled, hoping it didn't look as strained as she felt. "Would you like to come inside? Daniel and Will are out in the fields. I don't know exactly where though."

"That's all right, I mostly came to see you anyway." She followed Sara into the kitchen. "I had some errands to run and thought I'd come over and meet the woman who has finally captured Daniel's heart."

Sara rapidly grabbed the plates and glass she'd left on the table from her breakfast and put them into the sink. "Please, have a seat. Would you like some tea or coffee?"

Did Daniel even have any tea? She looked around the room, uncertain where to start. If she'd known her new mother-in-law was going to turn up out of the blue, she would have started her exploration of the farm in the kitchen.

She felt two hands rest on her shoulders.

"Relax," Abigail said, "I'm not here to judge you. You have a seat. I'll make the coffee. I'm guessing I'm more familiar where everything in here is anyway."

"Oh no," Sara gasped, mortified, "I couldn't let you make the coffee. You're the guest."

Abigail guided her to a chair and gently pushed her down onto it. "Whenever you come to my home you will never be just a guest, and I expect the same in yours."

Sara's shoulders slumped. This was not how she'd envisioned her first meeting with Daniel's mother. "I so wanted to make a good impression."

Abigail's bright laugh calmed her nerves, just a little.

"You've made my son happier than I've ever seen him.

46

You couldn't make any better impression than that."

Sara watched her mother-in-law light the stove, realizing she didn't even know where the matches were. Attempting to make the coffee herself would have been extremely embarrassing.

Abigail Raine looked much younger than the fifty-three Sara knew her to be from Daniel's letters. Daniel and Will had clearly got their dark hair and eyes from their mother, and their looks. Although her hair was now peppered with silver, it was still thick and lustrous, and she looked as strong and slender as any woman in her twenties or thirties. Sara hoped she'd look as good in thirty years.

"Daniel has made me very happy too," she said, voice filled with sincerity.

"I should hope so, what with you coming all this way just to marry him." Abigail placed the kettle onto the stove and came to join her at the table. "I wanted to be at the wedding, we all did, but Daniel said he didn't want to overwhelm you, with you having just arrived. He's very..." she paused, looking up at the ceiling as she searched for the right word, "concerned that you be happy here, right from the start."

"It wasn't much of an event. There were three couples. We couldn't have been in the church for more than half an hour. Not that I minded," she added rapidly, in case it sounded as if she was complaining.

"I can't imagine what it must be like to marry someone you've just met. I know you had to do it for propriety's sake, but still. Daniel's father and I knew each other for ten years before we finally married."

Sara looked at her hands folded in front of her on the table. "I felt like I knew Daniel from his letters. They always seemed to me like they were from his heart. And now I've met him and spent a little time with him, I think I was right. I know he's the only one for me."

Abigail patted her hand. "He feels the same way." She rose to fetch a tin of ground coffee from the pantry. "I admit, I came here specifically to talk to you. Maybe a little bit to find out how you feel about Daniel. He's been so excited for you to get here that I worried he might have been..." She glanced back at Sara before returning her attention to preparing the coffee.

"Disappointed?" Sara volunteered.

Abigail laughed. "I guess so. Sometimes reality doesn't measure up to our expectations."

"I worried about that too, before I got here. About if we'd like each other, if we'd get along, if we'd be able to talk easily or would it be all awkward silences. If he'd be attracted to me."

"If you'd be attracted to him?" Abigail said.

Sara winced. The last thing she wanted was for her mother-in-law to think she was overly concerned with appearance. "Maybe a little," she admitted. "Not that I had any reason to worry about that."

"Goodness, no." She brought two steaming cups to the table and took her seat. "One thing I managed to do right with my boys was pass on the Raine good looks. I was besotted with my husband from the first moment I saw him." She smiled. "Even though I was only nine at the time, and him eleven."

"Actually, I was thinking Daniel and Will look a lot like you," Sara said.

Abigail erupted into laughter. "I think you and I are going to get along wonderfully."

Sara took a sip of her coffee. Maybe meeting her mother-in-law this soon wasn't so bad after all. "Can you give me any advice about being Daniel's wife? What his favorite foods are," she lifted her cup, "how he likes his coffee, what he'd

48

like to see me wearing, anything he particularly doesn't like, that kind of thing?"

She wasn't sure if it was strange to ask a woman she'd only just met those sorts of things, but she didn't want to waste this opportunity to gather any information she might need to get her marriage off to a good start.

"Well, first I should say that I don't think there's one thing you could do that will make my son think any less of you. And as for food, if you knew what they've been eating with just the two of them here you'd realize that anything you cook will be no end of an improvement." Her smile faded and she studied her coffee for a few seconds. "The one piece of advice I will give you is for your benefit, not necessarily his. Daniel is very much like his father, him and his older brother both. My husband is the most loving, wonderful man you could hope to meet, but he also has very deeply ingrained ideas about the role of the man in a family. A man is the provider and protector. It's his job... no, more than that, his *purpose* to look after his wife and children and make sure they are safe and have everything they need. And Dan's mind works that way too. Now I don't want you to get the wrong idea, there's nothing wrong with that. But there will be times, believe me, when you'll need to remember it. Now Will," her smile returned, "he's completely different. But that's a whole other story."

Sara simply nodded, wondering what to make of what Abigail had said. She supposed if that was Daniel's only fault, if a fault it was, it didn't seem like a bad one.

"Now," Abigail said, "tell me your plans for this place. Because I know you must have some. It's just weeping for a woman's touch."

Sara laughed and looked around her. "Well, I haven't had time to think about it too deeply, but I do have some ideas..."

CHAPTER 5

"Should I wake her?"

"I don't know. She's *your* wife."

"She looks so peaceful. I don't want to disturb her."

"Then don't wake her."

"Doesn't she look pretty when she's sleeping?"

Will rolled his eyes. "You've been talking about her all day. You're smitten with her; I get it."

Daniel would normally have countered Will's teasing with some of his own, but since he *had* been talking about Sara all day he couldn't really do anything but smile. He freely admitted he couldn't get her out of his mind. And she was exceptionally pretty sleeping as she was now on the settee, sitting sideways with her head resting on the back and her feet tucked up beneath her. A book lay open on her lap, as if she'd fallen asleep reading.

A curl of red-blonde hair had escaped from her chignon and lay against her cheek and he had the strongest urge to wrap it around his finger. He was only distracted by Will's amused expression and he shooed him away. Will, smiling, walked into the kitchen.

Left alone with his sleeping wife, Daniel wasn't sure what to do. After some thought, he crouched down beside her and gently touched her shoulder. She drew in a deep breath, slowly opening her eyes, and he was again struck by the color. They were the most beautiful shade of pale, luminous turquoise. He wondered how long they would have to be married before he could gaze into them without making her feel uncomfortable. Was a day too little?

She smiled sleepily when she saw him. "I just meant to read for a while."

"You're still tired," he said. "You should rest. I can give you a tour of the farm tomorrow..."

"Oh, no."

She sat up, dislodging the book from her lap, and he caught it as it fell. As he handed it back to her their fingers touched sending a shiver up his arm.

"Thank you," she said, her face betraying no hint that she was aware of the effect she had on him. "I want to see the rest of the farm, I really do."

Sitting had brought her face to barely more than a foot from his and suddenly gazing into her eyes felt less like a choice and more like an irresistible compulsion. It was only when her cheeks turned pink and she dropped her gaze that he realized he'd been staring again. For how long, he had no idea.

Clearing his suddenly arid throat, he rose to his feet and backed away until his calves hit an armchair and he had to stop. "Well, I'm ready whenever you are."

She swiveled her legs off the settee and pushed her feet into her shoes, her skirt rising a little. At the flash of an ankle Daniel rapidly looked away, which was ridiculous because they were married and it was perfectly acceptable for a man to see his wife's ankles. Except now he was deliberately looking at the window and if he looked back at her it would seem like he was doing it specifically to see her ankles.

It seemed there was a wealth of nuances to being a newly married man that he hadn't anticipated. Maybe he should just have a frank talk with her. 'Sara, as your husband, would you mind if I ogled your ankles?'

Or maybe not.

51

"I'll just get my shawl," she said, standing. "Will we be going in the wagon?"

"No, we'll walk. It's a nice day. If you don't mind."

She flashed him a smile as she passed. "I don't mind at all."

He watched her disappear into the bedroom, let out the sigh he'd been holding, and wandered into the kitchen.

"Smooth," Will said from where he was sitting at the table eating a slice of bread and honey.

"Stop spying on me."

"But it's so entertaining."

Daniel tried to cuff the back of his brother's head, but he ducked out of the way. "Don't you have tools to clean?"

"After my snack. And I'm sticking around to watch you be awkward with Sara some more."

Daniel sighed again. "Is it that bad?"

"No. Well, yes. I don't know what's wrong with you. I don't have any trouble talking to her. She's great."

"That's because you aren't falling..." He stopped, surprised at himself.

"Are you falling in love with her?" Will said, his eyebrows rising.

Daniel didn't answer, but to his horror he felt his face heating.

"Oh my goodness, you're blushing."

"I am not blushing!" He was, he knew it. "Leave me alone."

"You-" Will stopped abruptly as Sara walked into the kitchen.

Daniel fervently hoped she hadn't heard their conversation. To his relief, she didn't look embarrassed.

"Hello, Will," she said, her eyes going to his impromptu snack. "I would have had something ready for you to eat, but he wouldn't let me cook." She indicated Daniel with a quick flick of her head and smiled at him.

"We've made it this far on our inexpert culinary skills," Will said. "I can survive a bit longer. Not that I'm not looking forward to getting decent meals, but a week on a train would be enough to knock anyone out, so I'm with Dan on this one. And you won't hear me say that often."

"Well, I'll make sure you'll always have something to come home to in future."

"I am going to love having you around," he said, grinning.

Sara smiled back at him. "Oh, by the way, your mother came to visit this morning."

Daniel almost swallowed his tongue. "She what?" he wheezed.

Will snorted a laugh. "Like you didn't see that coming. Were you seriously expecting her to stay away?"

"Until Sara was settled, yes! I asked her to give it a few days, at least."

Will took another bite of bread. "Have you met our mother?"

Daniel gave Sara an apologetic look. "I'm sorry. I begged her to not just show up, I honestly did."

Thankfully, she smiled. "I'll admit I was a little nervous when she arrived. OK, a lot nervous. But she was very nice. She stayed for a while and I enjoyed talking to her. I like her very much."

She liked his mother. One hurdle down. "Did she... um... give you any advice?"

Sara merely smiled and began clearing the honey and butter away.

Daniel groaned inwardly. "She did, didn't she?"

"Let's just say our chat was very... informative."

Still chewing, Will chuckled with his mouth shut.

A terrible thought occurred to Daniel. "Did she tell you

53

any embarrassing childhood stories?"

Sara's face lit up. "She has embarrassing childhood stories about the two of you?"

Will stopped laughing.

"No," Daniel said quickly, "none at all. Right, Will?"

"Uh, yes. I mean no." For someone who was so good at poker, Will's ability to bluff was terrible.

Sara looked like she was trying not to laugh. "Maybe I'll pay her a visit soon."

Daniel knew there was no way he was getting out of this. Maybe Sara would think his mother's tales of his misadventures as a child were adorable. "Just bear in mind that I was very young."

"And I was even younger," Will added, standing from the table and popping the final bite of bread into his mouth as he led the way outside.

Walking past Daniel on the porch, Will elbowed him in the side and whispered, "It's not a sin to fall in love with your wife." Then he said more loudly, "Enjoy your walk," and headed in the direction of the barn.

Daniel surreptitiously glanced at Sara to see if she'd heard, but her attention was directed out across the pasture. He liked having Will around and he had been a huge help with the farm, but sometimes he wouldn't have minded trying out being an only child.

"I think this is my favorite view in the whole world," Sara said as they descended the steps into the yard.

Daniel followed her gaze towards the distant mountains. "It was one of the reasons I decided to buy this place. It hadn't been lived in for years and it was badly overgrown and run down, but I could see the potential. And that view had me from the moment I stood here."

She turned to look back at the house. "Would you mind if I started a garden here? Just some grass and flowers? I used to love gardening back home. Not that I did a lot of the work, we had a gardener for that, but I did what I could."

He looked at the porch steps that led down into, well, nothing. He'd never really noticed before how the packed earth of the yard that stretched to the barns and the pasture beyond simply stopped at the house, featureless and dull. It would take a lot of heavy digging to get anything to grow in it.

"You can do anything you want." As if there was any question he wouldn't give her anything and everything she asked for.

She gave him a smile that made every aching muscle he knew it was going to take worth it. For him, at least. Will would be getting good cooking and a caring sister-in-law, so he couldn't complain. Well, he could, but Daniel wouldn't listen.

As they passed the open doors of the big barn, Bess raised her head from where she was lying on a blanket draped over a stack of hay. She'd spent most of the day chasing mice and butterflies while he and Will planted the first corn field. Evidently deciding that was enough exercise for the day, she lowered her head again and closed her eyes.

He and Sara took a track along the side of the pasture where the animals were grazing. He pointed to the odd one out in their mini herd.

"That's Peapod, our milking cow."

Peapod raised her head for a few seconds to look at them then returned to tearing up the grass around her. Daniel always got the impression she resented him in some way, although he wasn't sure for what.

"We met earlier, briefly," Sara said. "Why's she called Peapod?"

"She already had the name when I bought her. No idea why they called her that."

"Does her milk taste of peas?"

He laughed. "Not that I've noticed."

She stared at the cow. "I don't know how to milk a cow. There's a lot I don't know about farming." She looked up at him, her expression uncertain as if she thought he'd be disappointed in her.

He wanted to kiss away the lines of worry from her forehead so badly he had to swallow before speaking. "That doesn't matter, I can teach you everything you need to know. I'm looking forward to it."

She smiled. "I am too."

His heart shimmied around his chest. He wished he'd offered her his arm when they'd started walking so he could be as close to her now as he wanted to be.

"Lots of the advertisements from the men in the marriage service's pamphlet said they wanted a woman with experience of farm work. Some of them even listed the skills they wanted her to have. They sounded like they were advertising for a farmhand rather than a wife."

Daniel shook his head in disbelief. "Some men have their priorities badly wrong."

He couldn't think of anything he wanted more than the love of a good woman, her soft touch to soothe away the work of a long day, to be wrapped in her love the way he would wrap her in his. He'd grown up seeing it with his parents and it was all he'd ever wanted for his own life.

"That's why I answered you," she said, her eyes ahead of her as they walked. "You sounded like you wanted a *wife*, someone to share your life with, to raise a family with." She glanced at him quickly before looking to the front again. "To love."

She understood. He'd known she would. "That's exactly what I wanted."

She flashed him another glance. "Me too."

Now he *really* wanted to kiss her. He pushed his hands into his pockets.

As they walked a bee buzzed past, its flight catching Sara's eye.

"That's one of mine," he said, for something to say other than begging her to let him wrap her in his arms.

She stared into the distance where the bee had flown, even though it was far out of sight now. "How can you tell?"

"It had my brand on it. It's very difficult to see unless you know where to look. It's a tiny DR. Takes me an age to brand them all."

Her mouth opened and she gaped up at him in momentary astonishment before he could no longer keep his lips from twitching.

She pushed his arm. "You're teasing me."

He grinned and looked down at the path ahead of him. "I'm sorry."

"Don't be."

He raised his eyes and they gazed at each other until his heart was racing and she looked away again. Could this woman really be his wife? He felt as if he should pinch himself to make sure he wasn't dreaming..

"How many hives do you have?" she said after they'd walked for a while in silence.

"Twelve at the moment. I've just begun harvesting this year's honey, now the trees have been flowering for a while. The bees love the blossom. It makes the best tasting honey too."

"Was that what I had this morning? Because it was delicious."

"It was. I'm glad you like it." Glad was an understatement. He was thrilled.

"Is it difficult, the harvesting?"

"Not really, not if you know what you're doing and

you're careful. There's a book by a man called Langstroth that's been really useful helping me understand the bees. We get along a lot better now."

"Don't you get stung?"

He smiled ruefully. "I can't tell you it's never happened, but I've learned how to not rile them. The more relaxed they are, the less likely they'll sting."

They'd reached the farm's extensive orchard and Sara came to a halt, turning in a slow circle to take in the trees in their various stages of flowering and fruiting. "It's beautiful," she breathed.

He always thought the same thing, although right now it was hard for him to look at anything other than his wife.

"Having this many mature fruit trees was another reason I bought this place. Took me an age to get them all pruned right, especially at the beginning when I didn't really know what I was doing. Most of them were overgrown and weren't producing as much as all the books said they should have been. But the year after I moved in I had so much fruit I could barely keep up with picking it all. I lived on peaches and cherries and plums and apples for months. Now I sell more than I eat."

"Mrs. Gibson, our cook, made the most delicious cherry pie. I begged her to teach me how to make it. May I have some cherries when they're ready?"

"They're just about ready now." He pointed to a heavily laden cherry tree with its fruit beginning to darken. "We'll have to start picking in about a week. You can have anything you want. And make as many pies as you want. I'm serious, there can never be too many pies."

Her laughter made him feel like his feet had left the ground. He tried to think of something else funny to say.

"It smells wonderful." She closed her eyes and took in a deep breath. "And I can hear humming."

When she opened her eyes again, he pointed up into the branches of a nearby peach tree that was flowering. "Just keep looking."

She stared at where he'd pointed and after a few seconds her eyes widened. "I see them. They're everywhere!"

He forced his eyes from her face and looked up at the thousands of bees stripping the flowers of their nectar. The whole canopy was awash with movement. "They go elsewhere too, but they can't get enough of the fruit trees. That's why I have the hives nearby."

Her expression of delight helped ease some of the worry he'd been carrying with him for weeks; that she wouldn't be happy on his little farm. She'd lived in a large, fancy house in New York, with servants and everything taken care of for her. In comparison, the life he could offer her was nothing but hard work.

The truth was, he'd been astounded she'd had any interest at all in him, and he still wasn't entirely sure why she had chosen this life over the privilege she'd enjoyed at home. He wasn't sure why she had chosen *him*. For weeks, the joy of knowing she was coming had been tainted by the fear that she would be disappointed once she arrived.

And yet, here she was. She'd married him. And so far she seemed to be happy.

No one was more surprised than he was.

"I have wheat and barley and corn fields, a fairly big vegetable plot, and you know about Peapod and the chickens for eggs," he said as they carried on past the orchard. "It's really just a smallholding to give me some extra to sell so I can buy whatever else we need."

"You don't keep any animals for meat?"

He winced internally at her question. He'd hoped it wouldn't occur to her to wonder about the relative lack of animals on the farm, but he should have known she was too smart for that. "Uh... no. We buy all our meat from the other farms or Mr. Walker, the butcher in town." Daniel cleared his throat and looked at the ground, but he couldn't help noticing her scrutiny.

"I get the feeling there's more to this."

He glanced at her and smiled. Definitely far too smart to miss anything. "Well, the truth is there were fields on the farm when I bought it that had been used for grazing. When I moved in I bought a pregnant sow and a ewe with a couple of lambs, thinking I would be able to breed them and use the meat."

"And...?" she prompted when he didn't elaborate.

"And the pig had her piglets and they and the lambs grew up and eventually it came time that they were ready to be slaughtered. And..." he cleared his throat again, stalling for the right words to come, "it became apparent that I had a problem with becoming emotionally attached to my animals. I couldn't kill them. I couldn't even sell them to someone who would."

Her hand went to her mouth, covering a smile. Was she laughing at him?

"What happened to them?"

"I gave them to my parents and told them not to tell me what they did with them. You may have noticed I have a lot of chickens. They weren't all meant to be for laying. Couldn't kill them either." Might as well get all the embarrassing details out there. "I bet you didn't think you'd be marrying a farmer who doesn't even have the guts to kill his own food."

Expecting disappointment when he looked up, he was surprised to see her gazing at him with what looked very much like admiration.

"It doesn't take guts to kill something," she said, "but I think it does take guts to care. And, well, when I looked at the chickens this morning I was hoping I wouldn't have to learn how to kill any of them."

"So you don't think your husband is a poor excuse for a supposedly tough frontier man?" He had to know.

She smiled again, her cheeks coloring a little. "I think my husband is exactly what I hoped for."

He breathed out, relieved. And thrilled. But mostly relieved.

"Are those them?"

He had to look around him to find out what she was talking about. He'd momentarily forgotten why they were there.

"*Oh*, the beehives. Yes, that's them."

The twelve hives were spaced around a grassy area surrounded by shrubs, where they would get enough sun without overheating. He'd made them all himself, based on Langstroth's plans but with some tweaks and simplifications, and he was proud of them. The bees seemed to like them. He was hoping Sara would too.

"They're wonderful!" Her face lit up in excitement. "Could I see inside one day?"

"You sure can. We'll come back in a few days to check the combs, see if any of them are ready to harvest."

She stared at the hives in silence for a while. "I want to learn everything. I know it must seem strange that someone like me, with my upbringing, would want to do this, but I promise I'm not expecting to have everything done for me. I want to be a real farmer's wife and be a help to you. If you'll teach me."

Daniel fought the huge smile struggling to burst onto his face. "It would be my pleasure."

God had brought him the perfect wife. That's all there was to it.

CHAPTER 6

When Daniel walked into the kitchen through the back door the next morning, Sara was tying on her apron. She smiled as he entered sending a thrill through him that was becoming wonderfully familiar.

He leaned against the doorframe, attempting to look casual. "Good morning. Did you sleep well?"

She grimaced prettily. "Too well. I was going to make biscuits for breakfast, but I don't think I'll have time before we leave. Will eggs and bacon and bread be OK?"

"Don't bother with cooking. We can have bread and honey."

"I have time to cook, just not to bake."

"Well, actually, there's something outside I want to show you." He endeavored to be the picture of nonchalance.

She stared at him, a small smile creeping onto her face. "What's going on?"

Apparently, he was failing. "Come with me and you'll find out."

Looking uncertain but intrigued, she took off her apron and laid it over the back of a chair.

He led the way from the house, a little nervous and more than a little excited about what he was about to do. He'd been waiting a month for this moment, right from when he received Sara's letter accepting his proposal.

A mare he'd bought from his parents and got up extra early to fetch stood patiently tethered outside the barn.

"Her name's Rosie," he said as Sara approached. "I bought her from my pa. My niece named her, kind of. She was only two at the time so it came out more like Wosie, but my brother got the gist."

"She's beautiful," Sara breathed, touching her hand to the mare's golden neck. She laughed as Rosie turned her head to nudge her shoulder.

"She's yours," Daniel said.

Sara's hand stilled against the horse's creamy-white mane. "Mine?"

"You said you love to ride and what better place is there to ride than out here?" He swept one hand to encompass the mountains with their blue peaks touching the sky in the distance beyond the pasture. "And I thought you'd be missing your own horse."

He watched as she gazed up at the mare, hoping he'd made the right choice. Should he say he could get her another if she'd prefer?

"She's the most beautiful horse I've ever seen," she said, her voice tinged with awe. "You really got her for me?"

He breathed out in relief. Personally, the color of a horse didn't make any difference at all to him, but he knew these things were important to a woman. "I thought you'd want to ride. I don't mind at all if you ride River and I know Will wouldn't mind you using Ginger, but I hoped we could go riding together. Rosie's a good, strong, calm horse."

To his shock, Sara turned from Rosie and wound her arms around his waist, laying her head against his chest and murmuring, "Thank you. She's wonderful."

His heart racing, Daniel gently placed his palm against the top of her back. "I'm really glad you like her."

Too soon she stepped back, and he immediately missed the feel of her against him.

Wiping her fingers beneath her eyes, she gave him a

tremulous smile. "I'm sorry I keep getting emotional. It's just, I do miss my horse and this is the nicest thing you could have done for me."

He could have laughed for joy. He'd got it right, and even better, it had got him a hug. Today was shaping up to be one of the best days of his life and he hadn't even had breakfast yet.

~ ~ ~

Sara walked out into the sunshine, tucking a stray strand of hair into her bonnet. In front of the barn Daniel was hitching River and Rosie to the wagon.

He'd given her a horse, simply because he knew she would miss her own. She still couldn't get over it. An animal like Rosie would have been no small expense, not to mention the extra she would cost in feed. But he'd done it anyway, to make her happy. Just when she thought he couldn't be any more amazing, he proved her wrong.

Thank you for Daniel, Lord, she prayed silently as she watched him. *Thank you for bringing us together. I know I began to doubt after Henry that I would ever find a man I could love, but Daniel is perfect.*

She looked at the bunkhouse as she walked across the yard. There was no sign of movement and Will hadn't been at breakfast.

Daniel looked up as she approached, his eyes flicking down to her blue silk dress and back up again. She'd changed after breakfast, not wanting to risk spilling anything on her best Sunday clothes.

"That's a really pretty color," he said, returning his attention to buckling River's trace but darting glances at her. "It suits you."

She looked down at herself. "Thank you. This has

64

always been my favorite dress to wear to church."

He finished what he was doing and straightened, pushing his hands into his pockets and leaning against the side of the wagon. He was wearing black trousers instead of his usual denim, with a white shirt and light brown waistcoat. Dressing up looked exceptionally good on him. Although she had to admit, everything looked exceptionally good on him.

"Well," he said, "I probably shouldn't be thinking about this, it being a church service and all, but you'll definitely be the prettiest girl there."

She hoped she wasn't blushing again, but she suspected she was. "Thank you." Was it her imagination, or did she sound slightly breathless?

He pushed away from the wagon and held out his hand to her. "May I assist you into your carriage, my lady?"

She bobbed a curtsey. "Why, thank you, my lord."

If she hadn't been breathless before, she certainly was by the time he'd helped her up into the wagon, which seemed to involve a little more contact than was strictly necessary. Not that she was complaining at all.

Bess trotted up to them and Daniel rubbed her head before ordering her to stay and climbing onto the wagon. He picked up the reins from the seat between them.

Sara glanced at the bunkhouse. "Isn't Will coming?"

Daniel's smile faded. "He isn't home yet."

"Isn't home yet?" she said, confused. "Where is he?"

He heaved a sigh as they pulled around the house and onto the road that would take them into town. "I guess this is as good a time as any to tell you. You were going to find out soon enough anyway. My brother is a good man and there's no one I'd rather have working with me on the farm, but he isn't exactly what you'd call respectable." He paused as if reluctant to speak his next sentence. "He's a regular at Green

Hill Creek's saloon."

Sara tried to keep the shock from her face, but she wasn't at all sure she succeeded. "The saloon? You mean..."

"Gambling, to start with."

"He gambles his money away?"

"Oh no, he's actually very good at that part. Always could beat me at poker. He plays a few games, wins a lot of money," he glanced at Sara and then back at the road, "and then spends the rest of the night losing it on drink and women."

This time Sara gasped. "You mean..." She tried to think of a polite way to say it and couldn't. "Prostitutes?"

"Yeah." He sighed again. "Please don't think less of him. I meant it when I said he's a good man. You'd have to go a long way to find one better. He'll do anything for anyone. It's just that he's lost himself. I've been praying for him for a long time."

"Doesn't he believe in God?"

Daniel shrugged. "Used to. Gave his life to Jesus and everything when he was young, even before I did. But when he reached seventeen or so he got in with the wrong crowd, started doing the wrong things, and fell away. I think he still believes, he's just stopped following Him right now."

Sara was quiet for a while, trying to reconcile the kind, funny, hardworking brother-in-law she knew with the man Daniel had just described to her. It wasn't easy. "I think I'll be praying for him too."

His smile of gratitude warmed her heart. "I'd appreciate that. And I think, deep down, Will would too."

They reached the Green Hill Creek Emmanuel Church half an hour before the service was due to start, but the area outside the doors was still filled with people. Daniel brought the wagon to a halt at the fringes of the crowd and helped Sara to the ground.

"Will you be all right while I take the horses round the back?" he said.

She looked around and almost immediately spotted Lizzy in the throng. "I'll be fine. Lizzy's over there."

He followed her pointing finger with his eyes. "She draws attention, doesn't she?"

Lizzy's dress was bright yellow and matching flowers adorned her bonnet. Her arm was looped through her husband's and she was talking animatedly to the group of people they stood with.

Sara couldn't help but smile. "She certainly does."

As Daniel drove the wagon to the back of the church where River and Rosie would be watered and safe with the other horses, Sara wended her way through the small groups of chatting congregants. She was almost to her destination when she heard something that stopped her dead in her tracks.

"I've never known Mr. Emerson to behave in such a way. I wouldn't suggest anything untoward, but the whole situation is deeply disturbing."

Another woman joined the conversation. "I'm given to believe that back east Miss Watts was a..." she lowered her voice, "lady of low morals, if you know what I mean."

The first woman gasped. "I hadn't heard that!"

"It's no wonder that young man has been so beguiled. There's no telling what's been going on behind those post office doors."

Sara had heard enough. Burning with anger, she stepped up to the tight huddle of four women.

"You are so right. I..." The woman who was speaking saw Sara and stopped abruptly and the other three turned to see what had her attention.

"Uh... good morning... Mrs. Raine, I believe?" The second woman Sara had heard spoke. She was older, possibly in her fifties, wearing a dark green velvet dress that had probably been purchased several pounds ago.

"I couldn't help overhearing your conversation," Sara said, praying silently for restraint.

The other three women glanced at each other, clearly not wanting to meet her gaze.

"And I was put in mind of my Bible reading from this morning," she went on. "It was from the thirty-fourth Psalm; I'm sure you good Christian women are familiar with it. It speaks about keeping the tongue from evil and the lips from guile."

The woman in the green dress drew herself up. "I'm not sure what you're implying..."

"I'm implying that you are talking about my friend and circumstances about which you have no idea and about which you are completely wrong. So perhaps you shouldn't be talking at all."

The woman gasped in indignation. "Well, I never..."

"Then maybe you should," Sara snapped.

One of the other women slapped a hand over her smile.

Sara turned on her heel and stalked away, seething. It occurred to her she'd probably just made an enemy after only being in town for five minutes, but she never could stand gossip, especially when it was at the expense of a friend.

Lizzy and Richard had disappeared in the time she'd been berating the gossiping women and after a brief, fruitless search of the crowd Sara assumed they must have gone inside. She altered her direction for the door and spotted Jo's husband, Gabriel, standing a little way away.

"Mr. Silversmith," she said, waving to get his attention.

At first he seemed uncertain who she was, then his face brightened in recognition. "Mrs. Raine," he said, "real nice to see you again."

Sara looked around. "Is Jo inside?"

"Josephine isn't feeling well," he replied with a frown. "Said it was something she ate on the train. She's taken to her bed this morning."

"Oh, I'm sorry. Is there anything I can do to help?" Sara was disappointed. She'd so wanted to see the whole group.

"I'm sure she'll be just fine. All she needs is a few days to rest, she said. It was a long journey, but I guess you know that."

"It certainly was. I slept so late yesterday morning my mother would have been horrified," she said, smiling.

"Um... yes. Well, hope you enjoy the service." With a tip of his hat, Mr. Silversmith turned and walked into the church.

"Hmm," Sara murmured to herself. She hoped he was more talkative at home. Maybe he was just worried about Jo.

They'd all eaten the same meals on the train and the rest of them, as far as she knew, weren't sick. Maybe she'd ask Daniel or Will to take her to visit Jo during the week, just to check on her.

She made her way to the door where she found Mr. and Mrs. Goodwin greeting those entering.

"Oh, Mrs. Goodwin," Sara said, "your beef stew and dumplings were the most delicious thing I've ever eaten. Would you mind giving me the recipe? Although I can't imagine I'll come anywhere near making it as good as yours."

She could still remember the way the succulent dumplings had practically melted in her mouth. No wonder Daniel and Will had been so excited when Mrs. Goodwin had arrived on Friday.

The older woman's face lit up in delight. "Why thank you so much, I'm real pleased you liked it. It was my pleasure to welcome you to the town. And of course you can have the recipe."

"Thank you. I don't think Daniel and Will would forgive me if I didn't try it. They both raved to me about your cooking and I can't blame them one bit."

"You're such a dear for saying so." Mrs. Goodwin patted her arm, smiling. "By the way, someone was asking after you. Tall, thin fellow. Didn't say his name."

Sara tried to think of any tall thin men among the few people she'd met since arriving in Green Hill Creek and came up empty. "I can't imagine who it might be. Is he still here?"

Mrs. Goodwin looked at the people outside. "I can't see him. Can you, dear?"

Mr. Goodwin craned his head, scanned the crowd and murmured, "Nope," around the stem of his pipe.

Sara shrugged. "Never mind, I'm sure whoever it was will find me eventually."

Mr. Goodwin handed her a hymnal and removed his pipe just long enough to say, "Ma'am."

Inside the building was much the same as outside with groups of men and women standing and talking and children playing together. It seemed church was a much more social occasion here than Sara was used to, but she supposed when a scattered community came together everyone wanted to catch up with their friends and neighbors.

She stood up as tall as she could and searched the room for Amy's blonde hair or Lizzy's floral bonnet, but couldn't see either of them. She did, however, spot Louisa sitting at the front and so headed in her direction.

"So how is Miss Woods today?" she said as she took the empty chair beside her. "Or is it Mrs. Johnson yet?"

Louisa laughed and reached out to give her a hug. "Not yet. How is Mrs. Raine?"

"Mrs. Raine is very well." She couldn't help smiling. "And very happy with Mr. Raine. Daniel is wonderful."

Louisa was studying her face. "I can see that. You're practically glowing."

"I am not." She touched her fingers to her face. "Am I?"

Her friend grinned. "I'm afraid so."

"Well, what about you and Jesse? Is he here?"

"Yes, he's here." She nodded across the room. "I believe he's talking to your husband."

Sara twisted in her seat to see Daniel on the other side of the church. He looked over at her and smiled and her heartbeat speeded up a little, as usual.

"Um... has Daniel told you about Jesse?"

She dragged her attention from her husband back to Louisa. "Yes, he has."

"He asked me to give him two weeks and I said yes. I was shocked, I won't deny it, but I understand why he didn't tell me." A smile stole onto her face. "And we spent the most wonderful day together yesterday. He is an amazing man. And, well, very handsome."

"So you think you might be staying permanently?" she said, willing Louisa to say yes.

A small frown creased her forehead. "I don't know. I mean, Jesse's wonderful, but... did you know how small this place is?"

Sara looked around, confused.

"I don't mean the church," Louisa said, "the town. Green Hill Creek. I thought it would be... bigger. More... well, bigger."

"Daniel told me it was small in his letters. I guess coming from a big city we're used to more," she waved her hands outwards, "everything. But I like it. It's so clean! And don't you think it's beautiful? I could look at those mountains all day."

"Oh yes, it is lovely. Jesse took me for a drive to show me around. It's just, with the railroad here we thought, I mean I thought there would be more to it. But it's nice here, it really is." She gave a small shrug and smiled.

"I'm sure you'll get used to it," Sara said, hoping she

would.

"I'm sure you're right." Her eyes focused beyond Sara. "Isn't that Adam?"

Sara turned to see Amy's... well, she wasn't sure what to call him. Friend would probably be the best moniker, for now. "That must mean Amy's here. I wanted to speak to her about... well, you know. To tell her we support her."

"You go ahead," Louisa said, a soft smile on her face as she watched Jesse approaching. "I'll see you all afterwards."

Sara squeezed her hand. "Have fun."

She greeted Jesse as they passed each other, continuing to where she could now see Amy, sitting near the back and looking forlorn and alone.

Well, that was going to change. No gossiping busybodies were going to make any friend of hers sad, not if Sara had anything to say about it.

~ ~ ~

At the close of the service Sara expected everyone to go home quickly, but instead the churchgoers lingered, greeting each other and chatting in groups as they had been when she and Daniel arrived.

She enjoyed spending the extra time with Amy, Lizzy and Louisa. Even though it had only been two days since they'd last seen each other, she'd missed them. The train journey and the shared experience of travelling so far from their homes to find new lives had created a bond between them she'd rarely felt with other friends. She almost felt, as Lizzy had said to them earlier, that they were conquering the west, blazing a trail for women everywhere, and following their dreams. Albeit in a very small way.

She also spoke to Adam and Jesse, both of whom were sweethearts and almost as handsome as Daniel. Sara was relieved. She didn't want either Amy or Louisa to leave and if anyone could persuade them to stay it was those two men. Lizzy's husband was a little hard to read. Richard Shand was polite and friendly, but he seemed almost standoffish towards his new wife. Lizzy didn't say much about it, but it was obvious she was having a hard time getting to know him. Sara prayed they would find a way to become close and fall in love. She couldn't help wanting every one of her friends to be as happy as she was.

Eventually Daniel brought the wagon around and they left the thinning crowd in front of the church. Sara waved to Amy as they passed her and Adam on their way home to his post office.

"Don't tell Amy I said so, but Adam's crazy about her," Daniel said as he guided River and Rosie along the main road towards home.

Sara gasped in delight. "He is?"

"He really wants her to stay. She's your friend; do you think there's any chance she will?"

"I was just as surprised as anyone that she didn't intend to marry him when she got here. To be honest, I think she's not sure what she wants. She thinks she knows, but she doesn't."

Daniel glanced at her with a smile. "You sound very sure of that."

"It could just be wishful thinking because I don't want her to leave, but I've been known to have insight into emotional matters like this."

"Oh, you have, have you?"

"I'm extremely insightful. Ask anyone."

His dimple deepened as he chuckled. "I'm sure you are. And I hope you're right. Adam needs someone. I'd like him to be as happy as I am."

Her heart skipped a beat. "You're happy?"

73

He nudged her shoulder with his. "You're the insightful one. You tell me."

Sara's smile didn't leave her face the entire way home.

CHAPTER 7

When they arrived back at the farm, Ginger was in the pasture with Peapod. Sara left Daniel unhitching Rosie and River and went inside to check on the chicken she'd set roasting in the oven.

She found Will laying the table.

"I thought I'd get a head start on this," he said. "I found the potatoes and carrots you left so I put them in about half an hour ago. I hope that's what you meant to do."

"It was, thank you." She went to the oven to check on the food gently sizzling inside. "Shouldn't be too long now."

"Good. I didn't want to wait to eat once you got home. This delicious smell is driving me crazy."

She closed the oven and straightened, taking a surreptitious look at Will. After what Daniel had told her about him before church she was expecting... well, she didn't know what she was expecting. That he would have transformed into some kind of depraved wastrel? But he was the same Will who had made her feel so welcome on the day she arrived and whose company, even in the short time she'd known him, she'd come to enjoy. It was hard to imagine anyone like him would do the things Daniel described.

It wasn't until Will spoke that she realized she'd been staring at him.

"Dan told you, didn't he?"

She nodded, embarrassed, not knowing what to say.

Sighing, he pulled a chair out from the table and

dropped onto it. "It's not something I'm proud of, if you're wondering. It's just..." He shrugged and picked up a fork, his eyes fixed on it as it slid through his fingers.

"What you do is your business." It was true. All she could do was pray, like Daniel.

He put the fork down and stared at his plate. "I just don't want you to think... I mean, I wouldn't ever do anything to hurt you or Dan. I don't want you to think badly of me. You can trust me. If ever you need me, I'll be here."

Somehow, Sara knew it was true. What a person did wasn't necessarily who they were. Not so long ago she had almost agreed to marry a man she didn't love and become someone she wasn't.

"I believe you. And I'm not here to judge you. I'm your sister-in-law and your friend and nothing is going to change that."

He looked up from the plate and for a moment she saw the uncertain boy inside the man. Then he flashed her a roguish smile and the glimpse was gone.

"Dan had his head screwed on right when he asked you to marry him, that's for sure." He shook his head and chuckled. "That was an interesting night when he wrote that letter."

Curiosity grabbed her. She looked out the window and, seeing Daniel was still dealing with the wagon, sat down opposite Will. "What happened?"

He leaned back, a smile tugging at his eyes. "I'm not sure I should tell you. Dan might not want you to know."

She reached out and gave his arm a light smack. "Oh stop it. You wouldn't have mentioned it if you didn't want me to know."

He laughed and sat forward, shooting a glance at the door as he lowered his voice. "Well, he'd just gotten your latest letter earlier that day and spent about an hour reading and rereading and rereading and... you get the picture. Like he always did. Anyway..."

Sara's heart leapt. "He read my letters more than once?"

"Are you kidding? I'm surprised they're still in one piece with all the handling they got. The number of times I walked in on him reading one of your letters. Each time a new one arrived he'd be grinning for the rest of the week. If I ever did anything wrong, which was hardly ever I hasten to add, I'd wait until one of your letters arrived so he'd be in a good mood when I told him."

She found herself blinking back tears. So Daniel had treasured her letters the same way she treasured his. One day she would ask him if he'd kept them.

"Anyway," Will said again, "that night during supper he suddenly said, 'I'm going to ask Sara to marry me.' That wasn't exactly a surprise to me; I'd seen it coming for months. But then he asked me for my help with what to say, which *was* a surprise because while I know I got the lion's share of the charm among the Raine brothers, marriage isn't exactly my area of expertise."

On the heels of her tears, Sara was now trying not to laugh. "So I really got a proposal from both of you?"

"Ha! I guess you did. Although the actual part asking you to marry him, that was all Dan." A faraway look drifted over him as he stared at nothing in particular. "Hours we spent on that letter. Must have gone through fifty sheets of paper, at least that's what it looked like when they were screwed up all over the floor. At one point we almost came to blows over one thing Dan wanted to include. Can you believe he was going to use Pea as a selling point? 'Please marry me, I have a cow.' Usually he has more sense than that, but he always did get all addlebrained when it came to you. Anyway, we finally had a version Dan was happy with and I thought was reasonably sure to get you to say yes, and then,"

77

he laughed, shaking his head, "a gust of wind came in through the window we had stupidly left open and blew the thing onto the fire. Dan threw himself after it and he would have plunged his bare hands in to get it if I hadn't grabbed him. By that time I don't think either of us were thinking that straight."

Sara's giggles were escaping into the hand she'd clamped over her mouth. "Was it burned?"

Twinkling eyes belied his somber nod. "Every word. We had to do the whole thing over from memory and I'm pretty sure we didn't get it quite the same the second time round. Still, you're here so it must have worked."

She thought about that letter, the one she'd been waiting for since she and Daniel had begun corresponding. Of course she knew the proposal by heart after the many, many times she'd read it.

My dear Sara, these last few months of writing to you have been among the happiest of my life. Every time I find something particularly difficult on the farm, I remember why I'm doing it and I'm smiling again. You make me smile, Sara. Even from all the way across the country you fill my life with joy and I don't feel like I can wait another second to ask you the question that's been on my mind ever since I read your first letter.

Sara Worthing, you are everything I've ever dreamed of. Will you marry me?

I know life here is very different from what you're used to, but I can only promise that if you say yes, I will spend the rest of my days doing everything in my power to make you as happy as you've made me.

Of course she'd said yes. In fact, she'd grabbed the first piece of paper she could find and scribbled a huge 'YES!!' across it. Then she'd replaced it with a more demure response, the gist of which had, nevertheless, been that same 'YES!!' But if she was honest, if all the letter had said was, 'Dear Sara, will you marry me? From Daniel,' she would still have said YES!! And then danced around the room for joy.

"It was the most wonderful letter I've ever read," she said. "Even without knowing of the Herculean effort the writing of it took."

"Just call me Will Shakespeare," he said, winking.

The back door opened at that moment and Daniel walked in. At their abrupt silence he looked between the two of them. "Why do I get the feeling you've just been talking about me?"

"Because you have an inflated idea of your own importance?" Will said.

"Ha. Ha."

He walked to the sink, smiling as he passed Sara. After hearing the story of his proposal, she wanted to jump up and throw herself into his arms. As he washed his hands she couldn't tear her eyes from him.

No one said anything for a full twenty seconds.

Daniel finally spoke to Will while drying his hands. "All right, what were you saying about me?"

"You're being unreasonably suspicious," he answered, leaning back in his chair. "Maybe you should write your feelings down. Away from any fires and open windows."

Daniel froze and then slowly rotated to look at him. "You didn't."

Will shrugged one shoulder. "She was bound to find out sooner or later."

"It's been less than forty-eight hours!"

"So, sooner then."

He gave Sara an apologetic look. "I promise every word of my other letters was written completely by me. I was just so nervous about asking you to marry me. I only had one

79

chance to get it right and not mess up the rest of my life."

Even if she'd had the courage to throw herself into his arms now, her legs didn't feel like they would hold her up. "I think it's wonderful." *I think* you're *wonderful.*

Daniel's gaze held hers until her heart was thudding.

And until Will loudly cleared his throat. "I'm still here."

Sara felt as if she needed to gasp in a lungful of air. Daniel sauntered to the table and took a seat next to her.

"I would have said yes whatever you wrote," she said, gazing into his smiling eyes.

"*Now* she tells us!" Will said, shaking his head. "Is it time to eat yet?"

CHAPTER 8

Since Daniel hadn't let Sara cook at all the previous day and all they'd had for breakfast was bread and honey, the roast chicken dinner was his first chance to sample his new wife's cooking. It was as delicious as Daniel knew it would be.

He'd made up his mind long before they met face to face that he would adore everything about her, just as his own father adored his mother. Growing up, it had been obvious to him that the secret to a happy marriage was mutual respect and a lot of love. He'd seen it every day of his life and it was what he wanted more than anything. So far, Sara was everything he'd longed for, including a wonderful cook.

Will seemed to be in agreement as he had second helpings of everything and stopped just short of picking up his plate and licking it clean of the gravy, Sara clearly trying not to laugh as she watched him.

After the meal, Will retreated to the bunkhouse, probably to sleep off the previous night's activities. Daniel was relieved Sara seemed not to have any problems accepting Will after what he'd told her about his brother. With him disappearing several nights a week, there had been no other option but to tell her. But he'd been nervous about it. The last thing he wanted was for a wedge to be driven between his brother and his wife. Thankfully, that hadn't happened. In fact, they seemed to be even more comfortable with each other. Embarrassing stories about how he'd needed his brother's help in proposing to her notwithstanding, that was a good thing. He almost envied Will in the way he made being comfortable around her seem so effortless.

Daniel had been unprepared for the effect Sara had on him. Half of him felt like a schoolboy at his first dance; the rest wanted to sweep her into his arms and find out if those beautiful, rose-pink lips tasted as sweet as they looked. She was spinning him in exciting, frustrating, dizzying circles. And he was loving every minute of it.

"Would you like to take the horses for a ride?" he said as they sat on the porch bench after dinner. "There's a lake not too far away I'd like to show you, beyond the farm."

She looked up from her book and smiled. "I thought you'd never ask."

Daniel saddled River and Rosie while Sara changed her clothes. He never could fathom the amount of different clothing women seemed to need, although he did understand her explanation that she didn't want to risk damaging the dress she'd worn to church. That would have been a shame. She was breathtaking in the blue gown.

But when she walked from the house in a pale green calico dress, he had to admit she looked breathtaking in that too.

It wasn't the dresses, it was her.

"Is this new?" she said as she reached him and ran her hand over Rosie's saddle.

"If it's not OK, I can take it back and get another one. I wasn't sure if you'd want to ride astride or not."

Her nose wrinkled. "My mother thinks riding astride is unladylike. She used to make me ride side saddle when we were in town and I hated it. So this is perfect, thank you."

He stepped into position beside Rosie. "Can I help you up?"

Her smile turned mischievous. "Well, I don't need you to, but I wouldn't object at all if you did."

It was a few seconds before Daniel realized his mouth was hanging open. It was another couple before he remembered he needed to breathe.

Smiling, she placed her foot into the stirrup and he lifted her into the saddle, keeping his hands on her only a few moments longer than was absolutely necessary and resisting the desire to pull her back down and into his arms. His self-control deserved a medal.

The journey began at a walk through the farm. Daniel watched Sara as she rode, gauging her comfort in the saddle. As she seemed perfectly at ease, when they emerged into open countryside he nudged River into a canter that she easily kept pace with. And then she surprised him by breaking into a full gallop, her laughter drifting back to him on the wind. With a smile stretching his face, he urged River after her.

They finally slowed as they approached the lake. Sara's cheeks were red from the wind, her eyes bright. Tendrils of hair had escaped her chignon and curled haphazardly around her face.

Daniel longed to release the rest and watch it tumble over her shoulders.

"That was amazing!" she said breathlessly. "I haven't galloped in so long. Rosie is wonderful." She stroked her hand up the horse's neck and Rosie snorted and shook her head.

"You're a really good rider," Daniel said, dragging his eyes from her hair. "I could barely keep up with you."

She laughed and patted Rosie's shoulder. "Well, if that's true I think my beautiful horse deserves most of the credit."

Daniel led the way to the lake's edge and, when the horses had drunk, he and Sara guided them into a walk parallel to the shore.

Their conversation was easy and light; two people

getting to know each other, moving beyond the attraction of their letters to the more intimate, personal connection only talking face to face could bring. He'd often wondered if he would like Sara in person as much as he did in her letters, finding it hard to imagine that being possible. But she'd surprised him by being even better in person. He couldn't help hoping she felt the same about him.

After a while, they heard familiar voices.

Sara brought Rosie to a halt and pointed through the trees ahead to a clearing at the water's edge.

"Look," she whispered excitedly, "it's Amy and Adam."

Daniel followed the line of her finger and saw his friend stretched out on a blanket in the clearing, Amy sitting next to him and Stride, Adam's black stallion, grazing nearby. As he and Sara watched, Amy leaned forward and kissed Adam's cheek. He said something and she laughed, climbed to her feet and went to sit on a rock at the water's edge.

Adam's eyes looked like they were closed, but even from this distance Daniel could see he was still surreptitiously watching her.

"Let's not disturb them," Sara whispered. "They look like they're enjoying each other's company. The more she gets to know him, the more she'll want to stay. I know it."

"That's fine by me."

Much as Daniel liked Adam he had no wish to enlarge his own little group of two either. He wanted Sara all to himself this afternoon and he suspected Adam felt the same about Amy. Adam could thank him later.

They took a detour around the clearing, wide enough to not be seen by the not-courting couple, and rejoined the path skirting the lake's shore further along. Eventually they came to an open area of golden colored grass dotted with scrubby bushes covered with clusters of tiny pink flowers. They dismounted and let the horses graze while they wandered down to the water's edge. Sara drew in a deep breath and closed her eyes, tilting her head to the sky.

Being as he was her husband, Daniel knew that he had the right to look at his wife. But he still felt a little guilty for allowing his gaze to stray from her still unruly hair, along her jaw and down her smooth neck. He imagined reaching out his hand, brushing his fingertips along the path his eyes had taken, moving to cradle the back of her head. She would open her eyes, look up into his with longing. He would step in close, lower his mouth to hers and...

She opened her eyes.

Daniel snapped his gaze away so fast it made his neck click.

"It's so beautiful here," she said, looking across the sky blue water to the mountain beyond. "When you described in your letters what it was like, I have to admit that I thought you might be exaggerating to impress me. But now I can see it for myself, I know that you weren't."

"I can't say I didn't ever try to impress you, but this was the one time all I needed to do was tell you the simple truth. From your letters, I knew you would love it here. I would never have asked you to marry me if I'd thought otherwise." He couldn't have been more relieved that he'd never thought otherwise.

She darted him a glance and then looked back at the lake, smiling slightly. "Then I'm extra glad that I do."

Daniel felt a deep sense of peace settle over him. Being here with Sara by his side felt so... right. He knew bringing her all the way across the country to his farm had been the right thing to do, for both of them. It was so easy to see their lives together in front of them now. He would work hard on the farm so he could look after her and she would make their house a real home. There would be children, grandchildren, and a life filled with love and laughter. It was what he'd been dreaming of ever since he could remember, and it was finally happening.

Thank You for Sara, Father. Thank You for our life together that's coming, I know it's going to be everything I've ever wanted. Help me to be the best husband I can be.

"I've been praying a long time for a wife," he said. From the corner of his eye he saw Sara look up at him, but he kept his eyes fixed on the scene before them. "All the time I was building up the farm, making it work so I could one day support a family, I prayed every morning and evening for the woman God had in store for me, and I trusted that He would bring me a good wife. But I never thought..." He took a deep breath and let it out slowly, lowering his eyes to the shoreline in front of him. "That Bible verse that says God can do much more than we ask or think of? I've never truly appreciated what it meant, until now." He glanced at her and then back out at the lake. "You're more than I ever asked for or imagined, Sara. I just wanted you to know that."

He could feel her eyes on him and wished he knew what she was thinking. Maybe it was too soon for his little speech, but he hadn't been able to stop himself. He needed her to know how much her being there meant to him.

Following a few long seconds of silence, he moved a little closer and brushed the back of his hand tentatively against hers and then waited. After a few moments, her knuckles touched his. Barely able to breathe, he moved his hand again, slowly edging it around hers. And then their fingers were lacing together, the warmth of her palm settling against him, her small hand nestling in the cradle of his.

As they held hands and watched the water gently lap the lake's shore, Daniel couldn't ever remember being so happy.

CHAPTER 9

Sara pegged the final item of laundry on the clothesline, one of Daniel's shirts, and stretched her aching arms out behind her.

Laundry. She'd never before had to do it herself, other than the time a few weeks ago when she'd asked Elspeth to teach her how in preparation for becoming a wife. She'd thought she was prepared. She wasn't.

Hopefully it would get easier as she went along. It was after three in the afternoon and she was only now just finishing after working for practically the whole day. She was developing a new appreciation for how hard her family's servants had to work. But she was a farmer's wife now, which meant doing her own laundry.

Breathing a deep sigh, she looked along the line at the clean clothing swaying in the warm breeze. There was a certain satisfaction to it, she had to admit. Or maybe that was just relief that it was over.

She winced a little at the pain in her back as she bent to pick up the empty laundry basket and dropped in the bag of clothespins. A rest was in order. She'd made a lemon pie for supper and had intended to wait until then to have a slice, but there was no harm in having a piece now. She felt she'd definitely earned it.

"Miss Worthing?"

She jumped at the voice, her stomach knotting. She'd thought she was on her own. For the first time since arriving, fear gripped her at being all alone out here. Daniel kept a rifle in the house. Would she be able to reach it if she was in danger?

"Miss Worthing, are you home?"

A tall, thin man clad in a long, black coat which surely must have been too hot for the weather appeared from around the side of the house.

She breathed out in relief. Not a stranger. Not exactly welcome, but not dangerous.

He waved when he saw her. "Forgive me, I tried knocking at the front, but there was no answer."

She tried not to let her shoulders slump. "Mr. Pulaski, this is a surprise. I didn't realize you were in Green Hill Creek."

His ridiculous pencil thin moustache curled up and disappeared into the corners of his mouth. "Yes, I decided to remain for a while. I've taken a room in the hotel. Forgive me for turning up unannounced, Miss Worthing."

It was the second time he'd asked for her forgiveness, but since he was currently standing between her and a slice of lemon pie he was barking up the wrong tree.

"It's Mrs. Raine now."

His smile vanished. "Yes. Yes, of course."

"What can I do for you, Mr. Pulaski?"

"To be honest, I'm happy to see a familiar, friendly face, being new to the area and all. I'm sure you know how I feel, you being new here too." His eyes darted to the house as if he was expecting an invitation inside.

Sara sincerely hoped her face *wasn't* being friendly. On the train from New York she'd been unfortunate enough to find herself in conversation with Mr. Pulaski on several occasions, and on each of those occasions she'd done her best to keep it short. Two days into the journey she'd begun to actively avoid him. It wasn't that the man was objectionable in any specific way, it was simply that he was quite possibly the dullest person she'd ever met. If there'd been contests for being dull, he would be a winner every time. His favorite subject was buttons. They were his profession, he'd told her. He made them. They were fascinating, he'd claimed. He was utterly wrong on that score.

"Well," she said, "if you are planning on staying, I'm sure you will get to know everyone here. It seems like a lovely town."

"Yes, I'm sure it is." He looked at the house again.

"I'm sorry," she said, "I'd invite you in but as you can see, I'm in the middle of laundry and I still have so much to do before my husband and brother-in-law return."

She lifted the basket as evidence, offering a silent prayer for forgiveness for the lie. Then she wondered if it was wrong to ask forgiveness for something she'd do again in a heartbeat.

His gaze dropped to the basket. "Oh, yes. I can imagine it's very hard work out here in the middle of nowhere. To tell the truth, I was also hoping to see your," he paused, his mouth tightening for a split second, "husband. I'm looking for temporary work and it was suggested to me he might be hiring some help for his farm."

Sara couldn't stop her eyes darting to his feet and back up again. Of all the things his black coat, black trousers, polished black shoes and pristine white shirt said, it wasn't 'farmhand'. Although he had one of those faces that made it next to impossible to pinpoint his age, she didn't think he could be more than thirty-five, but he didn't look like he could lift so much as a shovel. Daniel must have been twice his size, all of it muscle.

"I'm sorry, but he hasn't mentioned anything to me about needing help. But I'll ask him when he returns. He can contact you at the hotel?"

"Uh... yes. Yes, the hotel. Albert Pulaski."

"I know, Mr. Pulaski."

He gave a short, nasal laugh. "Of course you do, after all the time we spent on the train together. I very much enjoyed our conversations, by the way. I don't know if I ever told you that. The time I spent in your company made a long journey a delight, if I may say so."

"It was my pleasure." She almost grimaced at her second lie in as many minutes.

This time his mouth stretched into a wide, open smile. One of his teeth was gold. It glinted in the sunshine. "Perhaps we'll have the opportunity to spend some more time in conversation while I'm here."

She tried to make her smile look genuine, she truly did. "Well, as you mentioned, there is a lot of hard work here. But perhaps."

He nodded, still grinning. "I'll look forward to it, um... may I call you Sara?"

I'd rather eat nails. "I'm sorry, I don't think that would be appropriate, Mr. Pulaski."

He nodded rapidly. "Of course, you're absolutely right. It was wrong of me to ask so early in our friendship. Please forgive me."

Friendship? She was beginning to feel uncomfortable, although she couldn't put her finger on exactly why. "Well, it was lovely speaking with you, but I do have work to do, so..." She waggled the basket a little to get her point across. That point being, please go away.

"Oh yes, of course. I'll be on my way then." He took a small step backwards. "I hope I'll have the pleasure of your company again soon."

Even though it was probably rude not to, she didn't reply. There was simply no polite answer that could have conveyed her true feelings at that moment. Instead, she just smiled and willed him to leave.

He took another step back. "Well, farewell, Miss Wor... I'm sorry, Mrs. Raine." He turned away and strode back around the house. A minute later, she saw his buggy disappear into the trees along the road.

"Well," she muttered to herself, "that was odd."

The whole exchange had been strange. She watched the trees for a few more moments, shrugged, and headed for the kitchen.

She could think about it later. Right now, lemon pie was calling her name.

~ ~ ~

Daniel stared in amazement at the lines of clean clothing and bedding shifting in the gentle breeze. "You didn't have to do all this."

Sara shrugged as if it was nothing, but he could see it wasn't.

"At home laundry day was always on a Monday so I thought, why not? If you'd like me to do it on another day in future..."

"Oh no, any day is absolutely fine by me," he said quickly. "I just meant, you're still tired."

She winced. "About that, I promise I won't get up so late again. I don't know what happened this morning..."

"I didn't mean that." He wanted to kick himself. Why was he saying all the wrong things? "I just meant that I don't want you to do too much. Will and I can look after ourselves, more or less."

Her face fell. "But looking after you is my job as your wife. You work to provide for us, I look after you so you can."

Now Daniel wanted someone else to kick him. "No. I

91

mean yes, I do want you to look after me. I just don't want you to tire yourself out doing it. I'm not doing this very well, am I?"

At least that got her to smile again. He loved seeing her smile.

Will wandered through the laundry, gazing at it in awe as he ran a hand over one of his now clean shirts. "It all smells so good. What did you use?"

"Um, soap?" Sara replied.

He clicked his fingers as if some great mystery had been solved. "So *that's* how you do it." Grinning, he marched over and threw his arms around her. "Thank you. You are my favorite person in the whole world."

She laughed and hugged him back. "You're welcome."

Daniel tamped down a twinge of jealousy. She was *his* wife; *he* should be the one hugging her. If he wasn't constantly unsure of himself around her, he would have.

"I washed everything that was in the laundry basket in the house," she said as Will released her. "And I just picked up everything that was on the floor in the bunkhouse."

At least he had the decency to look embarrassed. "I'll use a basket from now on."

She smiled. "That would be helpful, thank you."

Daniel pushed his hands into his pockets. "For the record, you don't have to do Will's laundry, he can do his own. You're under no obligation to look after *him*."

Will smacked his arm with the back of his hand. "Stop discouraging her."

"I'm not discouraging her from doing *my* laundry."

"I don't mind," Sara said. "You both work hard."

Will pointed at her. "Favorite person. Ever." He began removing his dry clothing from the line. "I'm going to take this inside and just breathe it in."

Daniel glanced at Sara as she took the pegs from Will

and dropped them into the pocket in her apron. He hadn't really been discouraging, had he? When Will had left them for the bunkhouse, he walked up beside her and began taking down the rest of the laundry.

"I didn't mean to sound ungrateful. I am, very."

"I understand." She kept her eyes on the underwear she was removing from the line. "I like how you're worried about me. It makes me feel cared for."

His heart beat harder as he considered his next words. "I do care about you. Very much." Why was it so hard to tell her how he felt?

Her hands stilled, her eyes finding his. "I care about you too."

How long should he wait before he told her just how much he cared about her, that he couldn't stop thinking about her, and just being around her made his insides do somersaults? Because at that moment he would have shouted it to the world if he'd been able to tear his gaze from her face.

When he failed to say anything further, she lowered her eyes and continued working on the washing. "I had a visitor today."

It was a couple of seconds before Daniel could gather his wits enough to grasp her meaning. "You did? One of the other ladies?"

"No, it was a man."

He stopped working abruptly. "A man? Who?" He should have thought of this. Sara would sometimes be on her own all day. He had to make sure she was safe.

"His name is Mr. Pulaski. He was on the train with us, all the way from New York. We spoke briefly a few times. I didn't even realize he was staying in Green Hill Creek until he showed up this afternoon."

"What did he want?" He tried to keep his tone casual. Who was this man who visited lone women unannounced?

"He said he was looking for work and had heard you might be hiring."

Daniel would have laughed if he hadn't been so concerned. "I don't know who would have told him that. Everyone in town knows this is just a small farm. Maybe if it was harvest, but not at this time of year."

She placed the last of the pegs into her pocket and led the way to the house. "He didn't say." Her brow furrowed. "He seemed... I don't know."

She held the back door open for him and he walked in and placed the mound of clean laundry onto the table.

"Seemed what?"

She stared unseeing at the table for a few moments then shook her head. "It's nothing. He just came as I finished the laundry and I was tired. To be honest, on the train I dreaded being caught in a conversation with him. I don't like to speak ill of someone, but he was awfully boring."

He couldn't help smiling at her longsuffering expression. "Sounds terrible. And you trapped on a train with him for a week."

"Sometimes I would duck into a compartment if I saw him coming, any compartment. Once there was a couple inside kissing. I was so embarrassed, but they were very understanding once I explained."

He burst into laughter, imagining the scene. "You've suffered so much just to come and marry me."

She shrugged and picked up one of his shirts. "It was worth it."

Daniel's stomach flipped. He longed to hold her. Was it too late to follow Will's lead and thank her for washing his clothes with a hug?

She stopped folding the shirt and stared across the kitchen. "Oh, that must have been him."

"I'm sorry?"

94

She placed the folded shirt onto the table and picked up a sheet. He took one end and they backed away from each other, stretching it out between them.

"Yesterday when I went into church Mrs. Goodwin said a tall, thin man had been asking after me," she said as they worked. "I had no idea who it could have been at the time, but it must have been Mr. Pulaski. That's a mystery solved."

The man was asking about her and then turned up while she was alone. Daniel was probably overreacting by being concerned, but still. "Have you ever used a gun?"

Her eyes widened. "A gun? No! Why?"

"You need to be safe here while Will and I are out. I'd like to teach you, just in case you ever need it."

She took the folded sheet from him, placed it onto the table, and picked up another. "You don't have to worry about Mr. Pulaski. He's harmless."

"Not necessarily for him. It's lonely out here and it's not just people. There are coyotes and bears and wolves. I've rarely seen them and they don't come near the farm, but I just want to know you're safe. I'm sure you'll never need it, but I'd be happier knowing you're prepared."

She looked uncomfortable, but nodded. "I didn't think of that. Not many wild bears in New York."

"So you'll let me teach you?"

"If you think I need to learn, then of course." She smiled. "Wouldn't do for me to come all this way only to get eaten."

He let out a relieved breath. "It wouldn't. I'm too young to be a widower."

She laughed and handed him a pillow case to fold. It occurred to him how natural working with her came, even if they were just folding laundry.

"Oh," she said, "I think possibly the real reason Mr. Pulaski bothered me was he turned up when I was about to have a slice of lemon pie."

All of a sudden there were more pressing issues than this Pulaski person or teaching Sara to shoot. He looked around the kitchen in what he hoped was a nonchalant manner. "You made lemon pie?"

CHAPTER 10

When Sara woke on Tuesday morning the sun was barely above the horizon. This time, she was determined to have breakfast ready for Daniel and Will before they began their day.

Even though none of them had to prepare it, her mother had instilled in her and her brother and sister the habit of rising early enough that they could eat breakfast with their father before he left each day for his office. Sara had decided before even coming to Green Hill Creek that she would do the same for her husband, not because she had to, but because she wanted to. Today was the first day she hadn't overslept.

She pressed an ear to the bedroom door and listened for signs in the living room that Daniel was already up, but she heard nothing. Hopefully, that meant he was still asleep. After washing, dressing and making herself presentable, she quietly eased the door open and peeked out.

She was slightly apprehensive that she might walk in on Daniel in a state of undress which was a mortifying proposition. Despite being married to him, she wasn't quite ready for that. But she was safe; Daniel wasn't even awake yet. He lay on his back on his bedroll, the blanket tucked around his tall frame and his chest rising and falling in deep, even breaths.

She walked on silent feet towards the kitchen, almost making it before her burning curiosity brought her to a halt. It took her a few seconds to build up her courage, watching Daniel to make sure he wasn't in imminent danger of waking, before she crept across the room. She lowered into a crouch at his side, thankful her dress was made of soft, silent cotton instead of the starched material of many of her dresses back at home that rustled with even the slightest movement.

Up close, his face was peaceful and serene in sleep. Sara counted herself more than blessed, and maybe a little lucky. She'd been smitten with his letters, but she'd known what was on the outside may not have matched up to what was inside. It worried her that she thought that way. In the first book of Samuel it said that God looked at the heart, not the outward appearance. Sara wanted to do that too, but it was hard not to want at least a small amount of physical attraction to the man she would be spending the rest of her life with. Thankfully, Daniel's face was easily as beautiful as his heart.

Deep in slumber, he looked even younger. Not that he looked old anyway, but his lightly tanned skin was smooth and unblemished. Thick, dark lashes brushed his cheeks and his hair tousled over his forehead. Sara wondered if it was as soft as it looked. One curl stood up, crying out to be touched. Did she dare?

Holding her breath and biting her lip, she reached out a hand, slowly edging forwards until her fingertips gently brushed against the dark, shiny lock.

Daniel's eyes snapped open. He gasped in a surprised breath.

Sara leaped backwards with a yelp, tripped over a low stool behind her, and stumbled onto the settee, landing in an ungainly heap with her skirts splayed around her. She rapidly pushed them down.

Daniel had pushed himself up onto his elbows, his mouth hanging open as he stared at her. To her acute embarrassment, his blanket had slid down and his shoulders and chest, his very bare chest, were now exposed.

"Sara?"

She scrambled to her feet, looking anywhere but at her half naked husband. "I'm sorry... I was... sorry... I'll go and..."

And then she fled into the kitchen and slammed the door shut behind her.

~ ~ ~

Daniel stared at the kitchen door in astonishment. After a few seconds, he closed his mouth.

Waking up to Sara's pretty face hovering above him, her hand touching his hair, was far from unpleasant. But it had been a surprise. Had she been watching him sleep?

A smile spread slowly across his face as he thought about it. She must have been. The smile threatened to escalate when he recalled her chaotic scramble to get away from him. He clapped one hand over his mouth to muffle his laughter. The startled look of horror on her face when he'd caught her in the act had been adorable. How he looked forward to the time when she would be the first thing he saw every morning.

He shrugged the blanket off and climbed to his feet, finding his clothes where he'd thrown them the night before. He was really going to have to be tidier in future. He was a married man now.

A married man with a wife who made him happier than he'd ever thought possible.

Truth was, he loved how she'd come along and changed his life. He loved how she occupied his thoughts almost constantly. He loved the way just thinking of her made him smile.

He loved... her.

He abruptly stopped buttoning his shirt, drawing in a

99

breath of realization. He was completely and utterly in love.

Closing his eyes, he slowly released the air in his lungs and whispered on the sigh, "Thank you, Lord."

Bringing Sara to him had been God's doing, he had no doubt of that. His dream of a wife and family to fill his heart was becoming a reality and the knowledge gave him so much joy he almost laughed out loud.

Thank you, Lord!

Dressed, he went to the kitchen door and knocked lightly, not wanting to startle her again. When there was no answer he opened it to find Sara sitting at the table, her head resting on her folded arms and her face hidden. He slipped onto the chair opposite and touched her elbow.

"I feel like such a fool," she said into the tabletop without moving.

"That's the most fun I've had waking up since, well, forever. It certainly beats Will's smelly sock draped across my face which I had on an almost daily basis when I was thirteen. Until I threatened to smash his favorite toy wagon if he did it again."

She snorted delicately and lifted her face to look at him. "I didn't mean to... I mean... I didn't think you'd wake up." She winced. "Not that I was intending to touch you while you slept." Her eyes widened and she dropped her head back onto her folded arms with a groan. "I'm going to stop speaking now."

Daniel couldn't help it, he burst into laughter.

She raised her head again and a few seconds later she was laughing with him.

"I'm sorry," he said when he'd caught his breath. "I'm not laughing at you. It's just..."

"I know," she said. "It was kind of funny when you think about it."

He looked out the window, considering if he should say

what he was thinking. "You know, I don't mind if you watch me when I'm sleeping."

She didn't answer immediately and he wondered if he'd made a mistake in being so honest.

Then she smiled. "We have a whole lifetime of marriage ahead of us. I imagine it might include times when I watch you sleep."

He caught his breath, staring into her shining eyes, the urge to wrap her in his arms so strong that he had to stop his hands from sliding across the table towards her.

Her cheeks turned pink and she lowered her gaze, a smile playing across her lips. Darting another glance at him, she pushed back from the table and stood. "I'd better get breakfast started."

He leaned back in his chair as she walked past him to the pantry, following her with his eyes. His wife. His beautiful, fun, incredible wife.

Oh yes, he was definitely in love.

And, without a doubt, he was the most blessed man in the world.

CHAPTER 11

Sara swirled the soapy cloth slowly around a cup as she watched Daniel walk across the yard through the kitchen window.

He reached the small barn and looked back at her and smiled and she melted. At least, that was what it felt like. She was a little surprised her legs were still holding her up. A sigh escaped her lips as he walked out of sight into the barn.

She had spent an inordinate amount of time sneaking covert glances at Daniel over breakfast, despite Will being at the table with them. Once or twice she'd even caught him looking back at her. Was this love, she wondered, this thrilling feeling of happiness and excitement? If it wasn't, it had to be close.

She placed the wet cup onto the drainer, took the dishcloth from its hook, and picked up a plate.

She was still a little embarrassed about being caught touching his hair when he was asleep, but he didn't seem to mind. In fact, if she was reading him correctly, he rather liked it. She laughed quietly at herself. Being married to a man she was still getting to know was a strange situation to be in. Not that she wasn't thoroughly enjoying every moment.

A blast cracked the atmosphere. Black smoke spewed from the barn door.

The plate shattered on the kitchen floor.

Sara dropped the cloth and ran outside, almost stumbling down the porch steps in her haste, screaming

Daniel's name.

Bess stood in the middle of the yard, barking frantically.

Will burst from the bunkhouse and raced for the barn. He and Sara reached it together. He caught hold of her as she was about to run in, pushing her aside.

"Stay here," he yelled, dashing into the building.

Smoke and heat billowed from the open door. Sara's heart thundered in her chest as she blinked into the gloom inside. *Please, Lord, please let him be all right.*

Fifteen seconds that stretched into an eternity later, Will emerged from the door coughing, Daniel's limp body slung over his shoulder. He carried him away from the barn and gently lowered him to the ground, leaving him to rush to the well pump.

Sara threw herself down beside Daniel. She rested a palm on his chest, desperately praying for movement. To her immense relief, she felt his chest rise and fall. His clothing and skin were blackened and she felt a lump on the back of his head. The skin on his face was an angry red.

"What do I do, Lord?" she whispered, blinking back tears. "Please, tell me what to do."

A memory came to her of a neighbor being burned a few years before and the doctor placing his injured hand in cold water. She leaped up and ran inside, grabbing the cup and filling it with water.

Outside, Will was running buckets of water between the pump and the barn. Sara returned to Daniel's side and pulled her apron off, dipped the edge into the water and gently dabbed across his face. She repeated the process three times before laying the material over his eyes and slowly trickling the water over to soak it.

Will emerged from the barn, dropped the bucket and leaned his hands on his thighs, coughing violently. He looked on the verge of collapse, but before Sara could go to him he straightened.

"Fire's out," he panted. "I'll hitch up the wagon. We need to get him to the doctor."

As Will went to fetch the horses, Daniel groaned, his head lolling to one side and dislodging the wet apron.

"Daniel?" She took hold of his hand. "Daniel, can you hear me?"

There was no response.

By the large barn, Will was hitching Ginger and River to the wagon. Smoke drifted from the door of the small barn. A blackbird sang somewhere. Sara wondered how it could make such a beautiful sound while Daniel lay hurt.

Placing her hand on his chest and closing her moisture-filled eyes, she did the only thing she could. "Father in heaven, please lay Your hands on Daniel and heal him. Whatever is happening in his body, take away the damage. Lord, please, make him wake up." Tears rolled down her cheeks, but she ignored them. "Please don't take him from me when we've only just found each other. Please, Lord. In the Name of Your Son, Jesus. Amen."

At the sound of the horses approaching she wiped her eyes and looked up. Will brought the wagon around, set the brake and jumped to the ground.

"It's going to be a bumpy ride," he said, crouching next to his brother and pushing one arm beneath his shoulders and the other beneath his knees.

Sara watched in amazement as Will, obviously straining, picked Daniel up from the ground and carried him to the wagon bed.

She shook herself into action. "I'll get pillows."

Inside the house, she grabbed his bedroll from the living room floor and took all the pillows from her bed. She carried them out to the wagon then ran back inside for clean cloths and a canteen of water. It was the only way she knew to help his burns and she needed to help, somehow.

When she got back outside Will had finished placing Daniel onto the bedroll in the back of the wagon. He reached down to help her in. She batted his hand away.

"I can do it. Just get going."

She didn't mean to be short with him, but he seemed to understand as he nodded and headed to the seat up front. Bess jumped into the wagon and Sara followed her up. As Will got the horses moving she arranged the pillows around Daniel to cushion him from the ride. He'd need it.

Once round to the front of the house, Will shouted "Yah!" and snapped the reins and Ginger and River leaped into a gallop.

Sara grabbed the side of the wagon as it lurched into motion, bouncing along the uneven dirt road towards the town. She settled herself more securely and pushed the pillows in tighter around Daniel, trying to protect him from the worst of the wagon's movement.

Bess seemed to be coping better than Sara was. She lay beside her master, resting her head on his arm and staring at his face.

Since his groan back in the yard he hadn't made another sound. Checking for breathing was impossible with the wagon jostling them around so Sara took his wrist and felt for a pulse. When she found it she breathed a sigh of relief and murmured, "Thank You."

The previous times Sara had travelled between the town and the farm it had taken twenty minutes. This time it took less than ten but seemed like fifty. She spent the entire time keeping Daniel's burned eyes damp, trying to stay upright in the jouncing wagon, and praying. Always praying.

"We're almost there," Will shouted over the pounding of the horses' hooves. "How is he?"

She wished she had a different answer. "The same."

They slowed as they reached the main street and Will steered them straight to the doctor's office, bringing them to a halt at the front of the two storey wooden building that served as the doctor's office downstairs and his living quarters above.

She helped Will move Daniel to the back of the wagon where he again picked up his brother's limp form.

"Are you all right?" Sara said, watching him stagger under the weight.

He nodded. "Just get the door, please. Bess, stay."

She ran ahead and pushed open the door without knocking. "Doctor?" she shouted when all she found was an empty room filled with chairs and a desk. "Doctor, we need help!"

A door in the back wall opened and a man stepped through. He wore eyeglasses and had graying brown hair and a neatly clipped moustache and beard. "What..."

"There was an accident," Sara said, rushing up to him. "My husband's been hurt and he's unconscious. Please help him."

When he saw Will standing beyond her with Daniel he stepped back into the room. "Bring him through, Will."

A man was sitting on a chair, half an unwound bandage hanging from his hand. The doctor beckoned Will to an examining table in the center of the room.

"Mr. Prescott, would you mind if we finish up later?" he said as he and Will positioned Daniel on his back on the table.

"Ah, no, doc. I'll get Peg to do this. Hope he's all right." He nodded to Sara and, looking slightly queasy, made a quick exit.

Daniel groaned, the first sound he'd made since the farm. Sara rushed to his side and took his hand. "Daniel?"

"What happened?" the doctor said.

"Some kind of explosion in the barn, Doc Wilson," Will

said. "Smelled like kerosene in there. When I got inside Dan was on the floor like this." He paced short lengths back and forth across the small room, his eyes never leaving Daniel's face. One hand ran through his hair. Now he'd got Daniel to the doctor, he didn't seem to know what to do.

"Did he bang his head?"

"There's a lump," Sara said, "at the back."

Doctor Wilson lifted his head just enough to feel underneath. Daniel moaned again. "Has he been conscious at all?"

"No."

He studied his face. "What did you do to his skin?"

Sara swallowed, afraid she'd made a mistake. "I kept it wet. I saw a doctor do that once with a burn. Was that wrong?"

"No, you did exactly the right thing." He gave her a small smile and went back to his examination.

She breathed out. At least she hadn't made it worse.

Daniel moaned again and his fingers tightened around hers. "Sara?" he slurred.

She wrapped both hands around his, almost bursting into tears at the sound of his voice. "I'm right here."

Will rushed to her side. "We're both here, Dan. We're at the doc's. You're going to be OK." He glanced at Doctor Wilson as if seeking reassurance.

"Daniel," the doctor said, "can you speak to me?"

"Sara, are you all right?" His voice was stronger this time.

"Yes, I'm fine."

"I'm fine too, if you were wondering," Will said, the humor sounding a little desperate.

Daniel smiled faintly and then winced in pain. Sara noticed he hadn't made any attempt to open his eyes.

"Tell me where the pain is, Daniel," Doctor Wilson said.

107

"The back of my head, my left elbow. The worst is my eyes."

Sara rolled up his sleeve to check his elbow. A graze had opened the skin, but it looked superficial.

Doctor Wilson fetched a magnifying glass from a drawer and pushed Daniel's hair back from his forehead. "Can you open them for me?"

She saw Daniel's neck undulate as he swallowed and she tightened her hold on his hand, praying for strength for both of them.

His jaw clenched as he slowly forced his eyelids open. Sara stifled a gasp at the sight of the redness beneath. No wonder he was hurting.

"Good," the doctor said. "That's good." He used the magnifying glass to study Daniel's eyes. "Is the pain concentrated in one place or just a general ache?"

"General."

"Well, I can't see any foreign objects in the eyeballs so it must be the burning causing the discomfort. I'll give you something for the pain and eye drops for the burns. Now, let's have a look at that bump."

His fingers tightened around Sara's. "There's something else."

Doctor Wilson paused in the process of lifting Daniel's head. "What is it?"

He stared at the ceiling, his eyes unmoving.

"I can't see."

CHAPTER 12

"Do you need anything else?"

"No, I don't need anything else!" Daniel sighed when he heard Sara gasp in a breath. "I'm sorry, I didn't mean to snap at you." He held out his hand and her soft fingers slipped around his. It helped to be able to touch her. "Forgive me?"

"There's nothing to forgive. I shouldn't keep asking. I just..." She paused and he could feel her hand trembling. "I want to help and I don't know what to do."

He knew she was afraid for him, he didn't need his eyes to tell him that. If their positions were reversed he would have been frantic with worry.

"You're here. That's all I need." He imagined her smiling at his words and wished he could see it.

He was seated on the settee with his legs stretched out and a blanket over him. He didn't need the blanket, but Sara had brought it for him and he didn't have the heart to take it off. He'd taken a dose of the laudanum Doctor Wilson had given him, partly to make Sara feel better and partly because he was in a lot of pain, but his head was still throbbing where he'd hit it. And his eyes, they were on a whole other level. The laudanum blunted the worst of it, but he still wanted to rip the bandage off and press his hands to them for some kind of relief. He would have if the doctor hadn't told him to not touch them and keep them covered. It felt like someone was branding his eyeballs.

His eyes.

The loss of sight could be temporary, Doctor Wilson had said. Daniel was holding onto that. God wouldn't bring him all this way to simply leave him blind. The farm, Sara, all his dreams were coming to fruition. He knew his sight would return. He'd probably wake up tomorrow and see the sunshine and the mountains and Sara's beautiful face. He could wait that long.

"Are you in much pain?" she said, not for the first time.

"It's not bad." Relatively speaking, it was probably true.

A door opened and closed somewhere, the back door from the direction, and the sound of footfalls entered the room. He'd spent enough time around his brother to know they were Will's.

The clicking of Bess' nails on the floorboards came with him. Daniel reached out his free hand and her nose nuzzled his palm.

"I found the remains of the lamp," Will said, dropping into an armchair. "I just have no notion how it ended up lit during the day or why it exploded like that."

Daniel could hear the armchair creaking. He'd never noticed how heavily Will sat down. He'd have to talk to him about it before he broke their only comfortable chairs with his tall, heavy body.

"How's the barn?"

"OK. A bit of scorching here and there, but I got the fire out quick enough. I just wish I could work out what happened. If we have one faulty lamp, we could have more. I should speak to Lamb about it." Frustration tainted his voice. "We only bought those from the store in December. You could have been-" He stopped abruptly.

Daniel knew what he'd been about to say – he could have been killed. He wasn't even sure how he hadn't been. He didn't remember much about the explosion, just walking into the barn, wondering why it was so light inside, and then

110

waking up in Doc Wilson's office. God had undoubtedly been looking after him today. His injuries could easily have been much more serious. Even worse, it could have been Sara or Will who'd gone into the barn instead of him.

If only his eyes hadn't taken the brunt of the damage. Without his eyes...

But they would heal, he was sure they would. God would heal him.

"Anyway," Will was saying, "if you'll be OK without me, I'll get started on planting the rest of the corn. I want to finish that by tomorrow so I can get to the cherries soon."

And without me it'll take far longer. Daniel started to push back the blanket. "I could come and..."

"Oh no," Sara said, placing one hand against his shoulder to stop him from rising. "The doctor said you may have a concussion and you should keep still. You're staying right here and I'm going to spoil you rotten."

Despite his frustration at being confined to the house when there was work to do, Daniel couldn't help but smile at her bossy tone. "But..."

"No buts. Doctor's orders. And wife's orders."

"I'd add brother's orders, but we both know that would mean nothing." The armchair creaked again as Will rose and a few seconds later Daniel's hair was ruffled.

He blindly batted at his brother's hand in good natured annoyance.

"Besides," Will said, "we both know I do ninety percent of the work around here anyway. Admit it, you're pretty much dead weight even when you can see. You just get healing while the bigger, stronger, better looking Raine brother does the work."

Daniel would have rolled his eyes if they weren't so painful. "Are you sure you weren't hit on the head too? You seem to be suffering from delusions."

111

Will patted his shoulder. "Just enjoy your day off. You know, I should tell Ma and Pa..."

"No," he said immediately. "I've got you and Sara to fuss over me, I don't need them too. I'll be better tomorrow."

Will huffed out a breath. "Fine, I'll wait. But if they find out anyway, you take all the blame for not telling them straight off."

Daniel listened to his footsteps cross the room and the door open and close.

"Promise me you won't try to do anything that could hurt you more," Sara said, her voice filled with worry. "I've heard that injuries to the head can be bad."

He squeezed the soft hand still in his. "I promise. But my head is fine, it barely hurts anymore." Compared to his eyes.

There were a few seconds of silence before she said, "I was really scared."

The vulnerability he heard in her voice pierced his heart. "But you were brave. Will told me how you looked after me, how strong you were. I'm so proud of you."

She sniffed, but when she spoke, he heard a smile in her voice. "Us frontier wives, we have to be strong. It's in the contract."

He grinned and employed his broadest accent. "Then ah reckon ah've got me a fine frontier wife in this here wild west frontier town."

She dissolved into giggles, to his delight. "Can I get you... sorry. Oh, would you like me to read to you? Or would you rather sleep? I can leave you alone."

He couldn't deny her eagerness to help him felt good. After almost five years of more or less having to look after himself whenever he was hurt or ill, it was nice to have someone care for him. Much as he hated being laid up like this.

"I wouldn't mind being read to."

Maybe a day off wouldn't be so bad. He'd listen to Sara's soothing voice as she read to him, they would spend time together, he'd have a legitimate reason to hold her hand. Maybe she'd even make another lemon pie, if he asked.

He'd get back to work tomorrow, when he could see again.

CHAPTER 13

Daniel woke in pain.

The night hadn't gone well. Sara had wanted him to take the bed, but he refused. If giving her the best place in the house to sleep was all he could do for her now, he would do it. Will had brought in a spare cot from the bunkhouse, so he wasn't uncomfortable. But sleep had still been difficult to find.

He'd tossed and turned for what could have been hours. When he finally did fall asleep, he kept waking as the pain from his head and eyes grew. He'd taken more laudanum before bed which had helped, but it hadn't lasted.

At least now his head was somewhat better than it had been the day before. But his eyes were throbbing.

Instinct told him it was morning. Part of him wanted to rip the bandages from his eyes and have the light flood in. The rest wanted to stay unmoving beneath the bedclothes and never come out.

If he stayed there, he could tell himself it was only a matter of taking off the bandages. Whether or not he could see was his choice. But if he removed them and the darkness remained it would no longer be in his hands.

He didn't want to be helpless.

He didn't want to know that he was blind.

How long he lay there, too afraid to find out what the morning had brought, he didn't know. It was only when he heard sounds from the bedroom that he stirred into action.

He didn't want Sara to be there when he found out if the night had made any difference. He didn't want to hear her pity if it hadn't.

Slowly, he sat up. It took a few seconds of steeling himself before he finally began to unwind the bandage from around his eyes.

"Please, Lord," he whispered as each layer peeled away.

Finally, only the pieces of gauze over each eye were left. He gingerly pulled them away, wincing as they tugged at his burns. The thick darkness remained.

Maybe it wasn't morning, he thought. Maybe it was still night. Maybe when he opened his eyes he'd see the dim outlines of the furniture in the inadequate glimmer of the moon. Maybe...

Slowly, he opened his eyes.

There was no moon, no furniture, no house, no hope.

He was blind.

"Daniel?"

He hadn't heard the bedroom door open. Soft footsteps crossed the room towards him.

"Is there any improvement?"

He turned his face in the direction of her voice and shook his head.

Her dress rustled softly as she sat in the chair next to him and her hands wrapped around his. "That means nothing. The doctor said it could take days for your sight to return. It's going to be all right."

Was she trying to persuade him or herself?

He immediately regretted having the thought. She was only trying to help. This had to be terrifying for her too. She had to be afraid that the man she'd come to marry, thinking he could provide and take care of her, would end up useless.

"You're right." He smiled, hoping it would make his words more convincing for both of them. "I just miss seeing your beautiful face."

It was true. He imagined her smiling, a blush staining her cheeks, which made him want to see her even more.

"I..." She gave a small laugh. "I don't know what to say to that."

"Just tell me you're smiling."

"I am. Very much."

~ ~ ~

Getting washed and dressed without being able to see what he was doing turned out to be much harder than Daniel had anticipated.

He knew he sloshed water onto the floor but couldn't see to clean it up. He put on a shirt but had no idea what color it was. At least he could tell the difference by touch between his denim trousers and the good ones he wore on Sundays. He forewent shaving altogether. There was a very real danger he'd slit his own throat if he tried to do it himself and there was no way he'd ask Will to help him. He could live with a little stubble for the day.

The process took so long that by the time he finished he was sure it must have been lunchtime. So he was a little surprised to smell the aromas of a cooked breakfast when he felt his way into the kitchen, only walking into three pieces of furniture along the way.

"Morning," Will said.

He didn't ask about his eyes. Sara had probably already told him.

He hadn't gone two steps before he felt Sara's hands take his arm to guide him.

"I can do it," he said, pulling away from her. He immediately regretted it. "I'm sorry, I didn't mean to do that. I'm just trying to learn how to do things by myself."

"I understand."

There was silence as he made his way across the kitchen, stopping when his leg bumped a chair. He felt for the table and pulled the chair out to sit. A few seconds later he heard a plate being placed onto the table in front of him. Sara's hand rested on his shoulder.

"Two fried eggs at six o'clock, a slice of ham at twelve o'clock, fried potatoes at nine o'clock and tomatoes at three o'clock. Knife and fork's by your right hand."

He found the cutlery and ran his hands around the edges of the plate, picturing the food as she'd described it. When he took his first mouthful he was slightly surprised to find it contained a quarter of a fried tomato and a chunk of ham, exactly as he'd meant it to.

"Think I'll stick around here today," Will said. "The corn's all done so I'll finish cleaning up the barn. And I've been meaning to fix that bit of fencing in the pasture. One day Pea is going to spot it's loose and we'll never see her again."

Daniel knew his brother was only staying by the house for his sake. The fence had needed mending for weeks. Much as he wanted to protest, however, he couldn't shake the feeling that Sara might need the reassurance of having a man around who had the use of all his faculties.

"OK," he said.

"I'll milk Pea once I'm done eating."

Daniel couldn't help but mention the obvious reason why he was usually the one to milk their cow. "Pea hates you."

"Pea hates everyone. I'll manage. It's time I showed that cow who's boss anyway."

"Yeah, her."

"If you teach me how to milk her, I can help from now on," Sara said. "I can collect the eggs from the chickens too."

"If you don't mind dealing with a belligerent cow, I can

show you how," Will said. "It'll mean I can get out to the fields sooner in the future. It'll also mean I don't have to start my day dealing with a belligerent cow."

Daniel's stomach dropped. He opened his mouth to object then closed it again. He couldn't teach Sara if he couldn't see what Pea was doing, or correct her if she got anything wrong. Or save her if Pea was in one of her bad moods. It made sense that Will taught her.

Except he'd wanted to be the one to teach her everything about his farm. He'd been dreaming of it for months.

"Thank you," Sara said. She sounded like she was smiling. Like she was happy Will would be introducing her to the new experience of milking a cow.

Daniel's cow. Daniel's farm. Daniel's wife.

He stifled a sigh.

"Is that all right, Daniel?" she said.

He'd never wanted to be anything less than truthful with his wife and now he was about to tell her his second falsehood of the day and it was only breakfast. "Yes, it's fine."

He smiled in an effort to make the lie credible. There would be plenty more to teach her when his sight returned.

At least Will couldn't teach her about his bees.

CHAPTER 14

While Will went out to the barn to move the horses into the pasture and muck out the stalls, Sara cleared the breakfast dishes and cleaned up. When she was done, she made sure Daniel had everything he needed and then followed Will outside.

She was a little nervous. Since her first meeting with Peapod four days previously she'd only seen the cow from a distance, either in the pasture or through the kitchen window as she was led to the barn for the night. Will's description of her as belligerent didn't fill Sara with confidence, but she was determined to help and that meant learning how to milk the cow. No matter how bad tempered Peapod was.

When she reached the large barn, Will was pushing the last wheelbarrow of what had been deposited in the stalls during the night to the manure pile around the back where it was some distance from everything else and surrounded by bushes. Sara resisted the urge to cover her nose. She was a farmer's wife now, unpleasant odors would be part of everyday life. Hopefully her nasal passages would develop some kind of immunity to it soon. Very soon.

She ventured inside and found Bess lying on a blanket draped over a stack of straw by the entrance. She wagged her tail as Sara scratched her ears.

Peapod stood in her stall eyeing Sara with what looked very much like suspicion. Although not having had much bovine experience, it was hard for Sara to tell what she was really thinking. Maybe she'd learn to read her moods eventually.

"Right," Will said, walking into the barn, "are you ready to risk life and limb to supply us with our daily milk, butter and cheese and all the other delicious foodstuffs that compel us to deal with these ludicrous animals?"

Sara didn't bother to hide her apprehension. "Is she really that bad?"

He laughed as he took a leather halter from a hook on the wall. "Don't worry, you'll be fine. Dan usually does this. For some reason Pea actually seems to dislike him less than me, although I have no idea why. Women usually love me."

"Maybe your irresistibility doesn't cross the species divide."

"That must be it." He walked up to Pea's stall. "The first thing you do is put the halter on her. That's very important. And always do that before you open the stall. I can't stress that enough." He showed Sara the buckles and how the whole thing fastened together, then reached towards Pea with the contraption. Pea backed away. "Come on, Pea, don't make me look bad. The less fuss you make, the happier we'll both be."

Backed into the corner, the cow looked unconvinced.

Tensed to leap away at the first sign of danger, Sara walked up to the stall. Peapod had let her touch her on Saturday morning, maybe she'd do it again.

She reached out her hand. Pea took a cautious step forward, clearly curious.

"Remember me?" Sara said in a deliberately calm tone, her hand still outstretched. "We met on Saturday. I told you then that our first milking would be awkward. Well, it will be, but I promise to be gentle and I'd appreciate it very much if you'd do the same. Is it a deal?"

Pea took another step forward and stretched her neck to

sniff at Sara's fingers. Apparently finding them acceptable, she walked to the stall door, forcing Sara to step back or be nuzzled by a very large, wet nose. She gave the cow a rub on the head instead.

Looking astonished, Will silently handed her the halter. She gently fitted it over Pea's head and buckled it in place, then attached the rope Will gave her.

"Well, I'll be," he breathed. "I've never seen anything like that. Must be all she wanted was a woman's touch."

Despite the relative victory, nerves still nipped at Sara's stomach. "What do I do now?"

"See that hook over there?" Will pointed to the wall by the door where a large hook was fixed next to a feeding rack full of hay. "You're going to lead her over there and loop the rope round it, then she'll eat while you milk. It's the only way we've found to keep her calm. Most cows will just stand still, but not Pea. But then maybe for you she will."

Sara held onto the rope as if her life depended on it and stepped back to give him room to open the stall door. Pea walked out and towards the hay, seeming to not need any leading, and Sara had to hurry to catch up. She secured the rope to the hook and looked at Will who was watching her as if she'd just grown wings.

"I have no idea how you're doing this, but we'll just go with it." He waved a hand at Pea's rump. "This is the back end of the cow. Stay away from it. Nothing good ever happens there."

Sara nodded fervently.

He picked up a small wooden stool and placed it beside Pea. "Have a seat."

She did.

His lips twitched. "Facing the cow."

She felt her cheeks heat. "Oh, yes. Of course." She swiveled round to face what looked like a ridiculously huge udder. "How much is in there?"

"About a half gallon, more or less. She gives about a gallon a day most days. Don't worry, once you get used to it, it shouldn't take you more than ten minutes. I have to warn you though, your hands are gonna hurt for a while until they toughen up. You sure you still want to do this?"

She looked at Pea eating the hay, then at the full udder.

When she'd decided to come to the farm to marry Daniel, she'd known there would be things that were difficult to do, and she'd made a promise to herself that she wouldn't shy away from any of them.

It looked like she was about to find out how much her promises were worth.

"Tell me what to do."

~ ~ ~

Daniel paced back and forth across the kitchen, wishing he'd gone with Sara to the barn. Even if he couldn't show her what to do, he could at least have been there.

Pacing blind wasn't easy in a small room. He kept walking into the cupboard and the chairs around the table. Eventually he limited himself to five small steps in either direction which wasn't very satisfying as far as pacing went. But still he paced.

After what seemed to be an unnecessarily long time, the back door opened.

Daniel came to a halt. "Sara?"

"I milked a cow," she said. "And now I can't move my hands."

"I couldn't believe how calm Pea was." Will sounded excited. "She just stood there patiently while Sara milked her. You should have seen-" He stopped abruptly and Daniel could almost hear him wince. "Sorry."

122

Daniel shook his head. "Don't you dare start getting awkward around me."

"Sorry," Will said, again. "Anyway, you *will* see it when your sight comes back. It was amazing. Sara's like some kind of... cow charmer. Pea loves her. Still hates me, tried to kick me when I was showing Sara what to do, but she loves Sara."

"Maybe it's because I warmed my hands first," she said.

Daniel heard a finger click.

"That must be it!" Will exclaimed. "You're a genius."

A burst of jealousy hit Daniel as his brother and wife laughed together. He wanted to be the one teaching her. Laughing with her. Seeing her.

"Could someone work the pump for me?" she said.

"I'll do it," he said, before Will could share that with her too. He darted forward and collided with a chair, sending it crashing into the table. Biting back a sigh of frustration, he made his way more slowly around the table to the sink.

"I'm going to get the eggs in and then start on the fence," Will said, "while Pea's still in a relatively good mood."

Daniel felt for the soap as his footsteps receded back outside. Sara came to stand next to him, her skirt brushing against his leg and her shoulder just touching his as she held her hands under the water. He lathered the soap onto his hands and held them out over the sink. Sara placed her hands on top.

"I didn't really notice it until I stopped," she said as he gently massaged her palms with his soapy fingers. "Is it always this painful?"

"Only at first. You'll get stronger and it will get easier. Will can milk her tonight and for the next couple of days so your hands can have a rest. But if you've changed your mind about the milking, I don't mind at all. You have so much to do as it is."

"No, I want to. I need to be able to do all of this. I'll be all

123

right." A smile touched her voice. "Just as soon as I can move my fingers again."

"Is this helping?" He desperately hoped it was because he very much didn't want to let go of her hands.

Her voice softened. "If I say yes, will you keep doing it?" Until his own hands seized up, if she'd let him. "For as long as you want."

She sighed and her head leaned against his shoulder. "I'd like that. It feels wonderful."

They stood for a while in silence as he gently worked on her palms, then each finger, and finally her wrists. He knew her forearms would be aching too, but he didn't press his luck. As it was, the experience felt incredibly intimate and he worried he was going too far. But she didn't make any move to stop him and her head remained against his shoulder.

Finally, when the soap began to dry, he rinsed her hands off and dried them with the dishcloth.

"Thank you," she said, taking his hands again. "That was amazing. I'd suggest you could charge people money to do that, but I think I'd like to be selfish and keep the experience just for myself."

He rubbed little circles onto the backs of her hands with his thumbs. "Anytime you want me to do it again, just ask. My fingers are at your disposal." He kept his tone casual, but inside he was leaping for joy at the thought he'd get to do it again.

"I'll look forward to it."

His heartbeat quickened. Would it be too forward to kiss the soft hands still nestled in his? Slowly, he lifted them towards his lips.

A bolt of agony shot through his head, behind his eyes. He dropped her hands, leaning forward and gasping in a breath, letting the air out on a grunt of pain.

"Daniel?" Sara said, her voice panicked as she grasped

124

his shoulders. "What is it?"

He straightened as the pain slackened to a sharp ache. "I'm OK. I've been getting these shooting pains behind my eyes, but it's going now."

"Here, sit." She guided him to a chair and gently pushed him down onto it. "I'll get the laudanum."

"It's really not that bad," he said, trying to keep the pain from his voice.

Her voice became firm. "Are you telling me the truth or trying to look tough?"

They'd only known each other a few days and already she could see right through him. "Well..."

"I thought so. You're having the laudanum and that's final."

He smiled despite the pain. "Yes, Ma'am."

His injuries had terrible timing.

Maybe he'd get a chance to kiss her hand later.

~ ~ ~

Sara watched Daniel fearfully for the rest of the day.

Even though he tried to hide it, she could tell he was in pain. She knew he didn't want to worry her and she was grateful that he cared, but it still scared her.

It didn't take any special observational skills to tell he was frustrated at not being able to do his usual chores or any of the work on the farm. Daniel wasn't the type of man to sit idle. It was an admirable quality in a husband, but a terrible quality in a patient. More than once she had to stop him from going outside to help Will. There was no way she was going to lose her husband just because he couldn't sit still, and she told him so. After that, he stopped his efforts to escape.

True to his word, Will stayed close to the house in case he was needed and Sara knew he was worried for his brother.

She was glad to have him around. If anything happened, she didn't know what she would have done if she'd been alone.

Around midday Mrs. Goodwin arrived with enough food to keep them fed for two days or more, along with an entire coffee cake. While Daniel and Will chatted to Mr. Goodwin outside, Sara stared, bewildered, at the huge spread laid out on the table. She didn't know whether to laugh, cry, or protest that it was too much.

Mrs. Goodwin came to stand beside her, taking her hand briefly. "It's no more than I know you and those two boys would do for me or anyone else round here if something happened to us. Don't you worry about a thing, me and Mr. Goodwin are pleased to help in any way we can."

Tears stung the back of Sara's eyes. "I don't know how to thank you."

"No need for thank yous. It's my pleasure."

Embarrassed at her emotional response, Sara wiped at her eyes and smiled. "I milked my first cow today. I was a bit worried I'd have trouble lifting the pans for cooking."

"Then the good Lord brought me at the perfect time. I remember my first milking. Couldn't do my chores for a week." Mrs. Goodwin winked. "At least, that's what I told my pa."

By evening Daniel's pain seemed to be easing, for which Sara was profoundly grateful, but there was still no sign of his sight returning. She'd taken to sitting beside him on the settee when she read to him, often holding his hand, and he seemed to appreciate the contact. She couldn't deny that she did too. At least his forced confinement was giving them extra time to get to know each other. All things considered, the day could have been worse.

But when Sara went to bed that night, her prayers were all for the healing of Daniel's injuries, the lessening of his pain, and the return of his sight.

CHAPTER 15

"It's been two days, Dan, I've got to tell them."

"But..."

"No buts. If they find out, they'll blame me for not telling them and I'm hardly the favorite son as it is. After we've been to see the doc I'm driving you over there and that's final."

Daniel took a bite of the cheese omelet Sara had made for breakfast. Will was right, he needed to tell his parents about his eyes. It was just that he didn't want to worry them. Or maybe it was more that he didn't want them seeing him so helpless.

"OK, but if Ma tries to persuade me to stay there, you have to get me out. You know what she can be like."

"You have my word, I'll mount a rescue mission."

"Are you sure you won't come with us, Sara?" For some reason Daniel couldn't put his finger on, he wasn't happy leaving her on her own.

"I'm sure. I've got things to do. But say hi to your parents for me. And don't forget to get more laudanum from the doctor for your pain. I know it's improving, but better to have it and not need it than to need it and not have it."

"Exactly how long did our mother visit with you Saturday?" Will said. "Because you seem to be turning into her."

"I think it's rather I'm turning into my own," she said, laughing. "Maybe all mothers are the same."

127

"Just make sure you keep the rifle with you," Daniel said. "And Bess."

He felt her touch his arm. "Don't worry about me, I'll be fine."

He placed his hand over hers, for her touch in his darkness as much as anything else. "I know you will."

~ ~ ~

Sara leaned the spade against the porch railing and straightened, pressing one hand to her aching back.

She was beginning to wonder why she'd chosen to do this, especially with her hands still aching from milking Peapod for the first time the day before. After digging for what felt like hours, but was in actuality less than one, she'd barely made a dent in the packed earth abutting the porch at the back of the house. Peering up into the relentlessly blue sky, she wondered if there was any likelihood of it raining in the next ten minutes and helping to soften the earth. Probably not.

A pickaxe might have been a better idea to break up the solid earth. Going to check if Daniel owned one would give her an excuse to take a break.

Bess lifted her head from where she was stretched out at the top of the porch stairs and looked at her.

"On reflection," Sara said to her, "I think you have the better deal between the two of us."

Bess' tail swished lazily back and forth across the wood a couple of times before she laid her head back onto her paws. Sara was tempted to join her.

The garden had seemed like a good idea, but doing it by herself wasn't going to be easy. In addition, she had to do it while both Daniel and Will were away from the house, which was why she was making a start now. If she did it while they were there, Daniel would feel bad for not being able to help and Will would insist on doing the digging for her. She couldn't let him do that. He already had a far bigger workload on the farm as it was while Daniel was convalescing.

She could have waited to start, but she'd woken with a yearning to do it today, to begin something that looked toward the future. A future when flowers would bloom in her new garden and Daniel would be able to see them.

A future when she didn't have to be scared for her husband.

For at least the twentieth time that day, she offered up a prayer for Daniel's healing. The verse in the book of Matthew about not using vain repetitions when praying came into her mind and she took it as God's assurance that He had heard her.

"But if you don't mind, Lord," she murmured, "I'll keep on praying. It makes me feel like I'm doing something." Somehow, she knew He understood.

As she was about to head to the barn to look for that pickaxe, Sara saw Bess lift her head and sniff the air. She turned to scan the yard but saw nothing.

"What is it, Bess?"

The dog rose to her feet, her head down and a low rumble emitting from her chest.

Sara looked round again, a shiver running down her spine despite the warmth of the day. Without really thinking about it, she picked up the spade and lifted it in both hands, ready to use as a weapon if needed.

A man appeared from around the barn. He strolled towards her, a smile that looked more like a leer plastered across his face.

"Good morning, Miss."

Bess' low rumble became a full on growl as she stalked

129

down the stairs to Sara's side.

The man stopped and held up his hands, his eyes fixed on the wary dog. "Whoa, easy there. I ain't here to hurt your mistress." He moved his gaze to Sara. "Would you mind callin' off your mutt?"

Mutt? Sara felt like growling at him herself. She tightened her grip on the spade. "Who are you?"

He took a step forward, stopping abruptly when Bess barked a warning. He pulled his hat from his scraggly brown hair. "Name's Ely. I was just passin' and noticed you have a fine horse in your pasture. Wondered if you'd be lookin' to sell 'er."

He rubbed one hand over the rough stubble shadowing his jaw and leered again as his eyes flicked down Sara's body. A shudder ran through her and she was suddenly very glad of Bess' presence.

"I'm sorry, Mr. Ely, but none of my husband or brother-in-law's horses are for sale."

"Well, maybe I can speak to them. Are they home?"

She thought about the rifle in the kitchen. Despite Daniel's warning at breakfast, she'd forgotten to bring it out with her. This was the second time she'd wished she had it nearer. The first time it turned out to just be Mr. Pulaski, but she really did need to start keeping it closer. She couldn't help wishing she'd thought of that earlier.

"You don't need to speak to them. None of the horses are for sale. Now, if you don't mind, I have work to do."

His eyes went to the beginnings of the flowerbeds behind her. "That's mighty tough work for a lady. Maybe I could help you, darlin'."

In spite of her fear, anger flashed through her. "It's Mrs. Raine. And I don't need any help. Now I'll thank you to leave my property." She'd read that in a cowboy novel once. She never imagined she'd be using it.

"Well now, you're a spunky one, ain't ya?" The leer returned as he stepped towards her. "I like some fight in a woman."

She stepped back, hefting the spade. Bess' growl morphed into a warning bark.

Sara was truly frightened now. Would she be better running for the rifle and hoping Bess could keep Ely busy long enough for her to get it? Or should she just stand her ground with the spade? He didn't appear to be armed, but she hadn't seen his back.

"Mrs. Raine asked you to leave the property, Sir. I suggest you do so." Mr. Pulaski strode around the side of the house, his angry gaze fixed on Mr. Ely and his chest puffed out.

She breathed a sigh of relief. Life was full of surprises. She'd never thought there would be a time when she was grateful to see Mr. Pulaski. Bess pressed her side against Sara's skirt, looking between the two men as if unsure which to turn her ire on.

Ely took a step back, raising his hands. "Me and the lady were just havin' a pleasant conversation. I didn't mean no harm."

"I don't care what you were doing. She clearly doesn't want you here. Now leave or I will have to get rough." Mr. Pulaski took a step towards him, glaring.

Ely took another step back. "All right, all right, no need to get all riled. I'm goin'." He placed his hat back onto his head and nodded at Sara. "Pleasure to meet you, Ma'am."

No one moved until he was out of the yard and striding away up the road.

Bess stared at Mr. Pulaski. She wasn't growling anymore, but suspicion radiated from her in waves.

Sara lowered the spade to rest on its blade on the ground. "Thank you, Mr. Pulaski. I have no idea who that

131

man was, but he made me nervous."

His chest, such as it was, puffed out even further. "I'm just glad I arrived when I did. No telling what could have happened if I hadn't been here." He glanced around the yard. "I'm surprised Mr. Raine allows you to stay here alone."

"Daniel and Will went into town to the doctor," Sara said, tamping down her annoyance at his condescending tone. He had, after all, just saved her from what could have been a dangerous situation. "They asked me to go with them, but I had things to do. Bess and I could have dealt with that man."

She reached down and stroked the top of Bess' head. Bess didn't move her eyes from Mr. Pulaski.

His smile didn't reach his eyes as he watched the dog. "I have no doubt."

"So what can I do for you, Mr. Pulaski?"

His attention flicked back to her. "Hmm?"

"What's the reason for your visit?"

"Oh, my visit, yes, of course." His face took on an expression of sympathy. It looked fake. "I simply heard about Mr. Raine's accident and wanted to see if there was anything I can do to help you."

Ah, so that was it. "You thought, as he's unable to work at the moment, that he might be hiring."

He jerked back as if struck. "What? No! Certainly not."

Now she was confused. "I'm sorry, I thought..."

He stepped forward and took her free hand. "Miss Worthing, I assure you that your wellbeing and happiness are my only concern."

A warning growl emanated from Sara's furry protector.

"It's Mrs. Raine." She extracted her hand from his slightly sweaty grip, resisting the urge to wipe it on her dress.

He smiled and stepped away from Bess. "Of course. My apologies."

The sound of hoof beats interrupted the conversation. Sara didn't think she'd ever been as relieved as she was when she saw River and Ginger precede the wagon around the house.

Mr. Pulaski took another step away from her.

"Sara, is everything all right?" Will said as they came to a halt. He jumped from the wagon's seat, waited for Daniel to climb down, and led him over to them.

"Sara?" Daniel said.

She moved to his side and slipped her arm around his. "This is Mr. Pulaski, I told you about him? Mr. Pulaski, may I introduce my husband and brother-in-law?"

"Mr. Pulaski, my wife told me you were looking for work on Monday."

Daniel held out his hand. Mr. Pulaski hesitated before taking it. He winced slightly as Daniel's hand engulfed his.

"Uh, yes, I was, but that's not the reason for my visit. I merely came to see if there was anything I could do after your accident. It was a good thing I arrived when I did too."

"What do you mean?" Will said.

Sara told them all about Ely, feeling Daniel tense as she spoke.

"I'm just glad I was here," Mr. Pulaski said. "It can be so dangerous out here for a woman on her own. Quite frankly, I'm surprised you would allow her to stay here by herself."

Daniel drew himself up to his full height which was a good two inches, maybe three, taller than the other man. "Mr. Pulaski, I'm grateful for what you did, but I'm not given to allowing or disallowing my wife to do anything. She is able to make her own decisions."

Sara wanted to hug him.

Mr. Pulaski pressed his lips together for a moment before seeming to realize that although Daniel couldn't see him, she and Will could. "Yes, of course," he said, his face

133

rearranging itself into a vague smile. "I didn't mean to imply otherwise. Well, if you'll excuse me, I have an appointment elsewhere." He nodded to them. "Mrs. Raine. Gentlemen."

"Is it me," Will said as they watched him get into his buggy and drive away, "or does he come across as a mite creepy?"

"It's not you," Sara said.

Daniel turned to her and took hold of her shoulders. "Are you all right?"

It felt good to have him close. She rested both hands on his chest. "I'm fine. Mr. Pulaski's harmless. The man he chased away though, Ely he said his name was, he scared me. Bess didn't like him either." She looked down, embarrassed. "I forgot to bring the rifle outside with me."

Daniel rubbed his hands down her arms. "He didn't hurt you, did he?"

"No, he didn't actually really threaten me at all, and Bess made sure he couldn't get near me. Still, something about him bothered me."

"I think I'll go and have a look around," Will said, "make sure he's not hanging about anywhere. Mind if I take Rosie? Can you manage with unhitching the wagon?"

"I can do it," Sara said quickly. "Daniel can tell me what to do. It's about time I learned anyway."

Will looked from Daniel to her and gave her a knowing wink. "Good idea. I'll be back soon."

~ ~ ~

"What did Doctor Wilson say?" Sara said as she worked on separating River and Ginger from the wagon.

The familiar sounds of metal against leather set Daniel's teeth on edge. He should have been the one unhitching the horses.

He should have been the one here when a man frightened his wife, instead of off finding out if he'd ever be any use in protecting her again.

He deliberately uncurled his fists which he couldn't remember clenching. "The burns are healing normally and the bump's gone down. He said it's good I don't have a headache anymore."

"And your eyes?"

He shrugged one shoulder, attempting to appear unconcerned. "He doesn't know why I can't see, could be the burns, could be hitting my head. He said it's just a matter of waiting."

"But your sight will return, won't it?"

He didn't need to see her to tell she was worried. It filled her voice.

"He doesn't know."

The sound of her movements stilled. "It's only been two days. You just need time to heal, that's all."

He didn't answer. It sounded like such a short amount of time and yet the past two days had dragged on for what seemed like forever. He wanted to get out to his fields and work. He wanted to not have to feel his way whenever he walked anywhere. He wanted to not have to ask if he'd finished everything on his plate at the end of a meal. He wanted to know he could protect his wife when someone scared her.

He wanted to stop feeling useless.

"I'm sure you're right."

Except he wasn't sure, not at all.

CHAPTER 16

"I'm going to start on the cherries today," Will said the next morning as he finished off his breakfast of fried eggs, ham, gravy and biscuits. "If I don't get started, it's going to get ahead of me."

Daniel pushed his ham around the plate. "I was hoping you'd be able to help with the hives today. I need to check if any of the combs are capped enough for harvesting. What with not going to market this week, I'm going to need everything I can get for next Wednesday."

"I can do it," Sara said. "I mean, if you tell me what to do, I'm sure I'll be able to pick it up."

Daniel stopped fidgeting with his food. "I... don't know. The bees can be dangerous. I wouldn't want you to get hurt."

Will finished his last bite of ham. "You'll notice how he doesn't care if *I* get hurt."

"You've never been stung by one of my bees," Daniel said. "You're just afraid to go near them."

"That's not fear, that's prudence. It's also why I haven't been stung by one of your bees."

"Please," Sara said, touching Daniel's arm. "I want to help. I'll be extra careful and do exactly what you tell me to."

He didn't reply for a few long seconds and Sara found she was holding her breath.

"All right. We'll go closer to midday, when it's warmer and the bees are more active."

"Thank you," she said, excited at the prospect of going

out with him.

She wanted to learn everything about the farm, and maybe this would be a good chance to get Daniel talking again. He'd been withdrawn since the incident the previous day with Mr. Ely and she was beginning to worry about him.

"Why do we need to go when they're more active?" she asked. "Wouldn't it be safer when they're less active?"

"Mm-mm," he said around a mouthful of ham before swallowing. "The warmer it is the more of them will be out gathering nectar and the less of them there are in the hive."

"I didn't think of that." Of course, it made sense when she thought about it. "I have a lot to learn."

"Better you than me," Will said.

"Coward," Daniel said.

"Prudent," Will shot back.

~ ~ ~

A few hours later, Sara and Daniel were walking the worn trail leading to the hives.

Daniel carried a canvas bag and a cane, with the rifle slung across his back. She'd never seen him take the rifle out before and it worried her that he felt the need to have it with them. It could have been that he thought Ely might return, even though Will hadn't seen any sign of him the day before. Or it could have been that Daniel no longer had confidence in his ability to keep them safe. That he would feel that way concerned Sara most of all. She always felt safe with him.

The cane belonged to Will. He'd sheepishly told Sara he bought it two years before after spraining his ankle badly while drunk one night. It was Doctor Wilson's suggestion during their visit to him the day before that Daniel carry something he could use to detect any obstacles in his way. Sara could tell Daniel wasn't keen on using it, but he took it anyway, sweeping it back and forth in front of him as he walked. With his left hand he held her arm so she could lead him. She got the feeling he wasn't too happy about having to do that either.

"Are you all right?" he said after a while.

"Yes," she replied, slightly mystified. "Why?"

"After yesterday, I mean."

"Oh." She thought about it. "I feel better that you're with me. I suppose I'll have to get used to that not always being the case, but for now I'm grateful for it. Although I'm not grateful you're injured," she added quickly.

The corner of his mouth twitched. "I'm glad to hear it. It's nice to know my wife doesn't wish me ill."

She touched his hand. "She doesn't."

His answering smile was wonderful to see. Maybe getting out and doing something was just what he needed to combat the melancholia she'd seen growing in him since the accident.

"So Will is afraid of bees?" she said.

"When he was sixteen he was climbing in an apple tree on our parents' farm to get to the fruit and he disturbed a honeybee nest. The bees weren't happy about it. I was working in the next field when I heard him yelling. Turned around in time to see him fall out of the tree, run to a pond the cattle used for drinking water, and throw himself in. By the time I got there the bees had given up and he was climbing out covered in mud. I took five stings out of his arms and head. He was hurting for a while. Ever since then he's been scared of them, although you won't get him to admit it. When I offered him the job here his exact words were, 'As long as I don't ever have to go near any of your bees.'"

"Poor Will," she said. "It's a good thing I'm not afraid of bees."

138

"If you hadn't offered, he'd have done it. But he wouldn't have liked it."

"Then that's another reason I'm glad I'm here."

He was quiet for a few seconds. "You're still glad you're here? Even after everything that's happened?"

"Of course I'm glad I'm here. I love being here on the farm with you. There isn't anywhere I'd rather be."

She was hoping for a response along the lines of he was glad she was there too, but he simply nodded. Whether that meant he wasn't glad she was there, she didn't know. He'd been glad she was there a few days before. Surely his feelings hadn't changed since then.

As they reached the orchard, Bess bounded up to them in a frenzy of tail wagging. Daniel reached down and she pushed her muzzle into his palm. "She probably wonders why I'm not out here with her and Will."

Having received her ear rub from Daniel, Bess moved her attention to Sara.

"You'll be back with them soon," she said, stroking the joyous dog.

"Hmm."

Will's voice called from amongst the branches some way into the forest of fruit trees. "Is it time for lunch yet?"

Sara spotted a ladder leaning against a trunk, his feet just visible at the top.

"Couple of hours," she called back.

"That long?"

"Have some cherries," Daniel said.

"I'm insulted that you think I would eat any of our profits," Will replied, sounding indignant. "That only ever happened that one single time you caught me doing it."

"Sure it did."

An arm emerged from the foliage and waved them away. "Go talk to your bees. And good luck. You'll need it against those monsters."

Bess trotted ahead of them as they headed for the hives. When they got within fifty feet she stopped and flopped down in the grass, stretching her head out on her paws.

Sara looked back at her. "Why has Bess stopped?"

"She knows not to go near the hives," Daniel said. "Dogs are smarter than humans."

She returned her gaze to the group of hives ahead of them, feeling a twinge of apprehension. "Oh."

He patted her hand. "I'm joking. Honeybees aren't dangerous unless they feel threatened. Some people don't even wear protection when they work with them, but I'm not that brave."

She wasn't completely reassured, but she tried to imbue her answering "OK" with more enthusiasm than she felt.

He slid his hands up to her shoulders and turned her to face him. "You don't have to do this."

Standing up straight, she said, "No, I love bees. Bees are my friends. I can do it." The last thing she wanted was for him to think she was incapable of doing anything he needed of her.

A rare smile curved his lips. "I know you can." He let her go and dug into his bag, pulling out two wide-brimmed hats and handing her one.

She turned it over in her hands, unsure what to do with it. "Um..."

"Like this." He donned his own hat and unrolled the attached veil to settle around his shoulders.

"Ohhh, that's what that's for." She put on the hat. With her face protected by the veil, she felt a lot less nervous about approaching the hives. "Clever."

He produced a pair of gloves from the bag and handed them to her. "Make sure there's no gap at your wrists between the gloves and your sleeves."

"These fit perfectly," she said in surprise as she pulled them on. She'd expected them to be a spare pair of his and therefore too large.

"I bought them specially for you. I was looking forward to introducing you to my bees." His smile faded. "I didn't think you'd be doing all the work though. I was going to bring you in easy."

Her reluctance disappeared. "No, I want to do it, I promise. And thank you for the gloves. I truly do appreciate them."

His smile returned. How she loved that smile. She'd missed it badly the past few days.

"All right," he said, "pick a hive and we'll get started."

She approached the closest of the twelve boxy hives with a little trepidation. Bees were constantly flitting in and out, flying every which way so that they were impossible to avoid.

"This is a movable comb hive," Daniel said. "I based the design on the Langstroth hive, with a few tweaks of my own."

"You have a book by him," she murmured, watching the bees fly in and out of the tiny entrance near the bottom. It was oddly mesmerizing.

"Yeah, I learned a lot from that book. I don't think my first couple of hives would have survived more than a few months without it. You see the different boxes placed on top of each other?"

She moved her focus from the bees to the hive itself. "Yes."

"Those are called supers. The lowest is the brood box. That's where the queen is, laying eggs into the comb the workers have built. We don't have to check that today. The shallower super on top of the brood box can have honey in, but I know all mine also have broods in there too, so we can

141

leave that alone. The top super is where the bees store the honey for the colony. I just need you to check if any of the combs in there are ready for harvesting."

"What do I do?"

"First, take off the lid."

She located the clips holding the lid in place, lifted it off and leaned it against the side of the hive. She looked into the box she'd exposed.

"There are bees in there." As soon as the words left her mouth she knew how stupid they were, but the sight of so many of the insects crawling over the wooden frames was unnerving.

He laughed softly. "I'm glad to hear it. There would be something seriously wrong if there weren't."

She was glad he couldn't see her blush of embarrassment. "What next?"

He handed her a short, flat metal tool, about an inch wide and curved on one end. "Use the curved end to gently lever beneath the top of the first frame to loosen it, then you can lift it out. If it's too heavy, I can do it. When they get full they can weigh quite a bit."

Following his instructions, she managed to extract her first frame, being very careful to not accidentally touch anything that was moving. There were times when she found she was holding her breath, she was so worried about harming a bee or stirring the whole hive into anger. She very much didn't want to have to run and find the nearest pond to throw herself into.

Finally, she slid the frame out and rested the base onto the top of the hive. All her nerves faded at the sight of the amazing construction. "Oh, Daniel, it's incredible."

He was grinning. "That's exactly what I thought the first time I saw one."

The perfectly shaped hexagonal cells filled the frame,

their honey-filled interiors glowing amber in the sunlight. Mesmerized as she was, she even forgot to be afraid of the bees crawling over it, refusing to stop working despite being removed from the hive. How could a simple insect have created something so perfect and so ingenious?

God, Your creation is amazing, she thought, turning the frame around so she could see the other side.

"How many of the cells are capped?" Daniel said.

She studied the cells sealed with cream colored wax. "You want me to count them all?"

"That's OK, just a rough percentage will do."

"Um... around seventy percent, I think."

He nodded. "I don't like to harvest until it's at least ninety percent, so you can put that one back."

They worked their way around all the hives, removing the ten frames in each top super one at a time to check them, making a note of the few that were full enough so they could return the following day when Will would be available to do the actual harvesting from the combs. He wouldn't go near the hives themselves, but he was happy to remove the honey back at the barn.

When Sara had replaced the final lid, she put her gloved hands onto her hips and looked around the clearing, feeling a sense of satisfaction. She'd learned a lot in the last couple of hours, enough to make her feel as if she could truly be useful on the farm. She wasn't going to be just cooking and cleaning and milking Peapod and gathering the eggs. She was going to be working at Daniel's side, helping to continue what he and Will had started.

It was the life she'd imagined when she'd said yes to Daniel's proposal. There would be no attending dinner parties and dances just to garner social favor, or spending hours primping and preening so she could look good on someone's arm. She wasn't a tool to further a husband's business aspirations. This was real. It meant something. It was the foundation of her and Daniel's life together, for them and their future family. It was just what she wanted.

"You did well today," he said as the two of them arrived back in the yard, Bess having decided to stay with Will. "I was afraid you'd be scared of the bees, but you were really calm."

Sara couldn't help feeling a sense of pride at his words. "Well, I was a little afraid to start with, but I enjoyed myself. I can see why you like the bees so much."

"They bring in a good income too. There aren't as many full combs as I was hoping for, but it will help with the mortgage payment next Friday. The cherries will too. No one else around here has them ripening as early as we do. That orchard gets us through the year."

"Oh, you don't have to worry about money," she said. "At least not for now. Would I be able to have some of the cherries for a pie tomorrow?"

"If Will hasn't eaten them all, sure. What do you mean, I don't have to worry about money?"

"I know you had to pay a lot for my train ticket, so I brought the money with me to give it back to you." She wondered if Will would bring the cherries he'd picked with him when he came home for lunch. If he did, she could make the pie today instead. She was eager to try out Mrs. Gibson's recipe.

She'd gone several steps before she realized Daniel's hand was no longer on her arm. She turned to look back at him.

"You brought the money to pay me for the ticket?" he said, frowning.

"Yes. I'm sorry I didn't tell you before. To be honest, with everything that's happened I completely forgot about it. I suppose you should deposit it with the bank so it's safe."

"I had the money to buy that ticket. I didn't expect you to give it back to me. I don't need help paying to bring my bride here."

"I know that, but I didn't bring a dowry because you said you didn't want one and you know my family has money. I just wanted to pay you back for the ticket, that's all. And my father said if we ever needed anything, he'd help."

His frown deepened. "You told your father I couldn't afford to provide for you?"

"Of course not! But he knows that life out here can be hard. What's wrong?"

"What's *wrong*? What's wrong is that my wife apparently doesn't trust me to take care of her and our family."

Sara's mouth dropped open. "I never said that."

"No, you just said you had to bring money with you to pay me for something that was my responsibility to provide as your husband. *And* that we need your father's money as a backup plan."

She couldn't understand why he was getting angry. "That's not what I meant at all! I've never said I doubted that you can provide for me."

"It sure sounded like it. And that was even before all this." He waved at his bandaged eyes.

She planted her hands onto her hips even though he couldn't see it. "Why are you making such a big thing out of it? I brought money with me, that's all. Why is that so wrong?"

He thumped his palm onto his chest. "Because it's *my* job to provide for my wife. That's what a man does; he takes care of his family. That's what all this is for, why I waited so long to get married, so I could be sure I could give my wife and children a good, stable home. We don't need your money!"

"Of all the..." She marched up to him and jabbed her

145

finger into his chest. "It's 1870, not the dark ages. This is my family as much as it is yours and if I want to contribute money to it, that's up to me."

He huffed out a breath. "I don't need you to contribute. Keep the money if you want to, but whatever you need, I will provide it."

A tight growl of frustration forced its way past her gritted teeth. "You're impossible!" Turning away, she marched towards the pasture. "I'm taking Rosie out."

"Where are you going?" he called after her.

"To visit Lizzy," she shouted back. "And since you're so determined to do everything without any help from me, you can get your own lunch!"

~ ~ ~

Daniel slumped onto a chair in the kitchen and dropped his head onto his arms with a groan. Outside, he could hear Rosie galloping away.

He'd had no illusions he and Sara would never have an argument, but he had hoped their first one wouldn't have come quite so soon. And it had been his fault.

The truth was, he had no objections to her bringing that money. But when she'd told him, it felt like she was questioning his ability to provide for her. There wasn't much that could have wounded him more, especially since it was what he himself had been doing for the past four days. And if he couldn't provide for her and keep her safe, what use was he?

Nevertheless, she hadn't deserved his anger. He probably deserved hers, however.

He rubbed at the edges of the bandage around his eyes, yearning to pull it off. It had started itching today. His ma always told him itching meant a wound was healing, usually

146

when she was trying to stop him from scratching one. He supposed it was a good sign, but that didn't make it feel any better. More than anything, he hoped it meant his sight would return soon.

If it returned.

Please, God, please give me my eyes back.

It wasn't much of a prayer, but it was all he'd been able to manage for the past couple of days.

Light didn't suddenly blaze through the bandage, no supernatural tingling heat signaled that God's healing hand was performing the miracle he needed. Not that Daniel was surprised. God didn't seem to be paying him much attention lately.

With nothing else to do, he sat thinking about how his life had so quickly gone downhill until he heard the wagon rumble into the yard. He couldn't do anything about it so he stayed where he was.

Will's footsteps entered the kitchen and stopped. "Where's Sara?"

"She's gone to visit her friend Lizzy."

"O...K. So what's wrong with you?"

Daniel considered not answering him, or at least lying about it, but it was true that misery loved company. "We had an argument."

"Your fault, I'm guessing."

This time, he didn't answer.

"I'm also guessing, by the lack of wonderful smells I usually walk in here to since she arrived, that we're on our own for lunch."

For some reason, that irritated Daniel more than anything else. "We've been coping with cooking for ourselves for two years, me for four. We can make ourselves lunch."

"How quickly you forget," Will said, his voice flat. "Should've saved some of what Mrs. G brought. I'll get the cans of beans I hoped never to have to touch again. And next time, could you save starting an argument with my wonderful cook of a sister-in-law until *after* she's made us food?"

CHAPTER 17

By the time Sara had ridden all the way to Lizzy's home, her anger had almost disappeared. Almost.

She walked Rosie around to the back of the two storey white clapboard house.

A young man with dark blond hair to his shoulders and a bright smile emerged from one of the barns and walked over to her. "G-g-good afternoon, M-Mrs. Raine."

"Good afternoon, Mr. Griffin. Is Lizzy in?"

"She is," he said, holding Rosie's halter as Sara dropped to the ground. His smile disappeared when he saw her close up. "A-a-are you O...K?"

She wiped a hand self-consciously across her face. The few tears she'd shed on the way evidently hadn't dried as well as she'd hoped. "I'll be fine, thank you. I'd just like to see Lizzy."

"She's inside." He indicated the house. "I'll take c-c-care of your horse."

"Thank you." She left Rosie with him, walked to the back door and knocked.

A few seconds later Lizzy's voice called out from above her. "Sara!"

She backed away from the door a few steps and looked up to see her friend leaning out of an upstairs window and waving.

"The door's not locked," Lizzy said. "Come on in. I'll be right down."

The kitchen of Lizzy's new home could have fit Sara's twice with room to spare. She stood next to the long polished wooden table in the middle of the room and turned in a slow circle, admiring the modern cupboards and cabinets and the large range stove with a separate bread oven and no less than seven hot plates. It reminded her a little of the kitchen at her home in New York, not so much in style, but in size and modernity.

An unexpected feeling of homesickness swept over her. For the first time since she'd arrived, the thought came to Sara – had she made a mistake in coming here? She pressed her lips together and shook her head. So she and Daniel had argued. All husbands and wives argued; it was bound to happen sooner or later.

"Sara!" Lizzy squealed, running from the door leading to the rest of the house and throwing her arms around her.

Sara found herself smiling. It was hard to feel down when greeted with such exuberance.

"How are you?" Lizzy said, pulling back to look at her. She gasped. "What's wrong?"

Was she wearing a sign? "Nothing. Well, OK, not nothing, but..." she sighed, "Daniel and I had an argument."

Concern took the place of Lizzy's smile. "Oh no! I'm so sorry. What happened? No, wait." She guided Sara to a chair at the table and headed for what turned out to be a larder. "These kind of discussions need cake."

She reappeared with a sponge cake which she placed onto the table and added plates, cutlery, napkins, and two glasses of milk. Finally she sat at the table next to Sara.

"So what happened?" she repeated, cutting two large slices of cake onto the plates and sliding one towards Sara. "Unless you don't want to talk about it because it's not my business, in which case I can just sympathize. I am a world class sympathizer."

"I know you won't repeat anything." She picked up a fork and pushed it into one corner of her cake. "We were on our way back from checking the beehives..."

"Beehives!" Lizzy exclaimed. "You got to see the bees? How wonderful! Sorry, go on."

"We were on our way back to the house and I told Daniel I'd brought the money for the train ticket with me to pay him back. I'd clean forgotten to mention it before today, what with the excitement of arriving and then the accident." She popped the first bite of cake into her mouth.

"I was so sad to hear about what happened to Daniel," Lizzy said. "I wanted to come see you, but I didn't know if he'd be up to visitors. How are his eyes? No, wait, tell me that later. The argument. Go on."

Sara swallowed the mouthful of moist cake. "This is delicious. Did you make it?"

A frown darkened Lizzy's usually cheerful face. "I should be so lucky to have the chance. Richard has a housekeeper who cooks and cleans for him. Mrs. Lassiter. She won't let me do anything, in the kitchen or anywhere else, no matter how much I beg. And I've been extra nice to her. At least she makes delicious cakes."

Sara couldn't argue with that. "Could you ask Richard to speak with her?"

"I did. He said he will as soon as he gets the chance." She glanced at the door to the rest of the house as if afraid she'd get caught. "To be honest, I think he's afraid of her. He always gets home after she's left anyway. If it wasn't for Elijah letting me help with the animals I'd be going out of my mind with boredom. Anyway, your argument with Daniel."

"Well, I didn't think anything of bringing the money, but he refused to take it. Acted as though I was somehow questioning his ability to provide for his family. He got angry so I got angry and, well, here I am." Now she talked about it,

151

it all seemed so ridiculous.

"Men," Lizzy said around a mouthful of sponge, imbuing the single word with a wealth of exasperation. "My mama said the secret to a happy marriage is to make the man think he's in charge while making absolutely sure that he isn't."

Sara snorted a laugh. "I have no idea how to do that."

"No, me neither. She said it was different with each man and I'd learn when I was married. She didn't say how long it would take."

Cutting another bite of cake with her fork, Sara gave it some thought. "I think I overreacted. He's suffering right now. I need to be more understanding."

Lizzy studied her for a few seconds. "And how are you feeling with all this going on? Truthfully."

She stared at the cake in front of her. "I'm..." A sudden wave of anguish seized her and she lowered her fork to the plate. "I'm scared."

"Oh, Sara." Lizzy edged her chair closer and took her hands.

"I'm afraid for him, that he won't ever be able to see again. He tries to hide it, but I can see he's losing hope. It's so hard for him and I don't know how to make it better and I'm scared it will come between us." Tears trickled down Sara's cheeks. "Things were going so well, but now it feels like he's pulling away. I'm just... I don't know what's going to happen and I'm trying to trust in God, I truly am, but it's so difficult to not be scared all the time."

"I'm so sorry," Lizzy said softly. "You deserve to be happy and have only good things happen for you. I've been praying so much for both of you." She straightened abruptly, her face lighting up. "I read something this morning that made me think of you. Stay here, I'll be right back."

She leaped up and disappeared through the door

152

leading to the rest of the house.

Sara wiped her eyes on her napkin and took another bite of cake, wondering how Daniel was. She regretted allowing her fear to get the better of her. She shouldn't have got angry with him. He was struggling too.

Abigail's warning about her son's need to be protector and provider came back to her. Now she understood what her mother-in-law meant. She would have to try harder to remember it in future.

Lizzy returned with a Bible and sat back down next to her, flicking through the pages. "I know it was in the Psalms somewhere... no, not that one... here it is. 'I was brought low, and He helped me. Return unto thy rest, O my soul; for the Lord hath dealt bountifully with thee. For Thou hast delivered my soul from death, mine eyes from tears, and my feet from falling. I will walk before the Lord in the land of the living.'" She looked up from her Bible. "I just know that's for you. God's going to get you and Daniel through this, I know He will."

She considered the words Lizzy had just read. *He'll deliver my eyes from tears.* Ironically, those were the words that caused her tears to begin again. She fluttered her hand at her face, waving them away. "You're right, Lizzy. You're a good friend. I really needed your cheerfulness today."

"Would you like to see some baby chickens?" she said, smiling. "They're just adorable. I'm sure it would make you feel better."

Sara gave a small laugh, wiping her eyes. "I would love to see baby chickens."

~ ~ ~

Sara spent the next few hours with her friend.

Much as she loved her new home, it felt good to have a

153

little time away from the farm, and she enjoyed spending the time with Lizzy and being shown around the house and ranch. She also stayed for lunch, feeling only a little guilty at leaving Daniel and Will to fend for themselves.

Lizzy was right, the myriad of fluffy yellow chicks in the chicken coop did make her feel better. She hadn't laughed so much in days. Lizzy's husband wasn't around, but she said it was normal for Richard to spend whole days out with the cattle, not returning until after dark. Elijah seemed more than happy for Lizzy to interrupt his work to give Sara a tour of all the other animals they kept.

By the time she returned to the farm it was mid-afternoon. Leaving Rosie at the barn, she went in search of Daniel, finding him in the living room on the settee.

For some strange reason, she found she didn't know how to speak to him.

"Are you all right?" he said.

"Yes. I had lunch at Lizzy's. Have you eaten?"

"Yes."

There were a few seconds of silence.

"I'm going to take care of Rosie. Can I get you anything?"

"No, thank you."

Swallowing a sigh, she turned to go.

"Sara?"

"Yes?"

"I'm sorry."

She longed to throw herself into his arms, but she was sure it was the last thing he'd want.

Instead, she simply said, "Me too," and walked out.

CHAPTER 18

Sara placed the final dish from breakfast onto the shelf, hung the dishcloth on its hook by the stove, and looked through the window at Daniel where he was seated on their bench.

It broke her heart to see such a strong, vital man reduced to just sitting. She knew he had to be bored, but since their argument the previous day he hadn't even wanted her to read to him and any conversation she'd tried was met with single word answers. She was desperate to fix whatever had broken between them, but she had no earthly idea how. All she could do was pray and she was doing that almost constantly. So far it didn't seem to be having any effect.

She winced and whispered, "Sorry, Lord."

God could see the big picture, she couldn't. Simply because she couldn't see the results of her prayer didn't mean there weren't any. The future could hold so much she couldn't foresee. It was just so hard not being able to do anything to make her husband feel better. He was sinking deeper and deeper into despair and she had no power to stop it. At their wedding she'd promised to stand by him in sickness and she took her marriage vows before God seriously, but what was she supposed to do when nothing she tried worked?

"Please help him, Father," she whispered, for what felt like the thousandth time.

She hung up her apron and fetched the milking bucket from the pantry. When she walked outside onto the porch

Daniel didn't react at all.

"There are clouds above the mountains," she said, looking into the distance. "Does that mean it might rain?"

"Maybe."

She bit back a sigh. "I'm going to milk Pea. Would you keep me company?"

He gave exactly the answer she knew he would. "I'm all right here."

She was glad he couldn't see her shoulders slump. "OK."

She walked down the steps from the porch and headed for the barn, trying to ignore the ache in her chest. Falling apart wasn't going to help either him or her.

Will had cleaned out the horses' stalls and put Rosie into the pasture before leaving for the orchard with Ginger, River and the wagon. Bess, as usual, had gone with him. Sara walked up to the fence and pulled an apricot from her pocket and Rosie immediately trotted over to greet her. She stroked her soft mane as she ate.

Despite her best efforts, she found herself blinking back tears. She so badly wanted to go back to the previous Sunday when Daniel had given her the beautiful golden horse and they'd ridden together and talked and he'd been happy to be with her. It seemed like an age had passed since, not just six days. How could everything have changed so much in such a short time?

"I need him, Rosie," she whispered to the only one she could tell. "Why can't he let himself need me?"

Rosie gently nudged her honey colored nose against Sara's arm, bringing a smile. At least someone loved her.

She rubbed the horse's muzzle. "I'll bring Pea out as soon as she's milked."

Inside the barn, Peapod was getting restless to join her friend in the pasture, shuffling around and nudging against the sides of her stall.

"All right, Pea, I'm coming," Sara said, fetching the milking stool and placing the bucket down beside it.

She brought the cow from her stall and tied her halter rope to the hook on the wall next to the rack of hay, and as Pea ate and she milked, Sara began to sing. She'd found, completely by accident, that Peapod seemed calmer if she sang as she milked her. Whether it was because she actually liked the singing or because the soothing sound reassured her of where Sara was, she didn't know, but it had become a routine in the last few days.

If Sara was honest with herself, she found singing made her feel better too. Without having to do it for Peapod, she probably wouldn't have sung at all.

This day she chose Abide With Me, feeling a need for the comfort of its words.

> *"Abide with me; fast falls the eventide;*
> *The darkness deepens; Lord with me abide.*
> *When other helpers fail and comforts flee,*
> *Help of the helpless, O abide with me."*

If the composer, Henry Lyte, could write those words when he was close to death, then Sara could believe that God was with Daniel in the midst of his darkness. And with her, helpless as she was.

Feeling more at peace, she opened her mouth to start the second verse.

"You have a beautiful voice."

She started, whirling round to see who had spoken.

At first she couldn't tell who the man was who stood framed in the barn doorway, silhouetted against the brightness outside. Then he stepped forward into the relative gloom of the barn's interior.

157

She'd thought she recognized the voice. "Mr. Pulaski."

He sauntered across the dusty floor towards her. "It truly is like listening to an angel."

She rose from the milking stool, fighting the urge to back away. Why did he make her feel so uncomfortable? "What can I do for you?"

He shot a brief glance back at the open door behind him. "I wanted to check on you after your ordeal on Thursday. Has Ely bothered you again?"

"Uh, no, I haven't seen him since."

His eyes darted around the interior of the barn. "That's good, that's good. Still, it's a worry. What if he comes back? You should be thinking about your safety and whether it can be guaranteed here. Don't you think that being in the town would be better? As you know, I'm staying at the hotel and it's an excellent establishment. I'd be happy to pay for a room for you." He smiled as if he'd made the most reasonable suggestion in the world.

Sara's mouth dropped open. Did he really expect her to say yes?

"Mr. Pulaski, I appreciate your concern, but I'm safe with my husband and brother-in-law. Besides which, it would hardly be appropriate for me to stay in a hotel room paid for by a man who isn't my husband. Now if you'll excuse me, I have work to do."

He looked at the ground, not speaking, and she waited, willing him to leave. Her eyes went to the door beyond him. Could she reach it first, if she had to? She silently berated herself for thinking that way. What was she worrying about? He was harmless, she was sure of it.

Mostly sure.

After at least twenty seconds of silence, he looked up. "A beautiful woman like you should be cared for, not left alone in a barn, milking cows." His eyes went to Peapod and his

158

face twisted in disgust. "This is all so beneath you, Sara. You deserve so much more. I could give you more, if you'd let me."

This time she did step back, placing her hand on Peapod's back. "I think you should leave."

"Sara..."

"It's Mrs. Raine," she said through clenched teeth.

"He doesn't deserve you," he snapped. "He can't look after you." He reached her in three long strides and grasped her hands. "I can give you everything you want. You don't have to stay with him. Come with me and I'll make you the happiest woman on earth."

Sara struggled to pull from his grasp. "Let me go!"

Sensing her fear, Peapod mooed, straining against the halter rope keeping her in place and kicking backwards. Standing behind her, Mr. Pulaski grunted in pain and let go of Sara's hands.

She backed away. "Why are you doing this? I don't know you and I certainly don't want to leave my husband. Please, just leave me alone."

"You don't understand," he said, lifting his hands towards her, pleading. "Just give me a chance. Let me show you that you belong with me."

He darted forward, grabbing her arms as she backed up against the stall.

"Let me go!" She fought to pull away, but his grip was like iron.

He pushed forward, pinning her against the stall door as she struggled, his breath hot on her face. "Please, Sara, you must know you're mine."

"*Daniel!*" she screamed. "Help!"

Anger flashed across Pulaski's face. "You're betraying me?"

She heard footsteps running outside. Daniel yelled her

name.

Pulaski finally let her go and stepped away, limping from Pea's kick and breathing heavily.

Daniel ran into the barn. "Sara?" He'd pulled the bandage from his eyes, but he still held his hands out in front of him, feeling his way.

"You see?" Pulaski scoffed. "He's useless."

At his voice, Daniel growled in fury and started forward. "Pulaski, if you harm my wife..."

Pulaski stepped towards him.

"Daniel, watch out!" she shouted.

His foot rammed into Daniel's shin, sending him crashing to the floor.

"This is what you want?" he spat, jabbing a finger at him. "A man who can't even stay on his feet?"

A pitchfork rested against the wall to her right. Sara grabbed it and raised it in front of her, advancing on him. "Get out!" she yelled. "Leave us alone!"

He backed towards the door, shaking his head in disgust. "He can't make you happy. Deep down, you know you belong with me."

With a final derisive glare at Daniel, he turned and strode out.

Sara ran to the door to see him leap into his buggy and drive off. When she was certain he had left for good, she ran back to Daniel and dropped to her knees at his side, taking hold of his shoulders as he sat up.

"He's gone."

He reached for her, grasping her arms. "Are you all right? Did he hurt you?"

"No, I'm OK. Are you all right?"

He turned his head away, clenching his fists and muttering, "I'm fine."

Tears sprang to her eyes. "I didn't know, I'm sorry. I

160

thought he was harmless. I never thought he'd..." She stopped, her voice failing.

Daniel turned back to her and raised his hand to her face, hissing in a breath when his thumb brushed across her damp cheek. Wordlessly, he held out his arms and Sara collapsed into his embrace.

He rocked her gently, holding her close as she trembled.

"I'm sorry I couldn't protect you," he said quietly.

She shook her head against his chest. "I just need you here, that's all."

CHAPTER 19

"We need to go tell Marshal Cade," Daniel said when Sara had stopped crying.

"I know." He felt her take a deep breath in and out and her face lifted from his chest. "Can I finish milking Pea first?"

He felt a small, unexpected smile creep onto his face. "You're becoming a real farmer's wife."

"I hope so."

As soon as he heard the smile in her voice, he regretted his words. It wasn't that he didn't mean it; it was that he didn't want her to think it. He didn't want her to miss the farm when she left it.

When she left him.

"All right, but hurry. We don't want Pulaski to get away."

They rode into town half an hour later. With River and Ginger out with Will, they had to ride together on Rosie. Daniel tried to ignore the feeling of Sara sitting in front of him, her back brushing against his chest, the rose scent of her hair filling his nostrils, but it took every ounce of self control he possessed not to wrap his arms around her and pull her close. The twenty minute journey was such exquisite torture he wasn't sure if he was relieved or disappointed when they finally arrived at the Marshal's office.

He listened warily to the sounds of the people around them. "Can you see Pulaski anywhere?"

"No," she replied. "I've been looking out for him since

we got into town. Do you think he'd come back here?"

"I have no idea how that man's mind works."

If he was honest with himself, Daniel wanted Pulaski to be here, where he could confront him and put a fist through his face. He'd always been taught that violence was never the answer, but when someone threatened his wife and made a fool out of him, how could he be expected to simply let it go?

Father, forgive them; for they know not what they do.

Jesus' words, said as He hung on the cross, came to Daniel. He shook his head. He was just a man and right now forgiveness wasn't on his mind. And what was more he didn't want it to be.

"Is something wrong?" Sara said in front of him.

"No. Let's just get inside."

The first thing Daniel smelled on entering the building was gun oil. Someone had recently been cleaning their weapon.

"Morning, Daniel, Mrs. Raine," Marshal Lee Cade said from somewhere ahead and to Daniel's left, probably at his desk. "What can I do for you? Please tell me it's something that involves leaving this office because I am just waiting for an excuse to take a break from writing these reports."

"I thought you were cleaning your gun," Daniel said as, his hand on Sara's elbow, he followed her in the direction of the marshal's voice.

"Twenty minutes ago I was," Cade said. "How'd you know?"

Daniel found a chair and sat. "I can smell the oil."

The marshal sniffed. "Oh yeah, I didn't notice. Anyway, why the visit?"

Sara detailed to Marshal Cade the events in the barn and about how she'd met Pulaski on the train from New York and his previous visits to the farm. The marshal interrupted to ask the odd question, his pencil scratching as he wrote.

163

Finally, when she'd finished, his chair scraped along the floor as he stood. "I'm going to check if he's still at the hotel. You can come if you want to, or stay here and wait for me."

"I'd like to go with you," she said.

Daniel merely nodded, not knowing whether anyone saw it. All he wanted to do was confront Pulaski and give him what he deserved.

It only took a few minutes for them to walk up the main street to the hotel at the head of the road.

"Hey Marshal, Daniel, Mrs. Raine." Daniel recognized the voice of Zach Parsons. Zach was a childhood friend, but he and Will were closer, being the same age and having grown up together. He worked on the hotel's reception desk during the week and at his father's livery at weekends. "What's up?"

"Zach," Marshal Cade said, "doesn't Art Porter usually work here Saturdays?"

Zach heaved a sigh. "Yeah, but his twisted ankle is still getting better. This is the second Saturday I've had to work. At least my pa won't be missing me so much at the livery, with Amy working there now. She's doing wonders in that place."

"Do you have a Mr...." The marshal hesitated.

"Pulaski," Sara said. "Albert Pulaski."

"Is he staying here? Would have arrived Friday before last."

"You say that as if you need to jog my memory," Zach said. "We've only had four check-ins in the past two weeks and yes, Mr. Pulaski was one of them. He's in seventeen. Came back about an hour ago looking really annoyed. Kind of creepy, if you ask me. Why, what's he done?"

"Thanks, Zach," Cade said, without answering his question.

Daniel followed Sara up the stairs and to the right for

164

roughly thirty paces. Someone, he assumed the marshal, knocked on a door.

Sara slipped her arm around Daniel's, holding onto him a little tighter than normal. With a flash of guilt, he realized she was afraid. He'd been so fixated on his own anger he hadn't considered how seeing Pulaski would affect her.

"You don't have to be here," he whispered to her. "We can go back to the marshal's office and wait."

"No, I want to be here."

Despite her fear her voice was steady and Daniel was proud of her. She had a strength that would put many men to shame. He placed his free hand over hers where it held his arm, trying to reassure her. Not that he expected her to gain any reassurance from his being there after all he'd been able to do in the barn was fall on his face. Her bravery was far likelier to come from the marshal's presence than her own husband's.

Heated anger again blossomed in his chest as he heard the door open.

"Are you Albert Pulaski?" Marshal Cade said.

Sara's grip on Daniel's arm tightened.

"I am. Mr. and Mrs. Raine, what's going on?"

At the sound of Pulaski's voice, Daniel's anger grew to full blown fury. If Sara hadn't been holding onto his arm with a vice-like grip he would have thrown himself at the man, no matter that he couldn't see him.

"Mr. Pulaski," the marshal said, "I'd like to talk to you about an incident at the Raines' farm this morning."

"Is that what this is about? My goodness, I didn't realize you'd feel the need to involve the authorities in such a minor matter. I assure you, Marshal, it was all just a misunderstanding."

"Misunderstanding," Daniel growled. "Is that what you call attacking my wife?"

165

"Attacking?" Pulaski said in a shocked tone that made Daniel want to punch his teeth out. "I would never do such a thing. Mrs. Raine, if you truly felt threatened by anything I did, I apologize unreservedly. It was never my intention to scare you in any way, I swear."

"Mr. and Mrs. Raine have told me their side of events," Cade said. "I'd like to hear yours."

"Of course. I went to visit Mrs. Raine, just to check on her. A dangerous man almost attacked her on Thursday, did they tell you about that?"

"Yes, they did."

"Oh, good. Well, since I drove the scoundrel off I've been worried for her safety, so I thought I'd visit just to check that everything was all right and that he hadn't come back. It wouldn't have done for him to return while Mrs. Raine was without protection, what with Mr. Raine being incapacitated and everything. I admit, in my eagerness to ensure her safety I may have been a little... overenthusiastic when I spoke to her. I didn't mean to scare her and I'm beyond sorry if I did. She called out for Mr. Raine, he ran in and in my haste to distance myself from the situation I may have inadvertently tripped him up. I am truly sorry for any harm I caused."

"He's lying!" Sara said.

"I assure you, Mrs. Raine..."

Daniel couldn't take any more. Blinding fury shattered his self-control. Shaking Sara's grip from his arm, he stepped towards the man harassing his wife, raising his fist.

A hand pressed against his chest, stopping him.

"Don't do anything you'll regret," Marshal Cade said quietly. "I don't want to have to lock you up. Your wife needs you."

Sara took hold of his arm again. "Daniel, please."

Only her pleading voice had the power to clear the fog of rage from his mind. Lowering his fist, he took a deep

166

breath in and out and allowed her to pull him back.

"Mr. Raine," Pulaski said, sounding shocked, "I didn't realize you had such a temper. I can't help but be concerned that Mrs. Raine isn't safe..."

"Is there a reason you are in Green Hill Creek?" Marshal Cade said, raising his voice to drown out Pulaski's.

Daniel's teeth ground together.

"Well, I was planning on finding work and possibly settling here. It's a lovely place. Very picturesque."

"And have you found work?"

"No, not as yet."

"Then I suggest you give serious thought to moving on to somewhere where you may have better luck."

There was a pause. "Are you telling me to leave town?"

"I'm *suggesting* that you look for work elsewhere," the marshal said, an edge to his voice.

"Well, I will certainly give your *suggestion* some thought," Pulaski said. "Now if there are no more questions, I have things to do. A pleasure to meet you, Marshal. Mr. Raine, Mrs. Raine."

The door closed.

Daniel relaxed his jaw and it began to ache. He felt as helpless as he had been lying on that barn floor.

"Come on, let's go," Cade muttered.

"So that's it?" Daniel said as they walked back along the corridor. "There's nothing else you can do?"

"I can arrest him, but I've got to say, I don't think any judge will convict him. It's your word against his and he hasn't actually broken any laws. Maybe, at a stretch, assault, but even then it's doubtful."

"Then what are we supposed to do?" Daniel said, unable to believe Pulaski could simply get away with what he'd done. "That man attacked and as much as threatened Sara and I can't..." He stopped as his voice broke. He had to

167

swallow before continuing. "I can't protect her when I can't see."

"I understand, but I can't do anything if he hasn't broken the law. I'm sorry, I really am, but there's nothing else I can do. Believe me, I would do something if I could. I can't put my finger on why, but even without knowing what you've told me, Pulaski rubs me the wrong way."

Daniel opened his mouth to give the marshal a reply he probably didn't deserve, but Sara spoke first.

"I know you're doing everything you can, Marshal. And I'm grateful you believe us. We'll be OK."

Afraid as Daniel knew she was, she was being far more gracious than he was. He wanted to march back to Pulaski's door, kick it down and do something he doubted he would regret.

Instead, he swallowed his anger and hoped Sara was right.

~ ~ ~

If the ride into town had been exquisite torture, the ride home was simply torture.

Daniel had never felt so inadequate, so impotent, in his entire life. Not even Sara's proximity could distract him from the depths to which he'd sunk.

Nothing he did mattered. He couldn't work, couldn't protect Sara, couldn't do one single thing about Pulaski. He wanted nothing more than to wrap his arms around his wife, bury his face in her sweet-smelling hair, and forget about all of it. But he couldn't even do that. What right did he have to touch her when he couldn't keep her safe? She deserved so much better than him.

When they arrived home, he stayed with her as she finished the rest of her morning chores then followed her

168

inside and sat at the kitchen table while she baked cinnamon cookies for dessert later. He may not have been able to protect her, but at least he could be there. If he'd gone with her to milk Pea when she'd asked him, maybe the whole thing with Pulaski wouldn't have happened. But he'd got that wrong too.

She didn't try to engage him in conversation, seeming to understand that he preferred not to talk. He was grateful for that. Right now, he had no idea what he would say.

"Would you like coffee?" she said as she slid the tray of cookies into the oven.

"No, thanks."

He heard her pull out a chair and sit at the table. After a few seconds, her hand pushed into his. He tensed at the intrusion into his self-imposed isolation before realizing how selfish he was being. He turned his hand over to wrap his fingers around hers.

"I don't know why he's doing this," she said. "I promise I didn't ever do anything to make him think I would welcome his attentions. The very first time we spoke on the train I told him I was travelling to California to get married. I didn't ever lead him on, I give you my word."

"It hadn't even occurred to me that you did," he said truthfully.

"Maybe I could have been clearer from the beginning and told him plainly I had no interest in him. But I had no idea of his intentions. If I'd known..." She sighed and lapsed into silence.

Without thinking about it, he began to rub tiny circles on the back of her hand with his thumb. "None of this is your fault, Sara. You haven't done anything wrong."

There was another period of silence when they simply sat, holding hands.

After a while, she said, "The way he looked at me in the

barn, as if he thought I somehow belonged to him, it scared me."

He lowered his head, his shame and anger returning. She shouldn't have to feel afraid in her own home. It was his responsibility to make her feel safe.

Releasing a deep sigh, he sat back and let go of her hand. "Pulaski was right."

She gasped in a shocked breath. "About what? Me leaving you to go with him?"

"No, of course not." He clasped his hands together on the table in front of him and frowned down at them. "He was right about me being useless. All I do is sit all day and stare into darkness. And when a man came here and threatened you," he swallowed, barely able to speak past his shame, "all I could do was fall on my face."

"That's not true. You couldn't... he wasn't..."

"What kind of man can't even protect his own wife? I *am* useless."

"Being able to see doesn't make you a man. And neither does being able to protect your wife."

"Then what does?" He threw his hands into the air in frustration. "Tell me, what makes a man a man? Because I can guarantee that, whatever it is, I can't do it anymore." Why couldn't she understand? Why did she keep trying to deny there was a problem?

"Not giving up," she said. "That's one of the signs of a good man."

He pressed his lips together and sat back. "That's not fair."

"Nor is what you're doing!"

"What *I'm* doing?"

"Yes! I've tried everything I can think of to help you, but you push me away. You barely talk to me or Will anymore. You're giving up on yourself and it breaks my heart to see it

170

and I don't know what to do."

"Well maybe you should give up on me too. I'm *blind*, Sara! How am I supposed to feel? Everything I've ever wanted is gone."

It was a few seconds before she replied. "I thought you wanted *me*."

His gut dropped at the hurt in her voice. "That's not what I meant."

Her chair scraped across the floor, her skirt rustling as she stood. "Are you sure about that? Because I'm not."

Before he could answer, she ran from the room. A moment later the bedroom door banged shut.

Daniel balled his hands into fists, pressing them into his thighs beneath the table until his muscles shook. He stood and walked into the living room, feeling his way along the wall to the bedroom door. He could hear Sara's sobs from inside and the sound ripped into his heart. All she'd done was support him and he had made her cry. What kind of a man would do that? He raised his hand to knock, intending to tell her how sorry he was and beg her forgiveness.

He stopped, his fist hovering in mid air.

Maybe this was for the best. If she saw how useless he was now, how he was nothing more than a pathetic excuse for a man who couldn't do anything but cause her pain, maybe she would divorce him, leave, find someone who could look after her like she deserved. His heart tore at the thought of her in the arms of another man, but what could he do for her now? She should have so much more than he could give her. Her future would be nothing but misery and hardship if she stayed with him.

Shutting out the sounds of her distress, he turned away from her door and walked back through the kitchen and outside to the porch.

Where he sat on the bench and stared into the darkness.

CHAPTER 20

"It will be nice to see Amy and Lizzy and Louisa, and I hope Jo is well enough to come to church this week. If you don't mind, I thought we could ask Pastor Jones to get the congregation to pray for you during the service. Since it says in the Bible if two people agree on anything God will do it, I think a whole church full of people in agreement should be more than enough."

Daniel tried to relax as Sara chatted. He wondered what color her dress was. Maybe it was the same one she'd worn last Sunday, but he couldn't remember that one either. He pushed the cutlery around on the table in front of him.

"The eggs are almost ready," she said, probably in response to his fidgeting. "Are you hungry?"

He moved his hands back to his lap. "No. Kind of."

"Well, I'm doing plenty so you can have as much as you want."

He didn't feel like replying, so he just nodded. Not that he had any idea if she was looking at him to see.

He heard the back door open.

"There are so many good things about having a woman around," Will said as he walked in, "but I think my favorite is the food. I can smell those eggs almost all the way to the bunkhouse. Good morning, Sara, Dan."

"I wasn't expecting to see you before we left," Sara said. "You look nice. Going somewhere?"

A chair scraped on the floor and the table nudged a little

as Will sat. He hesitated before replying. "Actually, I was thinking I'd come with you."

"To town?"

"To church."

Her reply took a few seconds to come. She was probably as stunned as Daniel. "It'll be nice to have you there."

Daniel didn't bother to hide his snort.

"What?" Will said.

"I go blind, you go to church. Maybe I should have tried this years ago."

"Daniel!" Sara said with a hint of reproach in her voice that he no doubt deserved.

"Well, someone got up grumpy today," Will said.

Daniel knew he should have been happy that Will was finally going to church, but that particular feeling wasn't in his emotional vocabulary lately. "You're just going to try to bargain for your crippled brother. Well don't bother. You think you have anything to offer that God wants? You think any of us do?"

Even the sounds of Sara's cooking stopped. Long seconds of silence followed.

Daniel pushed his chair back. "I'm not hungry. You can eat without me. And I won't be going to church. Get them to pray for me or don't, I don't care." He stood and felt his way back into the living room, pulling the door shut behind him.

By the time he reached the settee and collapsed into it, his hands were shaking. He clasped them together in his lap. He would have prayed, if he'd been doing that anymore.

Muffled voices drifted through the kitchen door, but he couldn't tell what they were saying. Not that it mattered. All he wanted was to be left alone to... what? Feel sorry for himself? Well, why not? If anyone had the right to a bit of self-pity, it was him.

No one came into the living room. After a while, he

began to feel sorry for himself about that too. He knew very well he deserved to be left alone, and that being left alone was what he wanted, but having them simply not come after him hurt. Stupid as that was.

After the amount of time it would take them to eat breakfast without him, he heard the door open. Footsteps he recognized as Sara's entered.

"I'm just going to get my shawl and bonnet," she said.

"Fine."

Her footsteps moved away to the bedroom and emerged again half a minute later. "Are you sure you don't want to come?"

At least she'd asked.

"I'm sure."

He heard her soft sigh. "There are eggs in the skillet if you're hungry. Be careful, it's still hot. And I left the bread and butter on the table." Her hand rested on his shoulder and a hint of her scent wafted to him. "I'll be praying for you even if you don't want me to."

She lingered a moment and then her touch left his shoulder and her footsteps left the room. A few seconds later, the back door opened and closed.

Daniel was left with his chest in twisted knots.

What was wrong with him? He didn't want to be like this to her, but his anger and frustration kept coming out and she was a convenient target. He despised himself for what he was doing. He'd been right the day before, she would be better off without him.

At the thought of Sara leaving, a pain stabbed through him so intense he doubled over, his head clutched in his hands.

"Why is this happening, God? What am I supposed to do?"

When no answer came, he curled into a ball on the

settee, buried his face in the cushions and screamed.

~ ~ ~

Sara was quiet as Will drove the wagon towards town.

"You all right?" he said eventually.

All right. She didn't know what all right was anymore. "I don't know what to do. I feel like somehow he blames me for all this." Tears pricked at her eyes and she drew in a deep breath. She didn't want to arrive at church with her eyes red from crying.

"Well you can stop thinking like that right now," Will said. "Dan doesn't blame you, he's just angry at the situation and you get the brunt of it, you being around him the most. He needs to get out of the house. I'll do something about that tomorrow. But don't you think for one second that he blames you, because he doesn't."

She knew he was right, but it didn't make her feel any better. "Everything I do just seems to make it worse."

Will sighed and looked up at the overcast sky. "Truth is, I don't know what to do either. I've never seen him like this, but then he hasn't ever faced anything he couldn't overcome by hard work and perseverance before. He's helpless and he hates feeling that way."

Will knew Daniel better than she did, but she was learning how Daniel relied on his strength. And now it had been taken from him. She couldn't blame him for being angry. As his wife it was her place to help him through the difficult times however she could, and if that meant enduring his frustration, she would, no matter how much it hurt. Wasn't that what for better or for worse meant?

"Are you really going to church to pray for him?" she said.

Will shrugged. "To be honest, I'm not sure why I'm

going. I just woke up this morning and knew I had to. And if it helps Dan, then it'll be worth it."

"You make going to church sound as if it's a great chore."

He looked uncomfortable. "I haven't been for a long time. I'll admit, I'm a mite nervous."

She patted his shoulder. "Don't worry, I'll look after you."

"I'd be obliged," he said, his tone mock serious. "Those churchgoers can be pretty terrifying."

~ ~ ~

Will offered to drop Sara off in front of the church before taking the wagon around to the back, but she declined.

If she was honest with herself, walking in completely alone felt a little daunting. People were bound to ask about Daniel and having Will with her would hopefully stop her from getting teary. She was also doing it so Will wouldn't have to walk in alone either. At least, that's what she told herself.

After Ginger and Rosie were settled with the other horses, Sara and Will walked around to the front of the church.

Immediately people approached them, asking how Daniel was ("He still can't see, but the pain is much improved. No, he's not here. He didn't feel up to coming."), how she was ("I'm fine, thank you. Everyone has been so good to us."), and if they could do anything to help ("That's very kind of you to offer. We are all right, but I won't hesitate to ask if I need anything.").

All the questions were directed at Sara. While they didn't specifically ignore Will and many of them greeted him by name, everyone seemed confused by and even a little

176

wary at his presence. Will, for his part, was unusually quiet. Sara felt for him. He looked even more daunted than she was. As they reached the door, she noticed him take a deep breath and swallow.

Mrs. Goodwin embraced Sara the moment she stepped through the door. "I'm so happy to see you here, Mrs. Raine." Her eyes went to Will and then searched beyond him.

"Daniel didn't feel up to coming," Sara said, before the inevitable questions began.

Mrs. Goodwin nodded and gave her a kind smile. "I understand. And it's lovely to see you here, Will. Are you staying?"

"Yes, Mrs. G, I'm staying."

Her smile grew. "Well, good. I've got the biggest chicken roasting in the oven at home. If you can stop by afterwards, I'll send you home with some."

"Oh, Mrs. Goodwin, that's so kind of you, but you've given us so much," Sara said.

"It's no trouble." She patted her hand. "There's far too much for just Mr. Goodwin and me."

Sara smiled and said, "Thank you," and hoped that one day she'd work out a way to pay her back for her kindness.

"Yes, thank you," Will said with a grin. "From the bottom of my heart and my stomach, thank you."

Mr. Goodwin handed them each a hymnal and nodded his usual greeting. "Ma'am. Will."

Sara wanted to be inconspicuous so she made a beeline for the back row, looking around for Amy as she did. She couldn't see either her or Adam, but she would save them seats.

A child's voice yelled, "Will!"

Sara spotted a dark-haired little boy of maybe three run through the maze of seats and legs and launch himself into Will's arms. Will lifted him up, laughing, and spun him around twice before settling him on his hip.

A slightly frazzled looking young woman bustled up to them. Sara vaguely remembered having seen the two of them in church the previous Sunday. The woman was wearing the black that marked her out as being in mourning.

"Have you met Daisy Monroe and her son, Nicky?" Will said.

Sara shook her head and held out her hand to the woman. "It's a pleasure to meet you both."

"Likewise," Daisy said, smiling brightly.

"Daisy, Adam, Jesse, Daniel and me and a bunch of us all grew up together," Will said.

Daisy looked Sara up and down. "Now I can see why Daniel is so smitten with you." She winked at Will. "Change your mind yet about finding yourself a pretty mail order bride too?"

He heaved an exaggerated sigh. "You sound like Dan. There will be no brides, mail order or otherwise, for William Raine. I value my freedom." He glanced at Sara and smiled. "No offence. You know I think Dan is lucky to have you."

She smiled back. "None taken."

Daisy shook her head. "You're impossible. It'll happen one day, mark my words. You'll find the perfect girl for you and realize how wrong you are and how right I am, as always."

He rolled his eyes. "Now you sound like my ma."

"Will you come sit with us?" Nicky said, turning pleading eyes on Will.

He glanced at Sara. "Well, I was planning on..."

"It's all right," she said quickly. "I'll be fine." Daisy and Nicky were the first people other than the Goodwins to treat Will like he belonged there.

"You're welcome to come and join us," Daisy said.

Sara looked towards the front of the church where Daisy

178

had come from. There were already lots of people sitting there, people who would no doubt ask her about Daniel. Just the thought made her feel exhausted.

"That's kind of you, but I think I'll sit at the back and wait for Amy and Adam. I'd like some quiet time to pray before the service starts."

Daisy reached out to give her hand a squeeze and lowered her voice. "I understand, believe me. Being around people while going through something so traumatic can be exhausting. If there's anything I can do, or even if you just want to talk, I'm here."

At the kindness in her voice Sara's chest tightened and she had to blink her suddenly burning eyes a few times. And she'd been doing so well with not crying. "Thank you."

Daisy let go of her hand and turned her attention to Will and her son. "OK you two, let's get back to our seats before someone steals them."

Will mouthed, 'You OK?' to Sara.

She nodded, adding a smile to reassure him.

"You can't steal in a church," Nicky said, his eyes wide. "God would see."

"God sees you wherever you are," Will said as they walked away. "Not just in church."

The little boy's brow furrowed in thought. "You mean, He can see everything we do all the time?"

"Yep."

"Oh." He continued to frown. It was clearly a concept he was going to be struggling with.

Sara found her way to the back row and sat, placing her shawl across the two seats next to her to stop anyone taking them. She opened her Bible to read but couldn't concentrate, the door drawing her gaze more often than not. Lizzy came in after a while, Louisa after her, and Jo when it was almost time for the service to begin. None of them saw Sara hidden at the back and she didn't do anything to attract their attention. She'd speak to them afterwards. For now, all she wanted was to sit quietly and see Amy when she arrived.

Finally, when almost everyone had taken their seats and Pastor Jones was up on the platform and Sara had given up hope, Amy and Adam walked in. She felt an indescribable relief as she waved them over and took her shawl from the seats.

"I saved them for you," she whispered to Amy as she sat beside her. "I'm glad you're here."

Amy's gaze moved beyond her to where Daniel would have been seated, if he'd been there. There was understanding in her eyes when she looked back at Sara. She took Sara's hand and the simple touch made her feel so much better.

Difficult as being here without Daniel was, at least she wasn't alone.

~ ~ ~

At the end of the service Adam diplomatically excused himself, leaving Sara and Amy to talk. Sara was grateful, although she couldn't help but feel self-conscious that everyone seemed to think she needed special consideration.

"I know you aren't staying, but he seems like a wonderful man," she said as they watched him walk away.

She thought a hint was in order. The thought of Amy leaving filled her with a desperate sadness. If Amy decided to stay with Adam, at least one thing would be going right.

"He is," Amy replied, her tone suggesting she agreed but would rather not discuss it. "How are you holding up?"

Sara looked down and tried to keep her voice steady. She wasn't particularly ready to discuss things either. "I'm all right."

Thankfully, Lizzy edged along the row in front of them and sat, taking the attention from Sara. Beyond her Louisa and Jo stood in the aisle.

"I would like to formally invite you two to lunch," Lizzy said. "Just the five of us. Pastor Jones and Mrs. Jones are going to be out for a couple of hours and they told Louisa we could use the house. I know it's short notice, but I think we could all use the time to talk." She reached over the back of her chair and took Sara's hand.

Again the assumption that she was emotionally fragile. Did she look that pathetic? "I don't know, I should probably get back..."

"Please?" Lizzy said, drawing the word out. "It wouldn't be the same without you. I for one could really use your sage advice and I think the rest of us could too. Jesse said he'd take you, me and Jo home afterwards."

"Lizzy's right," Amy said. "You're the most stable of all of us."

Lizzy nodded vehemently. "Exactly. The rest of us scatterbrains need you."

Sara couldn't help but laugh at their utter lack of subtlety. "All right, you don't have to lay it on quite that thick. I'll tell Will to let Daniel know I'll be back later."

Maybe it would do her good to spend some time with her friends. Daniel probably didn't want her around anyway. She felt as if he rarely had in the past few days.

Lizzy squealed in delight, clapping her hands.

"I'll go and tell Adam he can go without me," Amy said.

As she left to find Adam, Jo and Louisa came to sit.

"How are you feeling?" Sara said to Jo in an attempt to pre-empt anyone asking her the same thing.

"Much better," she said, pushing a strand of hair behind her ear. "I think I've just been eating too much wholesome food out here in the country."

Lizzy nodded, her expression somber. "All this fresh food and air and such., it's not natural. It's enough to make a person feel queasy all right."

As they all laughed, Sara felt glad she was staying. She'd missed them all being together like this.

In the aisle, Will walked past with Nicky in his arms. He disappeared out the door for a few seconds then returned alone. Sara excused herself and went to speak to him.

"The girls are having a lunch together and I said I'd join them, if you think you and Daniel will be all right without me for a few hours."

"We'll muddle through," he said. "You just enjoy yourself. I'll be stopping by the Goodwin house to pick up that chicken, so we won't go hungry. We'll try to save you some, but I can't promise anything, what with it being Mrs. Goodwin's cooking and all."

"I won't hold it against you," she said, smiling. "How did you like the service?"

He looked past her at the cross that hung on the wall behind the platform. "I'm glad I came. I didn't realize how much I'd missed going to the Lord's house. And the pastor's sermon gave me something to think about."

Pastor Jones had spoken on the prodigal son. Sara couldn't help wondering if God had inspired the subject choice, knowing Will would be there.

"Did a lot of praying about Dan," he continued, "although I've been doing that since Tuesday anyway. It's been a while since I've spoken to God too. I'm feeling a bit more at peace about it now."

Sara wished she could say the same, but she was happy for Will. "I'm glad. You think you'll come again next week?"

One corner of his mouth hitched up. "I just might."

When she returned to the little group of women at the back of the church, they were all watching her. She did wish

182

people would stop doing that.

"All set?" Louisa said.

"All set," Sara replied.

"My goodness," Jo said, fanning herself with her hand, "who was *that*?"

"Daniel's brother, Will. He works with Daniel on the farm and stays in the bunkhouse."

"Well, I'll say this for that family you've married into - they certainly know how to make them handsome."

Louisa gasped, her hand flying to her mouth. "Jo! You're a married woman!"

Jo smirked. "Married, not dead."

There were a few seconds of silence. Louisa's hand still covered her mouth, Sara assumed to contain her shock. But then a snort escaped from behind it.

Lizzy, her mouth pressed shut, began to giggle through her nose. Barely a second passed before they all burst into laughter.

Amy walked up to them. "What's so funny?"

Pastor and Mrs. Jones lived only a short distance from the church, on the same street, so they were there in only a few minutes. The five of them working together had the meal prepared and in the oven in under twenty minutes and they all gathered in the parlor with coffee to wait for it to cook.

As soon as they'd sat down Lizzy, Jo, Louisa and Amy all turned their sympathetic attention on Sara.

Poor Sara, who'd arrived with such high hopes and who was now struggling more than any of them.

Sara, whose husband may never see again and had all but shut her out.

Sara, who was losing her battle to keep herself together. As her friends gathered around her, she burst into tears.

CHAPTER 21

Daniel lay on his back and stared up at the ceiling. At least, he would have been staring at the ceiling if he could have seen it. He strained to find even the faintest hint of light, keeping his eyes wide open and unblinking, as if that would help. After a few seconds they began to burn and he had to squeeze them shut. Open or closed, it didn't make any difference to the complete blackness he lived in now anyway.

It was Monday morning. Usually on Monday mornings he'd be wishing it was Sunday so he could stay in bed for a bit longer. Today he would have given anything to *not* rest. Any more rest and he'd go insane.

"How are they feeling?" Sara said from somewhere to his left, her light footfalls and the soft rustle of her dress marking her progress towards him.

He opened his eyes. "There's no pain, but they feel a bit dry."

The bed dipped a little as she sat on the mattress beside him. Having her so close was almost physically painful. Half of him wanted to reach out and draw her to him, the rest wanted to push her away and tell her to leave him to suffer alone. He hated being so weak and helpless in front of her.

"Would you like to leave the bandage off for a while? The skin's not quite healed yet, but a bit longer shouldn't hurt."

"Yeah, I would. That bandage is starting to make me crazy."

He moved his hand to scratch at an itch, but Sara caught it in midair before he could. Her touch on his skin sent a shiver through his arm.

"Don't scratch though," she said, apparently oblivious to the effect her touch had on him. "You don't want it infected."

He managed to drum up a tiny smile. "Yes, Ma'am."

She hadn't let go of his hand and he found he didn't want her to, even though he knew he should. Every day he woke up in darkness he came one step closer to losing her. There was no way he'd be able to support a wife, much less a family, while blind. She'd be better off without him.

But he didn't want to let go of her hand.

They sat with their fingers entwined, not saying anything, for he didn't know how long. It was as if neither of them wanted to disturb the simple intimacy of the touch. And Daniel wanted more, so much more, than just holding her hand. He wanted to pull her into his arms, feel her breath on his face, experience the taste of her lips, the warmth of her body pressed against his, the caress of her hands, to take her to his bed. To become truly one with his wife, joined for the rest of their lives.

He jerked as if struck, wrenching his hand from her grasp. He heard her sharp intake of breath, but he couldn't bear her touch any longer, a reminder of what he couldn't have.

His dream could never be a reality. Not now.

"I... I need to go and milk Peapod," she said, her voice trembling.

And then she was gone and Daniel wanted to scream.

The back door opened again and for a moment he thought she'd come back. But the heavy footsteps weren't those of his wife.

"Get dressed," Will said, pushing his shoulder.

He wasn't sure whether to be annoyed or grateful to his

brother. "I am dressed."

"I mean in your work clothes. I'm going out to the orchard and you're coming with me. There are still cherries needing picking and I want your help with them."

Daniel frowned. Now he was just annoyed. "You know I can't help."

The bed bounced as Will sat with much less gentleness than Sara had. "I know no such thing. Only your eyes are damaged, nothing wrong with your arms and legs. Get your lazy backside out of bed and get ready."

Daniel glared in his direction. "Are you mocking me?"

Will huffed out a breath. "No, I'm dragging you out of this house. I'm tired of watching you feel sorry for yourself. The Daniel I know wouldn't let anything stop him, even losing his sight."

"Well maybe you don't know me as well as you think you do."

A hand cuffed his shoulder, making him jump.

"Don't be an idiot. You've been tormenting me since the day I was born. I know you better than I sometimes want to." The weight on the bed lifted. "Now get up or I'll drag you up. It's time you started facing this like the man you are. Or at least used to be."

The blanket was snatched from over him. Daniel reached for it blindly, flailed uselessly for a few seconds and then gave up and dropped his hands into his lap.

Maybe it would be better if he got out. At least then he wouldn't have the torture of being around Sara all day, not knowing how to be there without causing them both pain.

He swung his feet to the floor. "Sometimes I wish Ma and Pa had stopped having children after me."

"No you don't," Will said, a smile in his voice. "If I hadn't been around, you'd have had no one to irritate when we were growing up."

186

Daniel pushed his feet into his boots. "I think you've got that backwards."

~ ~ ~

Daniel turned towards the sun.

The warmth on his face felt good after being inside so much for the past six days. He was used to being outside most of the day, whatever the weather. But then there were a lot of things he was used to that he hadn't been able to do since his injury.

The wagon bounced over a hole in the track. He knew exactly where that hole was, could picture it in his mind. He'd been meaning to fill it in, back when the thought never even crossed his mind that he would ever be incapable of doing it.

"OK, we're here," Will said as they came to a halt.

Daniel could detect the faint fruity aroma of the orchard and hear the gentle hum of a million insects as they collected nectar from the flowering trees. "What on earth am I going to be able to do here?"

"We'll work it out."

His expression must have betrayed his doubt.

"It'll be fine, you'll see," Will said. "It'll just take some getting used to."

~ ~ ~

"Ouch!" Daniel threw the knife to the ground and clutched at his stinging hand. Sticky blood welled up between his fingers.

"Dan!" Will ran up to him. "Are you all right?"

"No, I'm not all right! I won't ever be all right." Tears of frustration and pain burned at the back of his eyes and he

187

turned away. "I can't do it! I can't do anything."

"Let me see your hand."

Biting back his anger, Daniel opened his fist.

Will took his hand for a moment. "It's not bad. I have to clean it though. I'll get the water."

"Don't bother," he said bitterly, "I'll do it back at the house."

"Dan..."

"Don't you dare tell me it'll be fine. It's not fine! Nothing is fine!" He knew it was unfair to shout at Will, but he'd had enough. "I've tried everything and I can't do any of it. I want to go back."

"It's only been a couple of hours..."

"A couple of hours, a couple of days, weeks, months, years. However long I give it, it's not going to change. I'm still going to be useless."

"Dan, you're not useless."

The certainty in Will's voice just made it worse. Why couldn't his brother give up on him the way he'd given up on himself? What was the point in denying it?

Daniel squeezed his eyes together, trying to stop the tears, but they soaked into his bandage anyway. He took a deep breath to calm himself. "Please, just take me home."

There were a few seconds of silence before Will sighed. "All right."

Bess pressed against Daniel's leg, whining and brushing her nose against his injured hand. He lifted it out of her reach and stretched down his good hand to stroke her. She never liked it when he got angry, which used to be such a rare event. Not anymore.

Will didn't speak to him on the whole ride home and that was fine by Daniel. He should never have allowed his brother to take him out there. What was the point? He hardly needed to be reminded of how everything he used to take for granted was now impossible.

He flexed his wounded hand and winced. He should probably have let Will clean it before they left though. Just another in the long list of simple tasks he could no longer do by himself. Couldn't look after himself, couldn't provide for a family, couldn't protect his wife. Everything a man should do, he couldn't.

His life was as good as over.

CHAPTER 22

Sara was somewhat surprised to see Daniel and Will drive into the yard as she prepared lunch. They'd barely been gone two hours.

She finished off the potato she was peeling, placed it into the pan with the rest and rinsed and dried her hands, ready to open the door as Will led Daniel to the porch.

"You're back early," she said as they walked in. "How did it go?"

She tried to keep her voice cheery, but neither of them looked like the morning had been a good one.

"I'll let Dan take that one," Will muttered before going back outside.

"Are you OK?" she said to Daniel.

He unfurled his hand and held it out to reveal a long cut across his palm, the dirt-encrusted blood beginning to clot.

"You're hurt."

Gently taking his hand, she led him to the sink and pumped out some water into a bowl. It took some time to thoroughly clean the blood and dirt from the wound and he was silent through the whole procedure, even when she knew it had to be hurting him. He was obviously angry and she longed to ask why, to help in some way, but she held her tongue. Lately he didn't seem to want her help with anything.

When the cut was clean and had stopped bleeding, she took him to sit at the table and fetched clean bandages and iodine from a drawer.

Finally, unable to stand the silence any longer, she said, "So what's wrong?"

He hissed in a breath through his teeth as she dabbed iodine onto the shallow cut. "What's wrong is I can't do anything anymore. I tried, but it's pointless. I'm never going to be able to farm like this."

The sheer hopelessness on his face broke her heart. "Maybe you just need to give it more time. There must be something you can do."

"You sound like Will."

She placed a pad of cotton onto his palm and held it in place with her thumb while she wound the bandage around his hand. "You can't give up hope that your sight will come back. It's only been six days..."

His free hand slammed onto the table. Sara jumped, startled.

"Six days!" he snapped. "You know the doctor said the longer I can't see, the more likely it is I'll be permanently blind. It's never coming back, Sara. I'm going to be like this for the rest of my pathetic life."

She touched her hand to his face, hoping to soothe his anger. "Your life isn't pathetic. I know you can learn to live with this and you have Will and me. I can help with the farming. Will can teach me what to do and I can..."

He shook her hand away and stood. "Don't you understand?"

Sara recoiled at the anger in his voice.

He turned his back on her and walked a few steps. "I don't want you to do it," he said, his voice shaking. "I don't want your help. I don't want you constantly telling me it will be all right. I don't want my wife doing everything for me. I'm the man! It's my job, not yours." He leaned his uninjured hand against the wall beside the living room door, lowering his head. "The best thing you can do is go. You have that money for the train ticket. Go home to New York and find yourself a man who can take care of you."

Her stomach knotted inside her. "You... you want a divorce?"

There were a few seconds of silence.

"Yes," he said quietly, bitterness in his voice. "I want a divorce."

She stared at his back, numb with shock, barely able to believe what he was saying. He couldn't mean it. Tears gathered in her lashes. "But..."

"Just leave me alone."

She wanted to say something, scream something. She wanted to run to him and throw her arms around him. She wanted to run to him and beat her fists against his immovable, unbending, frustrating frame.

But all she could manage was to push down the pain blooming in her chest before it escaped in a sob.

Shaking her head, she stood from the table and backed away from her husband, the man who had promised his life to her and now, less than two weeks later, was telling her to leave.

Tears spilling down her cheeks, she turned and fled from the house.

Wiping at her face, she ran across the yard to where Will was unloading a box filled with freshly picked cherries from the wagon.

"Could you saddle Rosie for me, please?" she said, desperately trying to keep her voice steady. She couldn't gather her thoughts enough to do it herself.

Will's eyes widened when he saw her. "Sara, what's wrong?" He ran over to her and took hold of her shoulders, ducking his head to see into her eyes. "Did something happen? Is Dan all right?"

She pressed her lips together, nodding and trying not to

burst into floods of tears. "Can you please just help me with the saddle?"

He frowned. "What did he do?"

When she didn't answer, he let out a deep sigh and let her go. Sara walked away and wrapped her arms around herself, staring at the distant mountains while Will fetched Rosie from the pasture.

"You know I'm here for you, whatever you need," he said when Rosie was ready. "And I'm going to have a serious talk with that idiot brother of mine."

A teary, desperate laugh escaped. "You're the best brother-in-law ever."

He nodded solemnly. "Yeah, I know."

~ ~ ~

Daniel rubbed the back of his hand over the bandage covering his eyes. What he really wanted to do was rip the loathsome thing off.

He raised his face to the ceiling. "Why have You done this to me?"

Heavy footsteps marched into the kitchen.

"What did you say to her?"

He turned away. "It's none of your business."

"It is my business when you make my sister-in-law, who has done nothing but be good to us, cry. You can shout at me all you want, but she's done nothing to deserve being treated like that."

A stab of guilt rocked him. "She was crying?"

"As good as. What did you say to her?"

When Daniel didn't answer, Will gripped his shoulder and spun him round to face him.

"What did you *say* to her?"

Daniel batted his hand away. "I told her I wanted her to

193

go back to New York and find another husband."

There were a few seconds of silence. It occurred to him that Will might be gearing up to punch him.

He was slightly relieved when all he did was shout.

"What is *wrong* with you?!"

"She should go. She'd be better off without me."

"I swear, Dan, you've done some stupid things in your life, but this may be the stupidest. Do you have any idea how lucky you are? That woman is the best thing that has ever happened to you and she adores you, although right now I have no earthly idea why. You finally have everything you wanted and you're trying to throw it all away."

Daniel rounded angrily on his brother. "I'm *blind!* Don't you get it? I've lost everything."

"No, all you've lost is your sight. I'm praying that you will get it back, but if you don't you can find a way to live with it. If you lose everything else it will be your own fault, and it would serve you right. It's time you stopped feeling sorry for yourself and dealt with this like the man you used to be."

Will's footsteps stomped away and the door slammed shut. Daniel wished he'd come back so he could shout at him.

Will had no right to tell him how he should be feeling or what he should be doing. Daniel couldn't *see.* How was he supposed to live like that? How could he be the man he used to be without his sight? How could he be the man Sara deserved?

You made her cry.

His fury ebbed as the realization of what he'd done began to truly sink in. He'd told her to leave him, to go back to New York, to find another man. When she did, she would take his heart with her.

He reached out his hand, found the back of one of the chairs at the table, and sank down onto it.

194

You made her cry.

Resting his elbows on his knees, he dropped his head into his hands.

"Please, Lord. Help me."

CHAPTER 23

Sara brought Rosie to a halt in front of a large two storey house with lilies in the garden and a porch like Daniel's, only bigger. There was even a bench that looked the same as theirs.

She'd galloped for the first half of the journey, the wind whipping against the moisture on her cheeks and burning her eyes, before slowing Rosie to a walk. Her tears had come and gone and now she just felt numb. It was a relief. Feeling anything else was too painful.

She hadn't known where to go when she'd asked Will to saddle Rosie. Several destinations had gone through her mind as the mare's steady gait lulled her raging thoughts. She'd considered both Amy and Louisa, and when she'd reached the turning that would have taken her to Lizzy's home she almost went there. But one destination had come to her over and over. She wasn't sure if it was God's guiding or her own desire to gain understanding from the woman who knew Daniel better than she did, but here was where she'd known she had to come.

As she climbed down to the ground and looped Rosie's halter rope around the hitching post in the yard, the door opened to the house.

"Sara?"

So much for feeling numb. With one look at Abigail's concerned face, she burst into tears.

In seconds her mother-in-law's arms were encircling her

shoulders and she was being led inside. Sara buried her face in her hands, unable to halt her great, heaving sobs. Without seeing where she was going, she let Abigail gently guide her to a seat where she wrapped her arms around her and held her for a long time.

When Sara's sobs finally petered out into sniffles, Abigail sat back and dipped her head to look into Sara's eyes. "Is everyone all right?"

Sara nodded, feeling guilty she hadn't thought to reassure her first, and fished a handkerchief from her pocket to blow her nose.

Abigail breathed out. "Good. So are you up to telling me what happened?"

Sara stared down at her hands in her lap, wrapped around the handkerchief. "It's Daniel." Just saying his name brought the hot tears back and she wiped her sleeve across her face. "He told me he wants a divorce. He said I should go back to New York and find a man who can take care of me." She raised her burning eyes to Abigail's face. "I don't know what to do. Everything I say or do just makes it worse. He's suffering so much and I don't know how to help him. What will I do if he sends me away? I don't want to be without him. I... I love him." It was the first time she'd said the words out loud, but she knew without a doubt they were true. She loved Daniel, more than she ever thought it was possible to love anyone.

"I am so glad to hear that." Abigail brushed Sara's hair from her face where it had stuck to her tears and smiled. "You know, he was always so focused, even when he was young. Could do anything he put his mind to. So when he bought that old, run down farm I knew he'd make it work, and he did. Worked from morning 'til night to get it going. Sometimes, in church, he'd be almost nodding off in his chair during the sermon, he'd be so tired. But he never gave up.

"Anyway, one day, about a year after he'd started, I asked him why he was working so hard, what it was all for. He told me that all he'd ever wanted was a happy family like he'd grown up in, with a wife to love and children to raise, and that was what would make his life complete. He was working to make the farm profitable before he took a bride, so he could provide for her like he felt he needed to.

"Four years later, he finally told his father and me that both the farm and he were ready and he'd asked Pastor Jones for help to find the wife he would share it all with. We were so happy for him, but as the months passed and he wrote to so many women and didn't find what he was looking for in any of them, I began to think he'd waited too long or set himself up for failure.

"Then one day I was helping Mrs. Jones with the flowers in the church and he came running in waving a piece of paper with the biggest smile on his face you've ever seen, and he said, 'I've found her.' That piece of paper was your first letter to him. He knew right from the start that you were the one for him.

"He thinks that everything he's worked so hard for, all his dreams for his life, are over because of what's happened to him. It's just like I told you, he needs to provide for you and now he thinks he can't, he's lost hope. But he loves you, Sara. I knew it the first moment I saw the two of you together; the way he looked at you, like he'd found something precious. I know he doesn't truly want you to leave and he needs you now more than ever. Be patient with him and the despair he feels will fade and he'll realize he still has so much to live for. Most of all you."

All Sara's tears had vanished. Daniel had never told her any of that, even in his letters. She remembered writing that first letter to him. It had taken her two days and eight false starts before she had something she was happy with. She'd been so eager to make a good first impression on the man who'd been able to so entrance her with just an advertisement in a newspaper insert.

But out of everything Abigail had said, there was one thing she needed to make sure of. "You truly think Daniel loves me?"

Abigail burst into laughter. "He hasn't told you already? Oh, Sara, my boy is head over heels, no doubt about that. A mother knows these things."

Sara wished she could be so sure. "So what do you think I should do?"

"I think you should go home and tell your husband that you are there for him whatever happens, and that you're not going anywhere, no matter what he thinks you should do. But that's just the opinion of the woman who raised him. And if he doesn't listen, you tell me. I'll come over there and set him straight."

A smile tugged at Sara's lips. "I think I might like to see that."

Abigail laughed, her eyes mischievous. "Just say the word."

~ ~ ~

Daniel lifted his face, feeling the sun shining on him. Its warmth was scant comfort, but it was pleasant.

He was out on the back porch. Funny how he'd never spent much time there before Sara arrived, had never really had any preference for any particular place in his home. Now he always seemed to gravitate to the porch. It was her favorite place.

His hands rested on the railing and he felt the wood warm against his uninjured palm. There hadn't been a railing around the porch when he'd first moved in. Or at least if there ever had been, it was no longer there. He'd had to build one from scratch.

The first two years had been tough. He'd been working the fields, tending the fruit trees and establishing the beehives on his own. It wasn't until the third year that he'd been able to afford to offer Will room and board and wages to come and work for him. It was backbreaking work and there were times when he'd doubted he could keep going, and then he would think about his dream of a family and it would give him the strength he needed. He didn't know it at the time, but he'd done it all for Sara.

Now he couldn't even picture her face clearly. She was fading from him, in more ways than one. Will was right, it was his fault he was losing her. But how could he ask her to stay? Everything he had to offer her was gone.

The door to the kitchen opened behind him and for a few seconds there was silence.

"Sara? Is that you?" Soft footsteps he knew were hers approached. "Sara?"

"Yes," she said, her voice quiet, "it's me."

Then the footsteps were moving and she ran into his arms, her face pressing against his chest. All the breath left him. He could feel her body shaking, her tears soaking into his shirt.

He couldn't do this; he couldn't keep causing her pain. "Sara," he said softly, "I'm so sorry. Please don't cry."

"Please don't send me away," she sobbed into his chest. "I can't leave you. I don't want to be anywhere else but here, with you. Please don't ask me to leave."

He lifted his face to the sky. His chest ached from the effort of fighting his emotions. Lowering his head, he brushed his lips against the top of her head.

"I don't know what to do," he whispered. "I don't know how to take care of you. I don't know how to take care of myself or the farm. I can't do anything anymore." He sucked in a trembling breath and it escaped again in a sob. "Without my eyes, I'm nothing."

Releasing her, he sank to the floor. Desperate sobs clutched hold of him, heaving through his body, wrenching his breath away. The last thing he wanted to do was cry in front of her, but he couldn't stop it as all the turmoil he'd been holding inside him poured out in a flood of anguished tears.

Sara lowered to her knees beside him and her arms wrapped around him. Too weak to fight the emotions anymore, he clung to her and wept, pressing his face into her shoulder, his tears soaking the bandages around his eyes.

She held him in silence for the long minutes he cried, until her warmth and strength seeped into him. It was only when his own tears stopped that he felt the wetness of hers on his forehead where her cheek rested against his skin.

"I don't want you to leave," he whispered. His voice trembled, but he was beyond trying to stay strong. He didn't have the energy anymore. "The thought of you with another man feels like I'm being stabbed through the heart, but I don't know what to do. I can't protect you and I can't look after you like I'm meant to. I only want what's best for you."

Her hold tightened around him. He hadn't moved from her shoulder and he found he had no wish to. As long as he stayed here, in her arms, he didn't have to face what had become of his life.

She turned her head and he could feel her warm breath on his skin as she spoke. "What's best for me is to be by my husband's side. Taking care of me isn't about money or even protection, it's about friendship and trust and support, for both of us. I know you'll provide for me for the rest of my life, whatever happens. Let me look after you now, while you need it."

"You shouldn't have to look after me," he said. "I can't promise you anything. You should have security and I can't give it to you."

"I had all the security in the world in New York, but it wasn't enough. I could have married a man who had everything, but I knew I'd never be happy with him. It wasn't until I got here that I truly understood why I said yes to you when I said no to him. It's you I've been waiting for, Daniel. Not money or security or even this farm. It's always been you."

He slowly raised his head. Could it be that she felt the same way he did? "Ever since you arrived, I've had this feeling that I've been waiting for you my whole life and that everything I've done, the farm, the house, has been for you. Even when I didn't know who you were."

"Like we were always meant to be together."

Inside him, a glimmer of hope breathed into life. "You feel it too?"

"Every second of every day." Her fingers touched his cheek. "You're it for me, Daniel. You're the only one. I can't leave you because I can't live without you."

He drew in a deep, trembling breath. What was wrong with him? He'd been waiting for her his whole life and he'd tried to send her away. "How can you ever forgive me? I've treated you so badly."

Her hand touched his hair, pushing it back from his face. It put him in mind of the morning less than a week before when he'd woken to her doing the same thing.

"I can't imagine we'll never argue again," she said, "or that there won't be times we'll drive each other crazy. But I will always forgive you. Seventy times seven."

"I'll probably need that many." Her soft laugh gave him such a deep desire to see her smile again that it made his heart ache. "I wish I could see you, just one last time. I can hardly imagine your face anymore. I feel like I'm losing you."

She took hold of his hands and brought them to her face. "You won't ever lose me. Even if you can't remember what I look like, I'm still here. I will always be right here."

Her closeness, her touch, made his heart thud. He slid the fingers of his right hand into her hair, marveling at its softness. The memory of the sun shining in her red gold tresses on the day she arrived was suddenly pin sharp, her face as clear to him as it had been then.

"You're so beautiful," he whispered.

He longed to draw her close, but after the way he'd treated her he knew he didn't have the right.

And then he felt her fingertips graze his face, brushing down his cheek to cradle his jaw. Her body shifted as she leaned forward, her breath caressing his lips.

He edged closer, the tip of her nose touched his, he tilted his head.

And then their lips met.

The first kiss was gentle, hesitant, and over before he wanted it to be. He waited, hoping he hadn't scared her, yearning for more.

She breathed his name, her lips found his again, and this time there was no uncertainty. He pulled her close, his heart soaring as she melted into his arms. With all the love in the world flooding through him, Daniel kissed his wife until he was breathless and elated and blissfully happy.

When they finally parted, she leaned against him and nuzzled her face into his neck with a sigh. It felt incredible.

"I'm so sorry for everything," he murmured into her hair. "I don't deserve you,"

He felt her smile against his skin. "There is no way for me to answer that without sounding horribly conceited."

Laughter bubbled up inside him and before he knew it he was laughing so hard his sides ached. And best of all, he

203

could hear Sara's laughter mingling with his own.

For the first time since he'd lost his sight, Daniel praised the Lord for his life.

~ ~ ~

By the time Will returned from the orchard, supper was cooking and Daniel was sitting on the bench with Sara. Their special place, as he now thought of it.

She was snuggled into his side, her head resting against his shoulder and his arm securely wrapped around her, holding her close. The relaxed intimacy felt almost as good as the kissing, which they'd done a lot more of during the afternoon. In fact, he'd been following her around like a puppy, but she didn't seem to mind.

Will was right, he'd been an idiot. He'd spent six days feeling sorry for himself when he could have spent the time getting closer to his incredible wife. Idiot didn't even begin to cover it.

He heard Ginger and River's plodding hoof beats enter the yard, the creak of the wagon, and the sound of Will dropping to the ground and walking up the porch steps. There was a long period of silence.

"Am I hallucinating?" Will finally said.

Sara kissed Daniel's cheek and slid from his embrace. "I'm going to check on supper."

As the door to the kitchen closed, Will took her place on the bench, if somewhat further away from Daniel.

"I'm sorry," Daniel said. "You were right."

Will made a choking sound. "Could you repeat that?"

He smiled a little. "I've been so busy feeling sorry for myself and thinking all my plans were ruined and that I've lost everything that I missed all the things I still have. I have an amazing wife who wants to stay with me no matter what, a God Who will give me the strength to get through this if I just let Him, and a brother who has stuck by me even when I've treated him badly."

"Hmm," Will said, "I'm glad to hear you've finally realized that. It certainly does sound like your genius brother has been right all along."

Daniel snorted a laugh. "You're not going to make this easy, are you?"

"Nope. Tell me again how I was right? I'd like to get it in writing too."

"Pity I can't write when I can't see."

"You can muddle through. I'll guide your hand."

Daniel reached out and found his shoulder. "Thank you for not giving up on me when I gave up on myself."

Will's hand touched his. "That's what brothers are for."

"Oh, *that's* what brothers are for. Good to know." He lowered his bandaged hand to his lap. "And I want to go out with you tomorrow and try again. You were right about me giving up too easily. I can do better."

"I could get used to you admitting I'm right all the time."

"Don't get carried away, I didn't say you were right *all* the time."

"Close enough," Will said, a smile in his voice. "So what happened between you and Sara? I just about fell off the wagon when I saw the two of you so cozy."

A grin slid onto Daniel's face. He couldn't help it. "Well, when I finally realized what an idiot I've been and apologized, she kissed me. Or I kissed her. We kissed."

"Ohhh. So that's why you look so pleased with yourself."

"And there has been plenty more since then." It wasn't meant to be a boast. "I may not be able to see, but there's nothing wrong with my lips." Maybe just a bit.

"I truly don't need to hear that."

"Kissing is so much better when you're in love. You should try it."

"Uh-uh, not me. You and Jimmy are the upright, family men. I am the roguish, devastatingly handsome one who all the girls want but none will ever pin down. No one will ever clip these wings. I'm an eagle that needs to soar in the clouds, free to ride the wind wherever he pleases."

Daniel gave his words some thought. "I think you may have overdone that a bit."

"Yeah, I did get carried away. It was a good metaphor though."

"Supper will be ready in five minutes," Sara called from the kitchen, "if anyone's hungry."

"Five minutes," Will said. "Better get the wagon unhitched. Want to give me some help?"

"I think I can do that."

As Will led him to the wagon, he patted Daniel's hand on his arm.

"It's good to have you back."

CHAPTER 24

Daniel sat on his bed, his Bible clutched to his chest.

He'd been praying ever since Sara went to bed, although he had no idea how long ago that was. It may have been hours, but he couldn't seem to stop. Now that he was finally ready to listen, it was as if God wanted his full attention, and He was taking the opportunity to show Daniel a few things.

Daniel had always thought himself a strong, steadfast Christian. He'd asked Jesus into his life when he was fourteen, he attended church regularly, read his Bible and prayed. There was no doubt in his mind that he belonged to God. He'd accepted Jesus as his Lord and Savior, knew his sins had been forgiven and wiped away through His death on the cross.

And yet when this terrible thing happened to him, when he lost his sight and with it all the capability and strength he'd always taken for granted, his assurance in his Lord had failed.

Daniel hadn't intended to push God away and he certainly hadn't intended to blame Him. But it had happened anyway, and God was showing him why - the confidence he'd always thought he had in God had really been confidence in himself. There was so much that was beyond Daniel's control, and yet he had been trusting in his own strength rather than his Creator's.

And when God didn't heal him as Daniel wanted Him to, Daniel sank into despair. He'd taken his eyes off God and turned them on himself. He now understood that he had been looking for the wrong type of healing; he wanted his body healed when what he really needed was healing for his soul. He had a lot to learn about what was really important.

Daniel longed to be able to read the Book in his hands and he'd prayed for that. Instead of receiving his sight back, however, verse after verse was coming into his mind. On and on it went, each verse a message from his Father about his life and what had happened to him. God was speaking to him, teaching him, and he listened. For the first time in a long time, he heard what God was saying to him.

He shed tears more than once during the long process, begged for forgiveness, and was comforted. And when the verses stopped he simply sat and prayed, pouring out his heart about his life, Sara, Will, the rest of his family and friends, the farm, his hopes for the future. He gave everything to God that he'd been taking on himself.

And finally, having given over every burden he'd been hoarding, he was able to fall into a deep, refreshing sleep, one final message from the Lord remaining with him.

Fear not: for I am with thee.

CHAPTER 25

Sara gazed through the kitchen window at the patchwork of grayish-white clouds scudding across a blue sky and exhaled a long, dreamy sigh.

A moment later she was forced to stop chopping the parsnip in her hand before she severed her own fingers.

Concentration had eluded her all day. All she seemed to be able to think about was Daniel. Specifically, the wonderful way she felt when he kissed her, or held her, or was anywhere in her general vicinity. She'd never experienced anything quite like it and she couldn't help wondering if he felt the same way.

Lowering her gaze, she was surprised to see Will by the barn, unhitching River and Ginger from the wagon. When had they got back and how long had she been daydreaming while staring into the sky?

Daniel was walking across the yard from the wagon, a smile on his face. In fact, he was practically striding, his footsteps sure as he swept the cane in front of him. When it hit the steps he grasped the handrail and walked up without stumbling, crossed the porch and stepped into the open doorway.

"Sara?"

"I'm here."

Something about him was different, a new confidence she hadn't seen since the accident.

He walked across the kitchen to her, grasped her waist

and lifted her into the air and she squealed and giggled as he spun her around. There was definitely something different about him.

"Just to warn you," he said, "I believe I'm about to claim my right as a husband to kiss my wife until her knees are weak. Or mine are."

"How about both?" she said breathlessly.

He lowered her to the floor and slid one hand up to cradle the back of her head, tilting his head down towards her. "Deal."

Her eyes fluttered closed and she wrapped her arms around his neck as he made good on his promise, his warm lips playing over hers until she felt like her legs would have trouble supporting her on their own. Kissing Daniel was fast becoming her favorite thing to do in the world. It was also a far smoother experience since he'd asked Will that morning to help him shave. The week's worth of beard growth he'd accumulated, while giving him a certain rugged attraction, had been a little rough on her skin.

"Do you mind? Not in front of the children, please."

Sara laughed as Daniel reluctantly broke away and heaved a sigh. "Must you?"

"I must," Will said, walking past them to the pantry. "It's shocking in here. I don't know where to look."

"There are freshly baked biscuits under the cloth," Sara said, resting her cheek against Daniel's chest since he didn't seem to be in any hurry to let her go. He kissed the top of her head and she smiled.

"Better hurry," he said. "I feel another bout of shocking behavior coming on."

Will emerged from the pantry holding a plate of three buttered biscuits and a jar of honey. "I'll be back for supper," he said, smiling at Sara as he walked out the back door.

"Is he gone?" Daniel said.

210

"Yes, he's gone."

He lowered his face to hers again. "Good."

They spent a further few blissful minutes engaging in Sara's favorite activity before she buttered two biscuits and joined Daniel on the settee, relaxing into his embrace as he ate.

"So what's got you in such a good mood?" she said. "Not that I'm complaining at all."

He swallowed a mouthful of biscuit. "I realized something today; I'm going to be all right."

She lifted her head to look at him. His face held a peaceful, even serene look she'd never seen, even before the accident.

"God's been teaching me a lot since yesterday," he said. "I've learned that I was relying far too much on my own strength, believing nothing could stop me if I just worked hard enough." He placed the biscuit down onto the plate and lifted both hands out in front of him. "This is where I put my faith, but I was wrong. We have no control over what happens to us. Anything can go wrong at any time, like the lamp exploding. I blamed God for not protecting me and I got angry with Him." He stroked one hand down her cheek. "And I pushed you away. I am so sorry for what I put you through."

"It's all right..." she began.

"No, it's not. You were suffering too and I made it worse behaving like I did. I don't know if I can make up for it, but I'm going to do everything in my power to be the best husband I can from now on. I can't promise I'll be perfect, but I'll try my hardest."

She wiped at a tear spilling down her face and stretched up to kiss his cheek. "Anything you do is good enough for me."

He found her hand and enfolded it in his. "I think

211

maybe God let this happen so I would learn that the only thing that will never change is Him and He's the only One I should put my faith in. I don't know what will happen with my eyes, but today I learned that I can still work, even blind. So even if I stay this way I know I will be OK, with His help." Bringing her hand to his lips, he kissed her palm. "And yours, if you'll have a blind man who makes more mistakes than he should."

She slid both arms around his neck and nuzzled into his shoulder. "I'll have you no matter what. You must know that."

His hand wrapped around her back. "I think I finally do. Thankfully."

CHAPTER 26

The wagon bounced along the road, causing a continual susurrus of tinkling as the glass jars of amber colored honey jostled against each other in their boxes.

Sara glanced back at them in concern. "Do they always make all that noise?"

"Yep."

"How do they not break?"

"We've learned just the right amount of packaging to keep them from cracking. I should probably admit it took a few tries to get it right. Honey is really hard to scrub out of a wagon bed, let me tell you."

His smile took her breath away. The orange sun was still fairly low in the sky and it shimmered in the waves of his hair and glowed over his skin. There were times when she was still amazed that she could be married to such a beautiful man.

She leaned her head against his shoulder and he circled his arm around her waist, gently tugging her against him.

She sighed happily. "What time do we have to be there?"

"Seven thirty. Why?"

"I was just wondering if we had time to... stop for a little while." She could feel her cheeks reddening at her own forwardness and was glad he couldn't see them.

"Why, Mrs. Raine, are you suggesting you want to take advantage of me? In public?" His arm tightened around her waist.

"There's no one else around," she said, her voice slightly breathless. "Besides, if anyone does come all they'll see is a man kissing his wife. Nothing overly scandalous about that."

His mouth moved to her ear and he whispered, "Stop the wagon."

A shiver skittered down her spine and she had to swallow before speaking. "But if we don't have time..."

He felt for the reins in her hands and pulled back, saying, "Whoa," while never moving the rest of his body away from hers.

As River and Rosie came to a halt, he wrapped both arms around her.

"We'll risk being late."

~ ~ ~

By the time they reached the town, most of the other market stalls had already set up.

Sara brought the wagon to a halt and patted her hair, making sure it was at least halfway tidy. She'd had to re-pin it after the prolonged pause in their journey, Daniel's roving hands having succeeded in thoroughly messing it up. She couldn't help smiling at the thought and hoped her face wasn't too flushed. Before Daniel she'd only ever kissed two other men, although she wasn't sure she could even compare kissing them to kissing him. She'd been thoroughly unprepared for the experience of having a man take her breath away with just the touch of his lips. She was certainly getting used to it though.

They'd barely finished setting up their stall of honey and fruit before Mrs. Goodwin bustled up to them.

"Oh, thank goodness, I thought you might not be coming and I'm in dire need of your delicious honey. If Mr.

Goodwin doesn't get his honeyed ham this Friday I think he might just up and leave me. I'll take four jars and twenty apricots. And throw in a pound of those cherries."

Sara dealt with the money while Daniel placed the jars carefully into Mrs. Goodwin's bag.

"Mr. Goodwin is far too smart to leave you," he said as he measured out the apricots and cherries, using his fingers to feel the pointer on the scales. "He's the envy of every man in Green Hill Creek."

She laughed and patted his hand. "You've always been a charmer, Daniel. No wonder you got yourself such a lovely wife." She smiled at Sara.

"Thank you, Mrs. Goodwin," she said, glancing up at Daniel next to her. "He certainly has charmed me."

The older woman stood back and cast a searching gaze over them. "You seem happier than you were last week."

Daniel slid his arm around Sara's shoulders and smiled down at her. "With God's help, I finally came to my senses and realized that no matter what happens, I am the most blessed man on earth to have Sara by my side."

Tears suddenly tingled at the back of her eyes and she leaned her head against his shoulder as she dabbed at them with her fingertips.

"Oh my, I think I'm going to embarrass myself and weep right here in the middle of the street," Mrs. Goodwin said, fanning her eyes with one hand. "I'm real happy for you both. And we're all praying for your sight to come back, Daniel."

"Thank you, Mrs. G," he said. "I know I'm going to be just fine."

The morning saw a steady stream of customers visit the stall. The fruit was popular, but it was the honey that went fast. After only an hour almost half of the jars they'd brought had been sold.

215

"So far I'm the only one who keeps bees around here," Daniel said when Sara asked him about it. "I'm thinking of setting up more hives for next year. I can barely keep up with the demand."

At just before nine Sara saw Amy and Adam approaching and she stepped out from behind the stall and ran to greet her friend.

"How are things?" Amy whispered as they hugged.

"Much better." Sara lowered her voice as she glanced back at Daniel and Adam where they were talking. "We had our first kiss on Monday."

"How was it?" Amy said, smiling.

Sara couldn't contain her long, blissful sigh. "Incredible. I don't know what the other two men who've kissed me were doing, but they definitely weren't doing it right."

Amy burst into giggles. "What happened to the proper New Yorker I travelled here with?"

"She married the man of her dreams and realized she was going to love life out here. But what about you? How are things with Adam?"

It was Amy's turn to look towards the two men at the stall. Adam glanced at her and smiled and her cheeks flushed. "To tell you the truth, I'm confused. I've had this dream of going to San Francisco for so long it's like a part of me, but every time I'm with Adam all I can think is how good it would be to stay with him. I don't know what to do."

"Stay," Sara said immediately. "There's a chance I'm not entirely unbiased in my opinion because I don't want you to leave, but if you're happy with him, stay. Being in love is the most wonderful feeling. Now that I am, I wouldn't give it up for anything."

A smile crept onto Amy's face. "Maybe you're right. But I don't know if he'd want me after what I did." The smile faltered. "All I've done is make his life harder."

216

"And yet his face still lights up whenever he looks at you."

Amy's eyebrows shot up. "It does?"

Sara shook her head in disbelief. How could her friend be so oblivious? The man was obviously crazy about her. But it wasn't her place to tell Amy. That was Adam's job.

"Come on. Let's..."

She was interrupted by a throat being cleared emphatically. Both she and Amy looked round. At the sight of Mr. Pulaski standing behind them Sara's stomach twisted. She took a step back, glancing at Daniel.

"Good morning ladies." Mr. Pulaski smiled and tipped his hat.

"What do you want?" Sara said, not bothering to hide her anger. Even in the midst of the crowded market he frightened her, but she wasn't going to let him know it.

"I wanted to check that you've had no more trouble from that ne'er-do-well I chased from your farm last week," he replied, either oblivious or uncaring about her animosity. "I still hate to think what might have happened if I hadn't been there to save you."

"From what I've heard, the only person Sara needs saving from is you," Amy said, glaring at him.

Sara silently applauded her friend.

Mr. Pulaski scowled at her. "And you are?"

"Mr. Pulaski," Sara said, taking courage from Amy, "after what happened on Saturday I don't wish to speak to you. Please don't bother me or my husband again."

She took Amy's arm and steered her towards Daniel and the stall. Before they'd gone two steps, Mr. Pulaski stepped into their path.

"Sara, I understand why you're upset at that unfortunate misunderstanding on Saturday, but truly I meant you no harm, as I explained to the marshal. Please forgive me anything I may have done wrong."

Sara gritted her teeth and spoke slowly. "It's *Mrs. Raine.*"

"Of course." He smiled.

She had no idea what to do. Whatever she did or said, he still didn't get the message. It seemed nothing would make him leave her alone.

"Do you mind?" Amy snapped. "You're in our way."

His eyes darted between the two of them before he stepped aside. "My apologies."

Sara pulled Amy past him before he had a chance to say anything more, only breathing out once she'd reached the stall and was back at Daniel's side.

"Awful man," Amy muttered. "I was *this* close to slapping him."

"Who?" Adam said.

"Mr. Pulaski."

Daniel's head whipped up. "He's here?"

"He spoke to us," Sara said.

He felt for her hand. "Are you all right?"

"My goodness, that honey looks delicious. I'd love to buy a jar." Mr. Pulaski walked up to the stall and smiled.

Sara's jaw dropped at his audacity. What was wrong with the man?

At the sound of his voice, Daniel stiffened. He put his arm around Sara and pulled her against him. At the other end of the stall, she saw Adam step protectively in front of Amy.

"Get out of here, Pulaski," Daniel growled.

"Now, now, is that any way to speak to a customer?"

"If you don't leave right now, I will..."

"You'll what, Mr. Raine? Tell me, what can you possibly do in the middle of a crowded street?"

"I don't care where we are."

Sara could feel Daniel trembling with rage against her. She put a hand on his arm in the hopes of calming him. While she wanted Pulaski to go away, she didn't want Daniel to get hurt.

"Well, perhaps you should," Pulaski said. "Because if you assault me I will have you arrested and there will be plenty of witnesses. And then Sara will be left alone with no one to protect her. Except for me."

For a moment Sara thought Daniel would launch himself across the table. Then he took a deep breath, relaxing ever so slightly.

"I think you should leave," Adam said, walking up to them.

Pulaski looked between him and Daniel, then he smiled. "Maybe I'll get that honey another time." He nodded to Sara and walked away, disappearing into the crowd of shoppers.

"He's gone," she said.

Daniel breathed out, but didn't let her go.

"So that's the Pulaski Amy told me about," Adam said. "He's creepy, isn't he?"

"That seems to be the prevailing opinion, yes."

"He's dangerous," Daniel said.

Sara hoped he was wrong. "He just did that to antagonize you."

"Well, he succeeded."

"Thought you were going to leap across the table at him for a moment there," Adam said. "That would have made things interesting. Maybe if you had, it would have given the local gossip brigade something to talk about other than Amy and me."

Daniel gave him a rueful smile. "Sorry you'll have to remain the talk of the town for another day."

"That's OK, I've gotten used to it now. Might miss the attention if it stopped."

"I'd better get going to the livery before George starts checking his watch," Amy said. She gave Sara a hug. "I'll see you Sunday. If you need anything, you know where to find me."

Sara leaned in close and whispered, "Sighing over Adam."

Amy giggled and pushed her away. Sara was sure she detected the hint of a blush on her cheeks.

"I'll walk you over there," Adam said.

"Don't you have to be at the bank soon?"

"There's time." He picked up the jar of honey he'd bought and held out his elbow. "Shall we?"

Amy slipped her hand around his arm and gazed up at him and Sara couldn't help but notice Adam wasn't the only one whose face lit up when the two of them looked at each other. Amy wasn't going anywhere, she was sure of it. After saying their goodbyes, they walked away arm in arm, talking.

With Amy and Adam gone, Daniel lapsed into silence as he ran his hands over the jars of honey to check how many were left.

When he hadn't spoken for a minute, Sara slipped her arm into his. "Let's not let Pulaski spoil this. I'm enjoying myself here. I want to just forget about him."

He sighed and ran his hand over hers. "You're right. I don't want to give him another thought. We're having a good day for sales, what do you say to having lunch at the hotel before we go home?"

The memory of going there on Saturday to confront Pulaski flashed across her mind, but she pushed it away. "If you think we can afford it."

Instead of insisting he could provide for them, as he would have before, he grinned and nudged her shoulder with his. "What's life if you can't have a treat every now and then?"

She nudged him back. "Not worth living."

As another customer approached, she thought she

spotted Mr. Pulaski watching them from across the street, but the customer distracted her and when she looked back he was gone. If he'd ever been there in the first place.

Shrugging it off, she continued serving at Daniel's side.

CHAPTER 27

Sara jerked awake. Heavy eyelids yearning to close again, she stared into the darkness of the bedroom and wondered what had wakened her.

Then she heard the barking.

Out in the living room she heard a thud and a muffled exclamation.

She scrambled out of the bed, pushed her feet into her shoes and grabbed her robe. Not bothering to light a lamp, she stumbled to the door and into the living room. By the light of the half moon shining in through the windows she could see Daniel trying to pull on his trousers and make his way to the kitchen at the same time.

"Daniel?"

"Something's wrong with Bess." In his haste he hit his shin on the edge of a chest and yelped in pain.

Sara hurried over to him and took his arm, guiding him through the kitchen to the back door. When she pulled it open the smell of smoke made her stomach lurch.

"Something's on fire," he said, pushing forward.

She only just managed to grab him before he plummeted down the steps at the edge of the porch. "You're at the steps. Let me lead you or you're going to hurt yourself."

"Can you see it?" he said as he held onto her hand, fear in his voice.

She peered into the darkness, searching for any sign of flames. The barking was coming from the large barn and she stared at it in the barely moonlit darkness. "I can't see anything. If you..." Something caught her eye. A sliver of flickering orange light framing the doors. "The barn. There's fire inside the barn."

"No!" He let go of her and started forward.

She ran into his path, pushing against his chest to stop him. "I'll go. You get to the pump and start filling buckets."

"No! I have to..."

"Don't argue with me!" Fear made her shout when she didn't intend to. "You can't do this, I can."

"But..."

"*Pump! Now!*"

For a moment she thought he would refuse, but he nodded, said, "Be careful," and turned in the direction of the well.

She didn't wait to see if he got there. Heart pounding, she ran for the barn. She glanced at the bunkhouse in case Will had returned home, but it was in darkness.

She could hear the fire now, mingled with Bess' increasingly more frenzied barking and the neighing and mooing of the terrified animals. The dog met her halfway to the barn and ran with her, dancing around her legs. Without stopping to think of any danger, Sara grasped the door handle and pulled it open.

Smoke billowed around her and she was immediately seized with coughing. She peered into the interior, struggling to see through the haze. Flames consumed a pile of hay to her right, already licking at the wooden wall nearby. Further back, another fire ate at a pile of old wooden boxes. A third blaze was taking hold of the back wall. A small part of her brain wondered how three fires could have broken out at once, the rest concentrated on what she had to do.

Holding the sleeve of her robe across her nose and mouth, she ran inside. The heat hit her instantly and she

223

almost turned around and ran back out, but the sound of the horses panicking in their stalls and Pea's frantic mooing drove her on.

She opened the cow's stall first, slapping her on her rump to get her moving before heading deeper into the barn's hot, smoky interior. As Sara had suspected, Ginger's stall was empty. Will wasn't home yet. Reaching the next stall, she fumbled with the latch before getting it open. Rosie burst out and galloped for the barn door and Sara moved to the final occupied stall.

Her lungs convulsed and she was forced to stop as a fit of coughing doubled her over. River kicked at the door trapping him, neighing frantically.

Managing to straighten, she unlatched River's stall and he launched himself for freedom, flinging the door open and into her. She stumbled back, grabbing onto the wall to keep from falling.

"Sara!"

She could hear Daniel calling her. Tears streamed down her face from the smoke. The roar of the flames surrounded her.

"*Sara!*"

She pushed herself away from the stall and staggered for the blackness of the barn door. Finally making it back outside, she gulped in the cool, fresh air and was gripped by violent coughs again. Bess was immediately at her side, whining.

"Sara." Somehow, Daniel had found her. He grasped at her shoulders, his face filled with fear.

"I'm all right," she wheezed, holding onto his arms and pulling herself straight. "I need water for the fire."

She expected him to argue, but he picked up a bucket from the ground and held it out to her, sloshing water over the sides. Taking the heavy bucket, she took a deep breath of the relatively clean air and ran back into the barn, throwing the water on the nearest fire. When she got back outside Daniel was back at the pump with another bucket. How he knew which way to go, she had no idea.

She lost track of time as they worked, desperately battling the fire, Daniel pumping the water and Sara throwing bucket after bucket onto the flames until her hands were raw and her arms exhausted.

Smoke rasped at her lungs and burned her eyes and more than once Daniel begged her to stop, but she wouldn't. After losing his eyes, she couldn't let him lose the barn too.

So she fought on with every drop of strength she had.

But it wasn't enough.

Sparks flew around the interior of the barn, igniting wherever they landed. Sara had to dodge around flaming clumps of hay drifting from the loft above. Eventually, she could no longer stand the heat and smoke and she stumbled back into the air and away from the barn, coughing, tears of frustration streaming down her face.

Daniel ran up to her, his arms outstretched. She reached out to take his hand.

"I can't do it," she sobbed. "It won't stop. I can't put it out."

In an instant his arms were wrapped around her, holding her close. "It's all right," he murmured into her hair.

She shook her head, clutching at his shirt. "It's not all right. Everything is in there, the hay, your tools, everything. You'll lose it all."

"No," he said, his voice steady. "Everything I need is right here."

Her sobs stilled and she looked up at him. The bandage around his eyes was blackened with smoke. Sweat sheened his face and his clothing was stained with dirt. But in his expression she saw only peace.

"How can you be so calm?"

To her astonishment, he smiled. "To be honest, I don't really know. But I do know the Lord is with us. He always has been, even when I couldn't tell. We're safe, that's all that matters."

This wasn't the same Daniel who had almost given up when he lost his sight. He truly had learned to trust in God completely. Maybe she needed to learn that too.

She leaned into him, taking comfort from the feel of his arms around her, and watched the flames licking at the walls of the barn and reaching into the star-speckled sky. Bess sat beside them, leaning her furry body against their legs. Sara reached down to scratch her head.

Father, she prayed silently, *I'm scared, but I know You're here. Thank you that Daniel has learned to trust you no matter what. Help me to do the same.*

"I hear something," Daniel said suddenly, lifting his head.

With the sound of the flames consuming the barn it seemed impossible to hear anything else. "I don't..." And then she heard it, faint but unmistakable.

Galloping horses and the rumble of cartwheels on a dirt road.

CHAPTER 28

A wagon rounded the house and came to a halt in the yard, its driver yelling, "Whoa!"

Mr. Ellery and his two eldest sons, Sara and Daniel's closest neighbors, jumped to the ground.

"Saw the flames and came right on over," he said, nodding to Sara. "Ma'am. Looks like you could use some help."

She could barely see through her tears.

"We sure could," Daniel said. "You're a real answer to prayer."

Mr. Ellery grinned and waved his two sons over. "Well, let's get that fire put out."

Daniel took his place back at the pump, filling bucket after bucket as the Ellerys threw the water onto the flames. A few minutes later another wagon arrived, this one with more of their neighbors, Mr. Bowman and his son and grandson. On their heels came another, this one bringing Lizzy with Richard, Elijah Griffin, and three of their farmhands.

Lizzy ran to Sara while Richard, Elijah and the farmhands joined the rest of the men in a chain between the well and the barn.

Lizzy threw her arms around her. "Are you and Daniel and Will all right?"

"We are," Sara said, hugging her friend. "And I'm even better now you're here."

She let her go to look at the barn. "Richard saw the

227

flames. What happened?"

"I don't know, Bess woke us up when it was already on fire. Will you help me find the horses and Pea?"

It took almost an hour for the men to completely extinguish the blaze, by which time Sara and Lizzy had rounded up Rosie, River and Peapod and settled them in the small barn, after having moved things around to make room. Sara could see they would need to rearrange the limited space even further, but at least for the night it was adequate. Bess found a place on a stack of hay in a corner and curled into a ball, clearly tired out. She was asleep within seconds.

Sara had made a batch of lemonade the day before and she and Lizzy served up glasses of the sweet liquid to the men when they finally came inside, slumping onto chairs and floor.

"Me and my boys can come back tomorrow afternoon and help with clearing the barn," Mr. Ellery said as they were leaving fifteen minutes later. "I'm not sure how stable it is right now. Probably ought to come down as soon as possible."

"Thanks, Silas," Daniel said. "I really do appreciate what you did here tonight. Will will be around tomorrow too."

Mr. Ellery didn't ask where Will was. His frequent night time activities were obviously common knowledge. "Nothing more than you would do for me." He clapped Daniel on the shoulder and walked out with his sons in tow.

Lizzy gave Sara a hug. "Are you sure you don't want me to stay?"

"It's good of you to offer, but we'll be fine. I'm just going to go to bed and sleep until Sunday."

"Sounds like a good idea," Lizzy said, smiling.

Elijah walked up behind her and touched her shoulder. "M-Mr. Shand is in the wagon, when you're r-r-ready to leave."

228

"Thank you," she said, smiling up at him.

"Thank you for your help, Mr. Griffin," Sara said. "We're so grateful for what you all did."

He nodded and smiled. "Any t-t-time, M-Mrs. Raine."

Lizzy gave Sara one last hug, said goodbye to Daniel, and followed Elijah out to the wagon where Richard was sitting in the driver's seat. Sara waited until everyone had left the yard then closed and locked the door.

Daniel's arms slid around her waist from behind. "Are you OK?"

She turned to face him and lay her head against his chest, closing her eyes. "I'm exhausted."

"So am I." He rested his cheek against her hair. "I pumped so much water my arms feel like they're about to fall off."

She reached behind her and brought his left hand in front of her to examine his palm. It was an angry red, nearly raw. Hers were almost as bad.

"You should have worn gloves," she said.

"It didn't occur to me while it was happening. It's all right, they don't feel too bad. I think right now I just want to sleep."

She felt the same, but she didn't want to leave his embrace. She tucked her head in below his chin. "Is it possible the fire started by itself?"

"I don't know how it could have, but anything's possible I guess. What else could have done it?"

Much as she didn't want to, she thought back to when she was fighting the losing battle against the flames. "When I first went into the barn there were three fires, all around the same size, like they'd begun at the same time."

He tensed in her arms. "*Three* fires?"

"Yes, in three different places. It's why I couldn't put it out. If it had been just one, I could have concentrated on that and I might have done it, but with three I couldn't keep up."

He shook his head slightly. "One fire I could believe started by itself, however unlikely it is. But there is no way three could have started at once."

She didn't want to think about what that meant, but she couldn't help it. "So you think someone did it deliberately?"

He was silent for a while. "I don't know."

She didn't believe him. He did know, and it frightened her. "Do you think Mr. Pulaski could have done it?"

"I think we should go to the marshal tomorrow and tell him there's a possibility Pulaski set fire to the barn."

"But why?" She was finding it hard to believe anyone would do such a thing, even Mr. Pulaski. "What reason could he possibly have?"

"Jealousy? Trying to get rid of me? Trying to scare you away from me? Some other twisted reason? Who knows how his mind works?"

She looked out the kitchen window into the darkness. "Are we safe here?"

Daniel's chest rose and fell against her in a long breath. "We're as safe here as we are anywhere else. We're in God's hands, all we can do is give it to Him."

Give it to God. Daniel had learned how to do that. Sara wanted to be able to too.

Father, help me to let go of my fear. And please keep us and the farm safe.

They walked into the living room and Daniel drew her into his embrace again.

"Don't worry about getting up to make breakfast," he said. "Sleep as long as you want. Whatever there is to do, it can wait." After placing a gentle kiss on her forehead, he headed for his bed.

Sara walked to the bedroom door and looked at her own, empty bed. Then she looked back at him.

"Daniel?"

He raised his head from where he sat, in the process of removing his shoes. "Yes?"

"I'm scared. I... I don't want to be on my own."

He froze for a few moments, then stood and walked over to her. Taking her hand, he led her into the bedroom and without saying a word climbed beneath the covers and held them up for her to join him.

She stepped out of her shoes, extinguished the lamp, and climbed in beside him. He wrapped his arms around her and she breathed out a long sigh, closing her eyes and leaning her head against his chest.

"Can I ask you something?" she said after a few seconds.

"Anything." So close in the dark, his low voice was like a soothing balm, stilling her fear.

"Why didn't you stop me? When I wanted to go into the barn to fight the fire, I mean. I could tell you didn't want me to."

He slowly stroked her loose hair as he spoke against her forehead, his breath warming her skin. "Because I knew you wouldn't stop. You knew you could do it, so I believed you. I will always believe in you, Sara."

A warmth that had nothing to do with the blankets over her, or even his arms wrapped around her, blossomed in her heart. "I'll always believe in you too."

He placed a soft kiss on her forehead. "Goodnight."

Safe in her husband's arms, the soft, steady sound of his heartbeat lulled Sara into a deep, dreamless sleep.

CHAPTER 29

It was the warmth Sara felt first on waking; the blissful sensation of Daniel's arm around her, his chest pressed against her back and the heat of his body radiating through the layers of clothing between them.

Keeping her eyes closed and lying perfectly still so as not to disturb him, she drank in the feeling of waking up in her husband's arms for the first time. After the events of the night, it amazed her that she could feel so wonderfully safe and content. This was what love felt like, and she never wanted it to end.

"Good morning," Daniel murmured behind her, his voice sending a not at all unpleasant shiver down her spine.

She couldn't help smiling. "I thought you were still asleep. How did you know I was awake?"

"Your breathing," he replied. "I've been listening to you sleep. The rhythm changed when you woke up."

She turned over to face him and he drew her into his embrace, his fingers rubbing tiny circles on her back that sent wonderful tingles of sensation sizzling through her skin. He smelled of smoke and wood and... Daniel.

She touched her fingertips to his stubble-roughened cheek and he smiled. Even with the smoke blackened bandage still around his eyes he was so beautiful it set her heart racing.

The words she hadn't yet said to him came almost of their own accord. "I love you."

The movement of his hand on her back stopped and for a few moments he was completely still. "I love you too," he said, his voice barely a whisper. "I don't have the words to tell you how much."

Sara's heart pounded in her chest as she gazed at her husband. Her strong, incredible, wonderful husband. He was everything she wanted, and she wanted him completely.

So she said the words she knew would bind them indelibly together as man and wife for the rest of her life. The life she didn't want to spend one moment of away from him.

"Then show me."

His breath hitched, his mouth opening in surprise. "Are you saying...?"

She leaned into him until their lips touched and whispered, "Yes."

~ ~ ~

It was after eleven when Daniel heard the sound of hooves galloping into the yard outside. Marshal Cade had already paid them a visit so he was pretty sure who it would be. His suspicion was confirmed when he heard Ginger whinny and River and Rosie return her call from the pasture.

He put down the shovel he'd been feeling for damage, walked from the small barn into the sunshine, and waited.

Running footsteps approached.

"I..." Will drew a shuddering breath. "I didn't find out until this morning. I came straight back. Are you and Sara all right?"

"We're fine."

There were a few seconds of silence. "Dan, I... I'm sorry. I'm so sorry." His voice broke on the last word and he touched Daniel's shoulder for a moment before striding away before he could answer.

233

He let out a long sigh. At least his brother was safe. When Will hadn't returned by the time Daniel and Sara reluctantly left their bed at around ten, he'd been worried.

Sara's footsteps hurried up to him and she took his hand. "Ginger's here. Is Will home?"

"Yeah. He told me he was sorry and then ran off."

She rested her head against his shoulder. "You should go and talk to him. I can unsaddle Ginger and put her in the pasture."

He slipped his arm around her waist and kissed her temple. "I'm wishing we'd stayed in bed."

She giggled and the sound shivered through him in the most wonderful way.

"Maybe tonight we can go early." Taking his face in her hands, she gave him a kiss that set his heart thumping.

"Definitely yes," he said. "Is after lunch too early?"

She laughed again and stepped away from him, making him long to draw her back into his arms. "Go and talk to your brother." With one final and far too brief kiss, she was gone.

Daniel breathed out and wondered if he was glowing.

After a few moments of enjoying the lingering feeling of Sara's lips on his, he called Bess' name. Within seconds she was pressing against his leg, her tail thudding against his calf as he ruffled her ears. "Take me to Will, girl. Where's Will?"

She rushed off and moments later gave a sharp bark. Daniel followed the sound to the closed door of the bunkhouse. Bess barked again and he opened the door, hearing the click of her claws on the wooden floor.

"Will?"

"I'll be out to unsaddle Ginger in a minute," he replied from inside.

Daniel walked in and pushed the door closed behind him. "Sara's doing it."

"What? No, I should be the one doing that." The

234

mattress squeaked as he stood.

"She told me to come and speak to you. I think we'd both be better off doing what she says."

"I think she may be smarter than both of us," Will said.

"You're not wrong there."

Will sighed and sat again. Daniel joined him on the bed and they sat in silence for a while. Bess lay her head on Daniel's knee for an extended ear scratch and then padded off, probably to Will for more of the same.

Eventually, Will said in a quiet voice, "I should have been here."

"I don't think you'd have been able to put the fire out any more than Sara could."

"That's not the point. Anything could have happened. You or Sara could have been hurt or killed while I was passed out drunk. I should have been here." He drew in a breath and when he spoke again there were tears in his voice. "What happened to me, Dan? How did I get like this?"

Daniel ached for his little brother. Even though four years separated them in age, they'd always been so close. When their parents asked him to take Will on in the hopes he would be a good influence on him, he hadn't hesitated to say yes. And he'd tried, he really had, but he couldn't help thinking he'd failed.

But maybe this was his chance. Maybe his injury could succeed where all the arguing and pleading and reasoning hadn't.

"For that which I do I allow not: for what I would, that do I not; but what I hate, that do I." Daniel quoted the verse from Romans easily. Every time he read it he thought of his brother. "This isn't who you are, Will. You've been caught up in the drinking and the women and everything else, but it's not what you really want. You're one of the best people I know."

His reply was tinged with bitterness. "You wouldn't say that if you could see me right now."

"What do you mean?"

"I got in a fight last night. A man in the saloon said something about... well, it doesn't matter. But I got angry and decided he needed to take it back. Turned out I was a lot drunker than he was."

Worried, Daniel reached out and found his arm. "Are you hurt bad?"

"Just a couple of bruises, split lip, and I've got one whopper of a black eye. Nothing serious. I'll live."

"Have you been to see Doc Wilson? Are you sure you're OK?"

"Someone patched me up. I'm just bruised and embarrassed, that's all. No need to fret about me."

Daniel remembered the frightened four-year-old little boy who climbed into his big brother's bed whenever the storms raged down from the mountains, the tearful nine-year-old who broke his arm falling from a peach tree as they climbed to reach the ripe fruit, the heartbroken twelve-year-old whose first crush danced with another boy at the hoedown. He'd been there every time Will needed him. How could he not worry?

"You're my little brother; it's my job to fret about you."

There was a long period of silence before Will spoke again. "I'm sorry for everything I've put you through."

"I've never regretted you being here, not once. You know that."

Will didn't answer.

Daniel tried changing tack. "Can I pray for you?"

"You mean now?"

He smiled. "Yeah, now."

There was a pause. "All right. Yes. Please."

Daniel reached out, found an arm and followed it up to

Will's shoulder. Then he bowed his head.

"Father God, thank You for keeping Will, Sara and I safe through last night when so much could have gone worse. And thank You for pulling me up and showing me how to trust You. And I especially thank You for Will and Sara, that they didn't give up on me even when I gave up on myself. Father, You know Will's heart and what he really wants; please give him the strength to break away from the path he's on and to follow You. Thank you that he's my brother, I couldn't ask for better. In the Name of Your Son, Jesus, Amen."

Will's "Amen" was barely audible and Daniel could feel him trembling. After a few moments, he sniffed.

Daniel squeezed his shoulder and lowered his hand. His sight would have been useful right then, if only to gauge how Will was feeling. He was slightly nervous that he may be crying and he wasn't sure what he'd do if that was the case. Would he want to be held? Daniel hadn't hugged Will since they were children.

"So, I'm..." Will stopped when his voice broke. He cleared his throat. "So I'm the best brother in the world."

Daniel couldn't help feeling relieved at the levity in his voice. He would do anything for his brother, but emotional moments between them felt... awkward. He knew it was ridiculous, but there it was. They were men.

"I don't recall saying that."

"Well, you did have a bump on the head only just over a week ago. Some memory loss is understandable."

"Nothing wrong with my memory. You're the one who got punched last night, must have caused hallucinations."

"Don't worry, I won't tell Jimmy. Wouldn't want him to get jealous."

Daniel shook his head at the thought. The supremely confident eldest Raine brother didn't get jealous of anyone.

"As if Jimmy would ever consider the possibility he wasn't both our favorites."

"Ah, so you admit I'm your favorite," Will said, a smile in his voice.

"Stop putting words in my mouth."

"Hey, remember when Jimmy tried to ask Felicity to the barn dance and that pig kept trying to eat his hat?"

Daniel snorted a laugh. "It was that cologne he insisted on wearing. It smelled like swill."

They spent some time laughing over their shared reminiscences of their growing up days on their parents' farm, and for a while Daniel forgot his troubles and simply enjoyed spending time with his brother. It felt good.

When they emerged from the bunkhouse over an hour later, his rumbling gut was telling him it was nearing lunchtime.

Beside him, Will's footsteps came to a halt.

"What?" Daniel said, stopping to wait for him.

"After lunch I'll start on the barn."

"I guess it looks bad." For once, not being able to see didn't feel like such a bad thing.

"It's... yeah, it looks bad. Most of the roof is gone, the back and side walls too. I'm not sure we can repair it. Might be easier to just take the whole thing down and start again. Some of the wood should be salvageable, but we're going to need a lot more. We'll have to fix up some stalls in the small barn for the horses and Pea."

"Took us an age to put it up the first time," Daniel said, remembering the blistered hands and long hours of hard work two years before. "And I don't know how much use I'll be now."

"Oh no, you're not using your eyes as an excuse to get out of the work. As long as you stay away from any hammers, you'll be fine."

Daniel grinned. "It was worth a try."

He chuckled. "Yeah." His tone turned serious. "It's the wood that's the problem."

Daniel turned his head in the direction of the small barn, seeing in his mind the timber stored there that he'd been collecting to extend the house. "There's what I've got to..."

"No." Will cut him off before he could go on. "You've been planning on adding those extra bedrooms ever since you started writing Sara. And once you pull yourself together and start living as man and wife, you'll need them for all my future nieces and nephews."

Daniel tried to stop the smile from creeping onto his face, but he wasn't entirely successful.

"Wait," Will said, "what is that look on your face?"

He could feel the corners of his mouth twitching with more determination. "Nothing."

"Well, knock me down with a feather, you mean you've actually...?"

Daniel would have rolled his eyes if his brother could have seen it. "Shut up."

"I'm so proud of you," Will said, mock tears in his voice. His arm landed around Daniel's shoulders and squeezed.

Daniel batted it away and tried not to laugh. "You are so immature."

"I almost can't believe it. My big brother, finally a man."

"Stop it!"

CHAPTER 30

Sara drew in a deep breath and let it out in a slow, contented sigh, nestling closer into Daniel's side. It was amazing how the space there seemed to be perfectly designed just for her.

He kissed her forehead and drew the blanket tighter around her shoulders. "Comfortable?"

"Mm hmm."

The sun had set ten minutes earlier and the temperature outside was beginning to fall, but she wasn't ready to leave their bench and go inside just yet. The sky was taking on a deep shade of turquoise and a handful of swallows were swooping back and forth across the yard, catching a last few insects before they returned to their nests to roost for the night. A golden glow silhouetted the distant mountains and stars were twinkling into life overhead.

The new view without the barn still seemed strange. What was left of the charred structure had been taken down two days before and it had opened up the vista to the mountains much more. Maybe when it was rebuilt she would ask Daniel to put it a bit farther to the side.

Across the yard, light glimmered from the bunkhouse window. Will was still home, as he had been every night since the fire three nights previously. It looked like he really was keeping to his word to change.

Daniel's fingertips traced lazy circles on Sara's upper arm, creating sensations that somehow managed to be both relaxing and stimulating at the same time. Other than having him able to see the beauty of the fading sunset with her, she couldn't imagine how the moment could have been any more perfect.

"I've been thinking," he said, his voice low in the comfortable hush surrounding them.

"Mm hmm?"

"Will and I need to rebuild the barn soon. The small barn alone isn't big enough to hold all the animals and the equipment and the harvest when it comes in."

"I could help," she said. "I've never built anything, but you could teach me."

With all the digging and planting she'd been doing, she had to be strong enough by now. That morning she'd actually thought she could see a muscle in her arm. Her mother would have been horrified, but Sara was proud of it. She was becoming a real frontier woman.

"I'd love to teach you," he said.

It made her smile. The old Daniel would have argued that it was his job to do the work. He truly was changing and she couldn't have been more proud of him.

"But there's something else you could do too, if you're agreeable."

The way he said it lit a spark of apprehension inside her. He sounded worried.

"Anything," she said. "What do you need?"

He shifted next to her, his fingers stilling their movements on her arm. "Well, we need wood for the barn and the only lumber I have is what I've bought to extend the house, and right now I don't have the money to buy more."

She breathed out, relieved. "You can use that, I don't mind at all. I love our little house and there's plenty of room." She smiled. "Especially now we're sharing the bed."

He chuckled, the vibrations in his body radiating wonderfully into hers. "So many good things about that situation."

She couldn't have agreed more.

"The thing is," he continued, "it took me a long time to save the money for that and it will probably be another long time before I can do it again. And now, well, if we have children we'll need more room. So I was thinking, if you don't mind, that once the barn is done maybe we could use some of that money you brought with you to buy more lumber for the house. But only if you don't mind. That's your money to do with as you please."

For a few moments Sara couldn't answer. She wiped at a tear rolling down her cheek. "I think that is the most wonderful idea."

"You don't mind?"

"Not in the slightest. You can use any of it, all of it. Whatever you need, it's yours."

He found her hand and brought it to his lips, kissing her palm. "It's ours. I was stupid to think I shouldn't need your help. I want to build our life together and, with or without my eyes, I can't do it without you."

More tears following the first, she flung her arms around his neck. "I love you so much."

He cupped her face in his large, warm hands and kissed her. Then he murmured, "Let's go inside," in a tone that made her insides quiver.

She sighed. "You are just full of wonderful ideas tonight."

CHAPTER 31

When Sara rushed into the kitchen the next morning, Will was already sitting at the table, finishing off a slice of bread, butter and cheese.

"I'm sorry, we didn't realize how late it was," she said, grabbing her apron from its hook on the back of the pantry door and tying it on over her dress.

"I figured that might be the case," he said.

Daniel sauntered to the living room doorway and leaned against the frame, a small smile on his face as he pushed his hands into his pockets. Will rolled his eyes.

Sara smacked the back of her hand into Daniel's stomach as she passed. "Stop it. And come help me."

His smile grew as he pushed away from the door and headed for the pantry.

"We'll make a quick sandwich each and eat them on the way," he said, handing her the bread and butter. "Will can drive." He grabbed Sara around the waist as she brushed past him, pulling her back against him and kissing her neck. "We'll cuddle in the back of the wagon."

"Do you mind? I'm eating here," Will said. "You two have five minutes or we'll be late. I've hitched up Ginger and River. You may thank me profusely later."

Sara broke away from Daniel and leaned down to kiss Will's cheek. "Thank you."

He lowered his head, smiling. "Worth it."

"That better not have been on the lips," Daniel said.

243

She breezed over to him, stood up on her toes, and kissed him briefly. "You're so adorable when you're jealous."

He grabbed her before she could walk away and brought his lips to hers, this time giving her a lingering kiss that sent heat all the way down to her toes.

Will rolled his eyes for the second time. "Don't you two ever stop?"

Daniel kissed her again before letting her go. "Not if I can help it."

She touched her fingers to his bandage. "This has been on for two days, but I'll have to change it later. We don't have time now."

"No, you don't," Will said, pushing his chair back and carrying his plate to the sink. "I'll bring the wagon round to the front. Don't want to be late."

"Used to be I couldn't get you to go to church for anything," Daniel said. "Now you can't wait to get there."

"Folks round here don't exactly think highly of me," he said. "Don't want tardiness to be another item on the list of reasons why I'm a reprobate. Hurry up."

Daniel shook his head as his brother walked out the back door. "I can't believe the change in him."

"I think the Lord's been changing more than one person around here," she said as she sat him at the table and guided his hands to the bread, butter and cheese.

He gave her hand a squeeze. "Thankfully."

"Three more minutes and I'm leaving without you!" Will yelled from outside as the wagon passed the door.

Sara burst into laughter.

Daniel sighed. "Did I really say thankfully?"

~ ~ ~

Eating cheese sandwiches while sitting on a blanket in the

244

back of the wagon with Daniel's arm around her turned out to be Sara's favorite way to travel. Much as she wanted to go to church, she was almost disappointed when the journey came to an end.

It felt like the entire town greeted them as they walked in, everyone telling Daniel how they'd been thinking of him and praying for them both. He thanked them all and told them they were just fine, but Sara could tell how touched by their concern he was.

Nicky ran to Will as soon as they got inside, tugging at his hand to join him and his mother. Sara waved to Daisy at the front.

"Daisy's little boy seems to love Will," she said as she and Daniel took seats towards the back of the congregation.

"Children always love Will," he said. "Probably because he's so much like them."

She laughed and swatted his thigh. Looking past him, she saw Pastor Jones approaching along the aisle.

"Good morning, Daniel, Mrs. Raine," he said when he reached them. "It's so good to see you both today. How are you?"

Daniel took her hand, entwining their fingers. "We're good. Actually, we're very good."

The pastor nodded, a smile on his face that made Sara think he wasn't surprised about that. "I'm really happy to hear it. Um... I have something I'd like to ask you, Daniel, but if you'd rather not, just say so. I don't want to make you uncomfortable at all."

"Fire away, Pastor."

He sat on a vacant seat across the aisle and rested his elbows onto his knees, leaning forward. "It's been coming to me for the last few days that the church should pray for you, for your eyes. So if you're agreeable I thought you could come up to the front and then the deacons and I would lay our hands on you and the entire church could be praying for you at the same time. What do you think?"

Daniel lowered his head. Sara tightened her fingers around his.

After a few seconds, he nodded. "I think I'd like that."

Pastor Jones smiled and stood. "Good. I'll call you up to the front after the first hymn."

"Are you really all right with it?" she whispered to him after the pastor had left.

"If Pastor Jones feels like God wants everyone to pray for me, then who am I to say no?" He rubbed her hand. "Yeah, I'm OK with it. Will you come up with me?"

"Of course I will."

Following the opening hymn, the pastor stepped to the front of the platform, looking out over the congregation. "I know you've all been praying for Daniel Raine and his family after the terrible accident which took his sight. It says in the Scriptures that if any of us are ill we should go to the elders of the church who will pray for them. But it also says in Mark that God can heal through every one of us, so I'm asking now that we, together, pray for healing for Daniel and the restoration of his sight." He looked at Sara and Daniel. "Daniel, Sara, would you come up here. And would the deacons come up too."

She took Daniel's hand and together they walked to the front of the church, followed by the Emmanuel Church's eight deacons.

As they stepped onto the platform, Pastor Jones looked at Will. "Will, would you join us up here in praying for your brother?"

Will's eyes widened and a murmuring started in the congregation. He glanced around him and back at Pastor Jones. The pastor smiled and gave him an encouraging nod. Clearly uncomfortable, he nevertheless lifted Nicky from his lap and passed him to Daisy then joined them on the platform, taking a place next to Sara as the group surrounded Daniel and the pastor began to pray.

"Father God, thank You for Daniel and his faithfulness and contribution to this community, and thank You for Your promise that we could lay hands on the sick and they would get well. We know that You are the God of miracles. So, Father, we are praying now that You would heal Daniel's eyes and restore his sight. We also ask that You would give him and Sara your peace and strength and bless them abundantly in their new life together. We pray in the Name of Your Son, Jesus. Amen."

A responding "Amen" murmured through those on the platform and expanded through the rest of the people gathered in the church.

A feeling of peace settled over Sara. She didn't know if it was from the Lord or if it was a result of the knowledge that these people truly cared for them, but for the first time since Daniel had lost his sight she truly knew without a single doubt that everything would be all right.

Next to her, Pastor Jones was speaking quietly to Will as the group broke apart.

"I know that wasn't easy for you, Will, so thank you for coming up. You belong here as much as anyone else."

"Thanks, Pastor," Will said.

He touched Daniel's shoulder, gave Sara a smile, and returned to his seat where Nicky immediately climbed back onto his lap.

It might have been Sara's imagination, but it seemed to her that her brother-in-law was sitting a little straighter than he had been before.

~ ~ ~

247

It was some time after the service finished that Sara and Daniel were finally able to leave. Practically the entire congregation seemed to want to wish them well.

Will walked up to them when they got outside. "I'm staying in town for a while."

Daniel opened his mouth.

"And before you ask, Dan, I'm not going to the saloon. Daisy's invited me for lunch as a thank you for the work I've been doing on her porch."

"I was just going to ask you how you're planning on getting home," he said with a smile that suggested it might not have been *all* he'd been going to ask.

"Yeah, right. Daisy said she'll give me a ride back when I'm ready."

"Have fun," Sara said.

As he walked away she saw Louisa, Lizzy and Jo approaching. Jo was watching Will leave and as they reached Sara and Daniel she blew out a breath through her pursed lips and winked at Sara. Louisa rolled her eyes and nudged her with her elbow.

"We're going to see Amy and Adam," Lizzy said. "Do you two want to come? We thought it would be nice for them to see some friendly faces. It must be so awful for them, locked up in a jail cell."

"Oh yes," Daniel said, smirking. "I'll bet Adam just *hates* being trapped like that with her. It must be torture."

Louisa's eyes widened and Sara did her best to hide her smile behind her hand.

Jo erupted into gales of laughter. "Oh, I like you, Daniel."

CHAPTER 32

Amy's trial was on Monday morning and Sara, Daniel and Will went to show their support for her and Adam. Afterwards, Will stayed in town to do more work for Daisy.

Sara took the opportunity to do some shopping, picking up material for a new dress and ordering a new pair of boots from Isaiah Smith, the cobbler who had a store a few doors down from Adam's post office. She also paid a visit to the bank to open an account for the money she'd brought with her. She would have been happy to simply deposit it into Daniel's account, but he insisted on her having her own. She was served by Mr. Vernon, the owner of the bank himself. After the scandal the bank had suffered in the past few days he was evidently eager to reassure any new customers, and most of the old ones, that the bank was absolutely secure in every way. Sara didn't trust him after the way he and his wife had treated Adam and Amy, but she did trust Jesse, so she left her money in the bank's hands. Besides, it being the only bank in town it was either that or hide it under her mattress.

As she and Daniel walked back out onto the street, Sara came to an abrupt halt.

"What is it?" he said.

She looked around, uncertain what had made her stop. "I... don't know. I just have a feeling..." She trailed off, not knowing how to finish the sentence. She felt uneasy, without having any idea why.

He placed his hand over hers where it entwined with his

arm. "What kind of feeling?"

She shook her head. "It's nothing. I don't know why I even stopped." A sudden desire to get out of the town swept over her. "Let's just go home."

When they arrived back at the farm Sara cleaned up the kitchen from breakfast and started preparation on lunch, while Daniel unhitched the horses from the wagon and got them fed, watered, and settled in the pasture.

She marveled at how, in only the few days since he'd been working again, he'd begun to adapt and learn to cope without his sight. The horses even seemed to understand, patiently waiting as he ran his hands over their harnesses and slowly worked out what he was doing.

Her husband was an incredible man. She couldn't have chosen better.

"I'm proud of you," she said as they relaxed on the settee together after they'd finished their chores.

"You are?"

"The way you're learning how to do things without being able to see. I know how hard it is for you, but you're doing so well. It makes me realize what an amazing man I married."

"Once I got past my stubbornness and spending a week feeling sorry for myself, you mean?"

She touched one hand to his jaw. "I mean I married an amazing man who's always been amazing for every second I've known him. You had every right to feel like that. Anyone else would be the same."

He cupped his hand over hers and pressed a kiss into her palm. "I'd still be like that if it wasn't for you. I married an amazing woman."

"The two of us are clearly an amazing couple."

He laughed, drawing her closer and kissing her forehead. "I guess we are."

She brushed her fingertips across the material over his eyes. "I should get to changing your bandage."

"It's fine, the burns have healed over anyway." He tangled his fingers in hers and rested his head on the back of the settee. "Maybe it's time to stop wearing it."

Sara pulled back to look at him, worried. "But the doctor said you need to keep it on to protect your eyes so they can heal. So you can see again."

He ran his hand up her shoulder and neck to the side of her face. "It's been almost two weeks. If God is going to heal me, He can do it with or without the bandages on. But I'm making my peace with it."

He may have been, but she wasn't. "No, you can't give up, not yet. The whole church prayed for you."

"I'm not giving up. I'm just trying to accept that it's possible I'm going to stay this way." He slowly caressed her cheek, his calloused palm warm against her skin. "Believe me, it's the last thing I want. More than anything, I want to see your face again, but I need to look forward to what is, not what I wish could be. It's the only way I'll get through this." He frowned as a tear slid down her face to touch his fingers. "Please don't cry. It'll be all right."

She placed her hand over his, holding it against her face. "I can't help being sad when the man I love is hurting."

A small smile touched his lips as he wrapped his arms around her. "I'd rather have you than be able to see a thousand miles."

He could always make her smile. She didn't think she'd smiled so much in her entire life as she had in the past two weeks.

He ducked his head, his nose brushing hers.

"I'm supposed to be changing your bandage," she protested without enthusiasm.

"It can wait," he murmured as his mouth found hers.

251

Barking erupted outside, interrupting the fledgling kiss.

"Bess probably just saw a 'coon or something," Daniel said. "She'll stop." He leaned towards her again.

Sara pushed him back. "I'll go check. And I'll bring back new bandages."

He heaved a sigh. "You're killing me here."

Laughing, she pushed herself up from the comfort of the settee and Daniel's arms and walked into the kitchen. Bess was still barking but Sara couldn't see her from the window so she opened the door and walked outside.

"Bess?" she called as she descended the steps into the yard. "What's wrong, girl?"

The barking ceased for a moment and then started again, even louder. Sara walked in the direction of the sound and found Bess to the side of the house, focused on something around the corner.

Sara stopped, suddenly wary. What if there was a wild animal there, a bear or a coyote or something?

She glanced back at the door to the kitchen, wondering if she should go back for the rifle. But concern for Bess prodded her onwards. She started forward again, intending to find out what had her attention and get back inside with her if it was anything dangerous.

But it was probably just a raccoon, like Daniel said. She'd been at the farm for more than two weeks and hadn't seen anything bigger than a possum, which Bess had also barked at.

Chastising herself for her nerves, Sara reached the corner and peered round.

Her heart slammed into her throat.

Mr. Pulaski stood in the shade of the huge oak tree that grew there, a revolver pointed at the angry dog.

"Get it away from me or I'll shoot it," he snarled.

Bess lowered her head and growled, taking a step

towards him.

Sara rushed to grab her and pull her back from danger. "Don't hurt her."

He moved his aim to Sara. "Shut that mangy mongrel up."

"It's all right, Bess," she said, trying hard to keep her voice calm and soothing. "Come on." She patted her skirt for the dog to come, lead her to the bunkhouse and shut her inside.

When she turned back to face Pulaski he had followed her and was only ten feet away. She glanced at the house. She wanted to call for Daniel, but she would die before she'd put him in danger. He couldn't do anything against a gun.

But Pulaski hadn't actually threatened her, as such. Maybe he was just there to say goodbye. With his revolver.

"What do you want?"

"I'd have thought that was obvious by now." He narrowed his eyes. "You really don't remember me, do you?"

Maybe she could somehow get back inside and grab the rifle from the kitchen. All she needed to do was distract him, keep him talking. "Remember you? From the train, you mean?"

"No, I don't mean from the train," he snapped. "From New York."

He'd known her in New York? She wracked her memory, trying to recall him. "I'm sorry, I don't remember meeting you. I met a lot of people in New York. Did you know my father?"

He shook his head angrily, causing the revolver to wave around. Sara flinched, wondering if he even knew how to use it.

"No, I didn't know your father! Morton's! You came in all the time."

Did he mean Morton's Dressmakers? She'd bought

much of her clothing there, but she didn't remember Mr. Pulaski at all.

Unless... buttons.

On the train he'd talked about making buttons. A vague memory came to her of a man she'd caught sight of on occasion at the back of the shop, surrounded by lace and ribbons, always working on something small and intricate. He'd smiled at her a few times and she'd smiled back, but he'd never spoken to her. They hadn't even been within fifteen feet of each other.

That was *Pulaski*?

"You worked in the back."

"I worked on all your dresses," he said, smiling slightly at the memory. "I made each one perfect, imagining the time when you'd notice and come and thank me." His smile disappeared. "But you never did."

She took a gradual step towards the house. "I... I didn't know you ever took any notice of me."

He shook his head slowly, as if unable to believe what he was hearing. "Took any notice of you. Took any *notice* of you?" He gestured at her with the gun and she froze. "Like you never saw my admiring looks."

"I swear, I didn't."

"When you finally got rid of that oaf, Hunt, I thought you would finally notice me. I followed you around, hoping you would see me on the street or in Fort Greene park or out at lunch. Once, you dropped your parasol and I picked it up for you, but you thanked me with barely a glance."

Sara suppressed a shudder at the thought that he'd been watching her. How long had he been following her around? "I'm sorry, I didn't know."

He went on as if she hadn't spoken. "And then I found out you were coming here?" His mouth twisted in disgust. "To become a mail order bride? I couldn't believe it. That you would choose this place instead of me. That you would choose *him* instead of me."

"I didn't know you!" Maybe she could run to the house. He wouldn't really shoot her, would he? She could run and get inside to the rifle.

Pulaski darted towards her, reaching her before she could react and grabbing the back of her neck. She cried out as he pressed the barrel of the revolver to her cheek.

"Well you know me now," he hissed into her face. "And when your cripple of a husband is dead, you'll finally want me the way I've always wanted you."

CHAPTER 33

Daniel's heart lurched at the sound of Sara's terrified cry.

He scrambled from the settee and raced across the room, arms stretched out in front of him. In the kitchen he clipped a chair as he dashed past and it spun away, grating across the floor. His left hand slammed against the far wall, his right found only air. The back doorway.

Throwing himself through, he shouted Sara's name.

"Daniel, *run!*" she screamed from somewhere ahead of him. "He has a gun!"

"*Sara!*" He rushed to where he knew the porch steps were and grasped the rail, only just managing to stay upright as he stumbled down to the yard.

To his left he could hear Bess' muffled barking. It sounded like she was somewhere inside.

"Stop right there, Raine."

He skidded to a halt at the all too familiar voice. "Pulaski," he growled. "If you hurt her..."

"You'll what? Fall on your face again?"

Daniel clenched his fists at his derisive snigger. "I will kill you."

Before Sara he would never have thought himself capable of killing another man. He couldn't even kill a chicken. But he'd never felt the kind of rage and fear that burned through him now. It drove every other thought from his mind.

"Kill me?" Pulaski laughed. "How are you going to do

that? Yet again, you are utterly inadequate. You see this, Sara? You see how unworthy of your affection he is?"

There was the brief sound of a scuffle before Daniel heard her voice, strained as if she had to fight to speak. "Don't you dare hurt him."

Pulaski puffed out a sharp breath. "What more do I have to do to show you that you belong with me? I rigged the lamp to blow up, hired that vagabond Ely to show you how unsafe you were, set the barn on fire. How much clearer can it be?"

It had been Pulaski all along. Suddenly it all made sense. How could Daniel have not suspected?

"You," Sara gasped. "It was all you."

"Because I love you. I've always loved you. From the first moment I saw you, I knew you were meant to be mine."

Daniel could hear her struggling. Anger filled her voice. "It's your fault Ely was here. He attacked Amy!"

Every part of Daniel wanted to run to her, to get her away from Pulaski, but with a gun the chance was too great that she'd be hurt. If Sara was killed, he knew he would die with her, whether or not he still lived.

"I don't want you!" she yelled. "If you were the last man alive on earth, I still wouldn't want you!"

A hand struck flesh.

Sara cried out.

Daniel jerked as if hit himself. He clutched at his bandages. *"Leave her alone!"*

"I'm sorry," Pulaski gasped. "I didn't mean to strike you. I would never hurt you, my darling." His voice hardened. "This is all *your* fault, Raine. She wouldn't be like this if it wasn't for your indoctrination of her woman's weak mind. I have to free you from his influence, Sara. You'll see I'm right, once he's gone."

"No, wait!" she cried desperately. "I'll go with you, I won't fight. Just please, don't hurt him."

Daniel thrust his fingers under the bandage around his eyes, tugging at it. *Please, Lord, help me.*

"No, you see," Pulaski said, "this is exactly why he needs to die. I have to break his hold over you."

"*No!*"

Sara screamed and Pulaski cried out. A gunshot cracked through the air.

A metallic ricochet sounded somewhere behind Daniel.

"*Sara!*" He tore the bandage from his face and opened his eyes.

Light slammed into his head, searing his retinas like a branding iron.

He clamped his eyes shut again, moisture forming around his lashes. It did nothing to improve the pain. Gritting his teeth, he forced his eyelids apart and wiped at his tears with the backs of his hands. Then he squinted into the first light he'd seen in thirteen days.

Everything was a blur. He wiped at his eyes again, trying to clear his sight. He needed to see. He had to save Sara.

Gradually, the world around him came into focus.

Twenty feet in front of him, Pulaski stood behind Sara with one arm wrapped around her waist, the other holding a revolver pointed at him. To Daniel's immense relief she appeared unharmed, although the fingertips of her right hand were stained red. Three long scratches on Pulaski's cheek were oozing blood.

She struggled against his grasp. "Let go of me."

Seeing Pulaski's hands on her made Daniel's skin crawl and he had to fight every instinct to keep himself from rushing forward.

"Keep still," Pulaski grunted, attempting to aim as she jostled him. Then he saw Daniel's bandage removed and laughed. "Come on then, let's see you make a fool of yourself

258

again. I'd enjoy some entertainment before I rid Sara of you."

Daniel immediately lowered his eyes as if still blind. He took a few steps forward, raising his arms in front of him to look like he was feeling his way.

Pulaski laughed again, his eyes going to Sara. "Look at him. Look at your pitiful husband."

Taking advantage of his distracted attention, Daniel looked straight at Sara. Her eyes met his and widened when she saw him focused on her.

"I see him," she said quietly, and he knew the words were for him. She turned to Pulaski, their faces only inches apart and her tone becoming calm and seductive. "What do you have to offer me instead?"

Pulaski swallowed and his hand moved across her stomach. "I... I have many skills that will earn me a good wage. You will never have to sully your hands with work again."

She touched the arm wrapped around her waist, sliding her hand slowly towards his. "Go on."

Daniel swallowed a wave of nausea as he watched her seduction of Pulaski. He knew she was only creating a distraction, but it still made him want to rush forward and rip them apart.

"I will give you a beautiful house," Pulaski said. "Not like this hovel you've been forced to live in here. You will have everything you desire."

She leaned towards him, her voice lowering to a whisper. "Everything?"

"Everything." His eyes dropped to her lips as her fingers reached his hand.

The gun pointed at Daniel wavered. He tensed to move.

Sara yanked back on one of Pulaski's fingers. He screamed.

Daniel launched himself forward, breaking into a run.

Pulaski shoved Sara away and brought up the revolver.

A gunshot exploded around Daniel. Pain shredded his arm.

He barreled into Pulaski, throwing them both to the ground. Letting out a wail, Pulaski flailed his long arms and legs, showering Daniel with a flurry of kicks and punches, forcing him to roll away from the barrage. Pulaski whipped the gun towards him again.

A screaming blur of blue rushed past Daniel's head and landed on top of Pulaski, grabbing his arm and pushing it up as he fired.

A window shattered. Bess' barking became even more frantic.

Pulaski swung his free arm at Sara, catching her across the face and throwing her off him.

Ignoring the agony in his arm, Daniel pushed himself to his knees and lunged for Pulaski, grabbing the gun and wrenching it from his grasp.

He shoved the barrel into his temple.

Pinned beneath Daniel's torso, Pulaski froze and swiveled his eyes towards the gun at his head.

"Give me one reason why I shouldn't kill you right now," Daniel growled, everything inside screaming for him to pull the trigger.

A soft touch brushed his shoulder. "Because you're not a killer," Sara said. "You're a good man."

No one else could have reached through his anger at that moment but her.

She was right, he wasn't a killer. He was just a man deeply in love.

He took a deep breath in and out, letting his anger drain away, and pushed himself to his feet.

Without the gun, Pulaski looked defeated, slumped on the ground and cradling the finger Sara had likely broken.

260

She stood over him, her hands on her hips. "Does it hurt?"

He squinted up at her. "Yes."

"Good. That's for saying I have a woman's weak mind." Her foot darted out, catching him in the ribs and making him grunt in pain. "And that's for everything else."

Daniel let out a bark of laughter. A significant amount of him was hurting and he was feeling a little lightheaded. Now he was no longer fighting for their lives, the full extent of the past few minutes was beginning to catch up with him.

Sara turned towards him and gasped, rushing to his side and touching his arm. "You've been shot."

For some reason her statement of the obvious made him smile. "Yep." He glanced down at his arm and saw what looked like a disturbing amount of blood soaking his shirt sleeve and dripping from his fingers into a small crimson pool on the ground. "Would you mind fetching some rope from the barn to tie him up with? I think I may need to sit down soon."

"How is it you can see?" Pulaski said, glaring up at him as Sara hurried off.

In all the excitement, Daniel had almost forgotten the miracle of his restored sight.

In spite of the circumstances, he couldn't help smiling. "Because God has perfect timing."

CHAPTER 34

With Daniel standing guard over Pulaski with the revolver, the first thing Sara did was release Bess.

The enraged dog burst out of the door and raced straight at Pulaski, growling and snapping. He cried out, throwing one hand over his face as she lunged at him.

Sara couldn't help noticing that Daniel waited until Bess had got her teeth around his forearm before calling her to him. She seemed disappointed to let go. She shook herself and trotted over to take her place alongside her master, glaring at the man still lying on the ground.

Sara fetched a length of rope from the barn and followed Daniel's instructions on how to tie a secure knot. It was a skill she had overlooked in her preparations for coming to the west, but she was able to get Mr. Pulaski into the wagon, hogtied and helpless. He looked extremely uncomfortable which Sara cared about not one bit. After everything he'd put them through, he deserved everything he got.

Leaving Bess guarding Pulaski, they headed for the back door.

Daniel stopped, staring at the areas to either side of the porch stairs where Sara had begun her garden. There wasn't that much to see, but she'd got most of the digging done, marked out the beds with a line of rocks and put in a few flowering plants.

"When did you do this?" he said in astonishment.

"Whenever I could. I haven't had a chance to plant much

yet, but I'd like to put in some climbing roses to grow around the porch and more flowers, maybe some grass. And I thought some pots to grow herbs and strawberries would be nice. I love strawberries and they're the one thing you don't have."

"Did Will dig it?"

"No, did it all myself. He did offer, but he already had so much to do with the farm that I wouldn't let him." She bit her lip uncertainly. "Do you like it?"

"I love it. I'm so proud of you. I never thought something so simple could make such a difference." He looked down at her and smiled. "It makes it look like a real home. A place a man would be proud and happy to raise his family."

Thrilled he was pleased with what she'd done, she took hold of his good hand. "Let's go and see to your arm. You're bleeding all over my new garden."

He looked down at himself. "Oh, yeah. Sorry."

The bullet had grazed his left upper arm, the wound relatively shallow but quite large. It was still seeping blood, albeit less than before. Sara was worried about the amount he'd lost. Daniel, however, didn't seem worried at all as he sat on a chair in the kitchen and stared at her as she worked, a small smile on his face.

"Isn't this hurting at all?" she said eventually.

"Sure is. Quite a bit." He continued to smile.

"Then why are you smiling?"

"Because I can see you again. You are the most beautiful thing I've ever seen. I never want to stop looking at you."

A smile of her own crept onto her face. "You can't look at me forever. We'd have to be together all day every day."

"Works for me."

She laughed softly as she tied the bandage in place. "I'm not going to say I can't see merit in the idea." She placed the scissors onto the table and stood. "I've done what I can, but we need to get to Doctor Wilson."

He reached up his hand and cupped her cheek, his expression becoming serious. "I love you and I will do everything I can to keep you safe, always. You don't have to be afraid."

Tears sprang to her eyes. And she'd been doing so well at keeping herself together. "I know," she managed to whisper.

He stood and put his good arm around her. "OK, let's go."

~ ~ ~

When they arrived in town Sara drove the wagon straight to the doctor, ignoring Daniel's protests. There was no way she wasn't getting him to help first.

Doctor Wilson opened the door, took one look at Daniel's bloody arm, and ushered him inside.

Her next stop was the marshal's office.

Marshal Cade's eyes widened when he saw Mr. Pulaski trussed up in the back of the wagon. "You found him I see."

Wanting to get back to Daniel, she related what had happened as quickly as possible while the marshal scribbled it all down and Deputy Filbert carried Pulaski, almost literally, to a cell.

"How's Daniel?" Marshal Cade said when she'd finished.

"I don't know, I left him at the doctor's. But he can see." That part was just beginning to sink in. A smile spread over her face. "He can see."

The marshal laughed. "Well, that's a bona fide miracle if ever I heard one."

"Do you need me anymore?" she said. "I'd like to get back to Daniel."

"No no, you go. We'll take care of Albert Pulaski. You go take care of your husband. And yourself."

She drove the wagon back to Doctor Wilson's office and ran inside without knocking. In the treatment room she found Daniel sitting shirtless on a chair as the doctor stitched the wound on his bicep closed. He looked pale, his good hand gripping the arm of the chair as the needle passed through his skin.

He looked up at her and smiled, pain glazing his eyes.

"Almost done, Mrs. Raine," Doctor Wilson said. "I've given the wound a good clean. Should heal up well."

She pulled a chair over to Daniel's uninjured side and wound her arm through his, leaning her forehead on his bare shoulder and silently praying for the Lord to ease his pain. She felt his lips press to her hair.

"I'm all right," he whispered, although the tension in his body said otherwise.

"All done," the doctor said, sitting back and dropping the needle into a small metal tray.

Daniel released a long breath and slumped back in the chair. "Don't take this the wrong way, Doc, but I hope I never see the inside of this room again."

Doctor Wilson chuckled as he dabbed the newly stitched wound with carbolic acid. "I don't blame you at all, Daniel. I've seen entirely too much of you over the past two weeks." He began winding a fresh bandage around his handiwork. "How's your face feel, Mrs. Raine?"

"My face?" She touched her hand to her cheek and hissed in a breath when pain flared.

"That's where Pulaski hit you," Daniel said. "Does it hurt a lot?"

"It's not so bad," she said. "Just bruised."

He frowned. "I should have let Bess work on him for longer."

The door crashed open and Will burst into the room. "I heard..." His eyes fell on Daniel. Daniel grinned at him. "It's true. You can see."

He nodded, still grinning.

Will closed his eyes for a few seconds, whispering, "Thank You." Then he blinked a few times and cleared his throat. "That's... um... great. That's really great. It's OK, isn't it, Doc? His eyes, they're OK?"

"As far as I can tell," Doctor Wilson said. "It's not unheard of for sight to spontaneously return after an injury like this, but I think we're all thanking the Lord for this one."

"Yeah," Will said. He looked at Daniel. "What happened to your arm?"

"Long story," he said. "The short version is Pulaski shot me. I'll tell you the extended version later."

"You gonna be OK?"

"It will take a while to heal," Doctor Wilson said, "but it's not a serious wound. I'd say Daniel should recover well. His wife is proving a very good nurse."

Daniel lifted her hand and kissed the back, staring into her eyes. "She makes me feel better just by being around."

"So you're going to be one-armed for some time?" Will said. "You know, I'm beginning to think this is all just a ruse to get me to do most of the work on the farm."

Daniel rolled his eyes. "You caught me."

"Can I have a raise?"

"I'll think about it."

"Because I could get another job tomorrow if I needed to."

"We'll talk about it when we get home."

"Smart, strong, skilled men like me are in high demand."

"For what, being annoying?"

A warmth growing in her heart, Sara shook out a shirt the doctor had brought for Daniel to use, his being covered in

266

blood and dirt, and helped him dress while listening to the brothers bicker.

It was the sound of home, and she loved it.

CHAPTER 35

Daniel's eyes snapped open as a sudden movement next to him snatched him from sleep.

"Sara?"

He could just see her in the darkness of their bedroom, sitting up and gasping for breath, her hands covering her face.

He immediately sat up beside her, his heart pounding in fear. "Sara, what is it? What's wrong?"

"I'm all right," she said, her voice soft. "It was just a bad dream. I'm sorry I woke you."

Ignoring the pain from his gunshot wound, he wrapped his arms around her. She turned to him, burying her face in his chest, and his heart broke to feel her so vulnerable.

"I'm here," he murmured, tightening his arms around her. "You're safe."

"It was him," she said. "It was dark and I knew he was in the house with me, but I couldn't see him. And you were outside and you couldn't get in. I was screaming for you and trying to get the door open, but it wouldn't open and you were calling me and I tried and tried, but I couldn't get to you and he was coming for me..." Her words faded as she clutched onto him, trembling in his arms.

Daniel couldn't remember ever feeling so helpless, even when he was blind. It had been less than twenty-four hours since Pulaski tried to kill him and abduct Sara and he knew it was too much to expect that it wouldn't affect her, but he hated to see her suffering.

"I'll do anything," he said quietly. "Just tell me what you need."

"I don't know what I need. I can't stop thinking about how he was watching me all that time and I never knew. He was following me. He knew everything about me. I know I shouldn't still be afraid now he's in jail and I'm trying to be strong, I really am, but I don't know how."

He stroked his hand slowly down her hair. "Then let God be strong for you."

She drew in a trembling breath and lifted her head. The faint moonlight shimmered in her eyes as she looked up at him, her lips pressed together.

He gently moved a strand of hair from her cheek. "There's no shame in crying."

A single tear grew in the corner of her eye and spilled over, drawing a gleaming track of wetness down her cheek. Another followed it.

He drew her back to him and she collapsed into his arms, dissolving into tears.

Closing his eyes, Daniel held her tight and began to pray. He didn't stop until long after she had fallen asleep again.

CHAPTER 36

It had been a good day.

Daniel's gunshot wound was healing well and he and Will had started construction on the new barn. Sara had even helped. They were still at the stage of planning and cutting the rough lumber to size, but she now knew how to join two pieces of wood together in five different ways and by the time the barn was completed she hoped to have acquired a whole host of carpentry skills.

They had also attended a wonderful wedding, with no less than a further three more due to take place in the near future. It was definitely the season for love in Green Hill Creek. Sara couldn't have been happier.

"You were right about building the new barn more to the right," Daniel said as they sat together on their bench, watching the swallows catching insects over the pasture, swooping at breakneck speed around Peapod and the horses. "The view is even better without the old one in the way. I should have thought of that the first time."

She smiled. "At least this way you don't have to move it for me."

His quiet laugh vibrated into her side where they touched. "If you'd asked me, I would have."

"I know." She had no doubt he would do anything for her. That was what love did to a person. "I'd move barns for you too."

"I believe you could," he said. "There's nothing you

270

can't do. Gardener, farmer, carpenter, and my personal favorite - baker of the tastiest cakes in the world. That was the best sorghum cake I've ever eaten."

Bess raised her head to look at them for a moment before lowering it back to her paws, thumping her tail lazily on the wooden floor of the porch.

Sara felt as if she glowed under her husband's praise. "There's plenty left if you'd like more."

He patted his stomach. "Better not or soon I won't fit into my clothes."

She shook her head, smiling. No one knew better than her that there wasn't an ounce of extra fat on him.

She leaned her head against his shoulder and he tightened his arm around her. Although she loved almost everything she did on the farm, bar laundry day which had yet to grow on her, these were her favorite times, when they would simply sit on their bench together, enjoying the view and each other's company. It was amazing how she'd spent so much time before she came imagining her life out here and yet the reality had turned out to be even better. She couldn't even have begun to imagine how deep her love for Daniel would grow. Among all the miracles she'd experienced since arriving, that might have been the greatest.

"Do you still have the letters I sent you?" she said.

"Every single one. Got them in a drawer in the bedroom. You never looked?"

"I didn't want to invade your privacy."

He pressed a kiss to her temple. "I don't have anything to hide from you. Besides which, I got rid of everything embarrassing before you arrived."

She laughed softly. "Glad to hear it. It's funny to think that just simple letters could have changed our lives so much."

"I'm not sure I would call them simple letters. I labored

over those letters. I wanted every one to be perfect."

She stretched up to kiss his cheek. "And they were."

"There's just one thing I've always regretted about them though," he said, unwinding his arm from around her and sitting back.

"There is?" She couldn't imagine what he meant. She didn't have any regrets at all.

He stood and faced her. "I never got to propose to you properly, like a man should."

Sara's hand flew to her mouth as he lowered to one knee in front of her, taking her hand.

"Sara, I think I've loved you since I read your first letter. I never imagined I could find someone as beautiful, as caring, as smart, as amazing as you are, and I thank God every day for bringing you to me. Would you make me the happiest man in the world by continuing to be my wife and letting me take care of you for the rest of our lives?"

She had thought there couldn't be a better proposal than the one he'd written in his letter all those months ago. She'd been wrong.

With tears in her eyes she nodded, laughed, sobbed a little, and said with all her heart, "Yes."

Eyes shining, he stood and drew her into his arms. But instead of the kiss she was expecting, he said, "I just have one condition."

"Oh?"

One corner of his mouth curled upwards. "You have to promise to take care of me too."

Sliding her fingers into his hair, she pulled his face towards her, gazed into his beautiful, deep brown eyes, and whispered, "Just try and stop me."

THE END

DEAR READER

Thank you for reading A Hope Unseen and I hope you've enjoyed Sara and Daniel's story! The series continues with The Wayward Heart. Lizzy dreams of falling in love. But when her new husband seems determined to avoid her, she begins to fear that coming to California has been a mistake. One from which she can't escape.

If you haven't yet read Amy and Adam's story, No One's Bride is also available on Amazon.

To receive an ebook of my novella *The Blacksmith's Heart* for free, as well as never miss a new release, sign up for my newsletter on my website. And if you're already subscribed, you are officially awesome!

If you liked Will in this book, I'll just say that this isn't the last we'll see of Daniel's brother, and he may not be as immune to love as he thinks he is!

If you have a moment, please consider leaving a review, even just a few words. Reviews are very important for independent authors like me and they really do help others find my books. I will be ever so grateful when you do!

If you'd like to contact me about anything, please do get in touch via my Facebook page or website or at nerys@nerysleigh.com. I love to hear from readers!

nerysleigh.com
facebook.com/nerysleigh

BIBLE VERSES

The following are the Bible verses either quoted or referenced in A Hope Unseen, this time from the New International Version (NIV) Bible, just to make it a bit easier to understand for people like me who aren't so used to the King James Version!

Chapter 1- The LORD does not look at the things people look at. People look at the outward appearance, but the LORD looks at the heart. 1 Samuel 16:7

Chapter 6 - Whoever of you loves life and desires to see many good days, keep your tongue from evil and your lips from telling lies. Psalm 34:12-13

Chapter 8 - Now to Him who is able to do immeasurably more than all we ask or imagine, according to His power that is at work within us, to Him be glory in the church and in Christ Jesus throughout all generations, for ever and ever! Amen. Ephesians 3:20-21

Chapter 10 - But the LORD said to Samuel, "Do not consider his appearance or his height, for I have rejected him. The LORD does not look at the things people look at. People look at the outward appearance, but the LORD looks at the heart." 1 Samuel 16:7

Chapter 15 - And when you pray, do not keep on babbling like pagans, for they think they will be heard because of their many words. Do not be like them, for your Father knows what you need before you ask him. Matthew

Chapter 17 - When I was brought low, He saved me. Return to your rest, my soul, for the LORD has been good to you. For You, LORD, have delivered me from death, my eyes from tears, my feet from stumbling, that I may walk before the LORD in the land of the living. Psalm 116:6-9

Chapter 19 – When they came to the place called the Skull, they crucified him there, along with the criminals - one on his right, the other on his left. Jesus said, "Father, forgive them, for they do not know what they are doing." Luke 23:33-34

Chapter 20 - Again, truly I tell you that if two of you on earth agree about anything they ask for, it will be done for them by my Father in heaven. Matthew 18:19

Chapter 23 - Then Peter came to Jesus and asked, "Lord, how many times shall I forgive my brother or sister who sins against me? Up to seven times?" Jesus answered, "I tell you, not seven times, but seventy-seven times." Matthew 18:21-22

Chapter 24 - Do not be afraid, for I am with you. Isaiah 43:5

Chapter 29 - I do not understand what I do. For what I want to do I do not do, but what I hate I do. Romans 7:15

Chapter 31 - Is anyone among you sick? Let them call the elders of the church to pray over them and anoint them with oil in the name of the Lord. James 5:14

Chapter 31 – "And these signs will accompany those who believe: In My name they will drive out demons; they will speak in new tongues; they will pick up snakes with their hands; and when they drink deadly poison, it will not hurt them at all; they will place their hands on sick people, and they will get well." Mark 16:17-18

Printed in Great Britain
by Amazon

39367030R00158